D11195558

"A sweet and interesting look behind the curtain of Hollywood as a girl-next-door and a famous actor realize that fake dating to save face may lead to real romance and mutual heartache. Shiloh offers a sweet romance with a strong dose of spiritual truth."

—Pepper Basham, award-winning author of *Authentically, Izzy*

"Toni Shiloh delivers another soulful, uplifting romance with *The Love Script*. Nevaeh and Lamont will have you rooting for their happily ever after. A swoon-worthy romance readers will adore."

—Belle Calhoune, bestselling author of *An Alaskan Christmas Promise*

"In *The Love Script*, Toni Shiloh once again proves she's a master of modern-day fairy tales, pairing a relatable heroine and a dreamy, honor-bound hero. This faith-forward romantic comedy is a refreshing and uplifting addition to the genre—a pleasant reward for readers looking for a true happily ever after."

—Janine Rosche, ECPA bestselling author of *With Every Memory*

"Fun and flirty, *The Love Script* provides a rich (and highly entertaining!) view of what it means to live a life of faith—even when the odds seem to be written against you. This fake-relationship story is a must-read for fans of contemporary romance!"

—Betsy St. Amant, author of *Tacos for Two*

"Toni Shiloh has taken the tropes of a relationship of convenience and fake dating and turned them on their head. Readers are going to be delighted by this endearing and adorable romance of star-crossed lovers set with a Hollywood backdrop. Fans of Becky Wade and Courtney Walsh will love this addition to the contemporary Christian romance genre."

—Sarah Monzon, author of the SEWING IN SOCAL series

the
LOVE
SCRIPT

the LOVE SCRIPT

Toni Shiloh

BETHANYHOUSE

a division of Baker Publishing Group
Minneapolis, Minnesota

© 2023 by Toni Shiloh

Published by Bethany House Publishers
Minneapolis, Minnesota
www.bethanyhouse.com

Bethany House Publishers is a division of
Baker Publishing Group, Grand Rapids, Michigan

Printed in the United States of America

Library of Congress Cataloging-in-Publication Data
Names: Shiloh, Toni, author.
Title: The love script / Toni Shiloh.
Description: Minneapolis, Minnesota : Bethany House Publishers, a division of
    Baker Publishing Group, [2023] | Series: Love in the Spotlight ; 1
Identifiers: LCCN 2023002263 | ISBN 9780764241505 (trade paper) | ISBN
    9780764241857 (casebound) | ISBN 9781493442164 (ebook)
Subjects: LCGFT: Christian fiction. | Romance fiction. | Novels.
Classification: LCC PS3619.H548 L68 2023 | DDC 813/.6—dc23/eng/20230202
LC record available at https://lccn.loc.gov/2023002263

Cover art and design by Jena Holliday

Author is represented by the Rachel McMillan Agency

Baker Publishing Group publications use paper produced from sustainable forestry practices and post-consumer waste whenever possible.

23 24 25 26 27 28 29   7 6 5 4 3 2 1

To the Author and Finisher of my faith.

One

The wind whipped through the car's sunroof, the sound competing with a serenade by H.E.R. on the R&B station as I drove down Coldwater Canyon. Privacy hedges created lush scenery against the clear sky peeking through the trees. Today's weather reminded me of the Southern California often portrayed in movies—abundant sunshine, not too hot and not too cold. The perfect temps made traveling across metro Los Angeles a dream.

My next client appointment was with Ms. Rosie Booker, one of the sweetest women I'd ever met. She'd overcome breast cancer while keeping her eyes on God, making her my hero and an inspiration all in one. As her personal hair stylist, I'd had the honor of keeping her hair healthy as it grew back into its former glory. She always imparted wisdom throughout our sessions, leaving me encouraged and ready to face whatever came my way. Working with her in the comfort of her home was a lot different from when I worked on set as a film hair stylist. Unfortunately, my last position working on a streaming show was about six months ago.

I'd been applying for more jobs in the film industry, but the rejections had me hustling to book freelance positions as a personal stylist and showing up to my part-time salon position at The Mane Do. Maybe one day I'd be able to tack on *key hair stylist* next to my name, Nevaeh Richards. Be the one who turned a normal actor into the next Carrie Fisher, known for her iconic hairstyles in the *Star Wars* franchise. Or maybe I could even be a part of the next blockbuster movie that had fierce warriors like the Dora Milaje in *Black Panther*. And I certainly wouldn't sneeze at an Academy Award win either.

I'd actually stumbled onto the job with Ms. Rosie. Lamont Booker—yes, *the* Sexiest Man Alive (SMA)—had been one of the actors on a Netflix show I'd worked on set with last year. Back then his mother, Ms. Rosie, had just shaved her head to combat the copious amounts of hair loss from chemo treatments. Lamont Booker overheard me talking about wigs, hair care, and the importance of a skin-care regime to one of the supporting actresses. Shortly after, he'd offered me the position of his mother's personal hair stylist. Now I came by their place once a week to style her curly tresses and pamper her as the locks grew back in. I didn't know a lot about the Sexiest Man Alive, but he sure did love his mom. Then again, she was an easy person to love.

The road curved, and I grinned as Lamont Booker's multimillion-dollar home came into view. The white structure gleamed in the California sunlight, the black trim adding a masculine touch. Though Lamont Booker—sorry, I can only say and think both his first and last names—lived with his mother. Well, *he* didn't live with his mother. He'd insisted Ms. Rosie move in to his home after learning of the treatment plan to target her particular type of cancer. From what she'd shared with me, she'd been wrecked by the chemo and was very grateful for her one and only child's devotion to help her.

Lately, she'd been making comments about finding her own place again, but the housing market in LA was absurd. I'd know. I shared a two-bedroom, one-bath apartment with my old college roommate because neither one of us could afford to live on our own income alone. Nora wanted to be an actress, and I wanted to make sure no actress got caught in a wig that looked more like roadkill than a million-dollar coiffure. Somehow our relationship continued to survive our nine-hundred-square-foot living space. But if she left an empty food package in the cabinets one more time instead of throwing it away, I'd need to pray the Holy Spirit intervened.

I punched the speaker button on the security box in front of the iron gate.

"Hey, Ms. Richards. Back so soon?" Kyle's voice sounded through the intercom.

"You know it," I called out.

Lamont Booker's security guard was a shameless flirt but completely harmless. He asked for my number every time I came by despite my assurances that I'd never fall for his charms. He was good-natured about being put in the friend zone—though could it be called that if I didn't actually consider us friends? More like work acquaintances?

The gate slid back into the stone wall, so I pulled forward onto the driveway, then waited for the gate to close behind my ancient MINI Cooper. Okay, not ancient, but a car made in 2010 might as well be. My parents gifted me the red hatchback as a high school graduation present. Since it still ran and the sunroof worked, I continued to drive it. And I would drive right on up to my high school reunion in it. But that was in a few weeks at the end of June and not my main concern.

After putting the car in park, I closed the sunroof. Sometimes my intense focus on the job caused me to forget to close the roof. I'd learned the hard way that seagull waste wasn't all that easy to get out of upholstery. Satisfied of its closure, I walked toward the hatchback to retrieve my supplies situated in my rolling stylist case. The all-black storage container looked like the old toy chests I'd seen in posts about the 1980s. My professional look, a nod to the '90s, came complete with a uniform consisting of black bib overalls that could perfectly hold hair clips and other various accessories. My dark blue tee would also conceal any water splashes.

I pulled my case behind me, heading for the lower-level garage entrance, where most of the help came in. After I pressed the buzzer, the door immediately swung open, and Kyle grinned at me. "Afternoon, beautiful." His gravelly voice held as much humor as the twinkle in his eyes.

"Hey, Kyle."

"Hey? That's it? Not, 'I missed you'?"

I placed a hand on my hip and a smirk on my lips. "Should I miss someone who doesn't sign my paychecks?"

"Ouch, girl." He clutched his muscled chest. "I thought we were better friends than that."

I laughed. "Not yet." I tossed a wave over my shoulder.

My rubber clogs fell silently on the light-colored wood floors as I traversed the hallway. The floor-to-ceiling windows let in copious amounts of sunshine. I sighed, thankful for the abundant light. I couldn't imagine living anywhere else in the world. Southern California held my heart.

The elevator entrance beckoned me. On my first day, Lamont Booker had taken one look at my styling case and shown me the boxed convenience. I'm not sure if he was concerned for his wood floors or genuinely worried that I couldn't lift the monstrosity up the stairs. Either way, I quickly became a fan of having an elevator in a house, as well as a tad bit envious, considering my entire apartment could fit into one of the rooms in this house, maybe even Ms. Rosie's closet.

Exiting the elevator, I made a right toward the mother-in-law suite. I rapped my knuckles on the door and heard a voice telling me to "Come in." Only darkness greeted me. Ms. Rosie lay in bed, her form hard to make out since the blackout blinds concealed all sources of natural light.

"Ms. Rosie?" I called softly.

Her face turned toward me, showing a furrowed brow and grimacing lips. "I'm so sorry, Nevaeh. I meant to cancel our appointment."

Her voice sounded thready to my ears. My stomach churned. "Are you okay? Should I go find your son?"

"No, please don't bother him." She tried to raise her arm, but it dropped limply onto her duvet cover.

"Does he know you're sick?" Was it the cancer? Had she relapsed? Did she need to go to the doctor? Get a scan or whatever it was medical professionals did to ensure cancer hadn't returned?

In all my time pampering Ms. Rosie, I'd never seen her look so bad. Then again, she'd canceled appointments before. Maybe moments like this had been the reason why.

"He does. It's just a stomach bug. I don't want you to get sick, too, so go." She turned her head the other way, a low moan filling the room.

I bit my lip. "I can make you some soup if he's not around. Is he on set?"

She nodded, groaning at the movement.

That was it. I couldn't leave her alone. "I'm making you some soup." From my understanding, Lamont Booker didn't have a personal chef. I think Ms. Rosie did most of the cooking, and she was in no position to make any meals today.

"You don't have to. I'll be fine," she murmured weakly.

Yeah, and I was the leading lady in the hottest new romantic comedy. Wait, no, it was Sandra Bullock. I had to give her two thumbs up for proving women in their fifties still had it. #Girlpower

"It'll be no trouble. Promise." I slid a hand on my hip, trying to show my sass instead of the worry snaking through me.

"Thank you, Nevaeh."

"Anything for you, Ms. Rosie." I closed her door quietly, leaving my suitcase outside the entrance.

Ever since I'd first seen Lamont Booker's gorgeous kitchen with its white marble counters and double oven, I'd wanted to create a meal fit for a queen. And since the Sexiest Man Alive was a prince in Hollywood, his mom surely fit the bill.

I slid my hands along the ridiculously large island that could seat five people comfortably before opening the stainless-steel fridge. Organic fresh fruits and vegetables gleamed in their open containers while sparkling water and choice cuts of meat filled the shelves. Of course Mr. A-Lister wouldn't have anything highly processed. After walking through his huge pantry, I had a better idea of what I had to work with. Now to find the perfect recipe.

After perusing BonAPPetit on my phone, I found the perfect chicken-and-noodle soup that called for enough ginger and garlic to evict any germs from one's body. This kitchen had every appliance, but it was the gas range stove I wanted to get my hands on. I washed my hands, then got to laying out the ingredients.

Before long, a fragrant aroma filled the kitchen. While the soup simmered, I brought an herbal tea to Ms. Rosie's room. The thermometer confirmed she was fever-free, but she still looked pitiful in her dark room.

"Do you want me to open the blinds?"

"Please don't."

I wanted to argue, but who was I to dictate her environment when she was obviously under the weather? Back in the kitchen, I stirred the large pot with a wooden spoon. I reached for the egg noodles and—

"What are you doing?"

I yelped, and noodles flew everywhere.

Lamont Booker folded his arms over his impressive chest, glaring at the pasta scattered across his marble countertops.

"Why are you cooking in my house?" He glowered at the mess, as if the spilled food would have the answers to his questions.

"Ms. Rosie's sick, and she forgot to cancel our appointment. I couldn't just leave her here all alone, so I made soup." My words rushed out as I struggled for air.

His gaze rose to meet mine, and I drew in a ragged breath. Whew, I could see why *People* had dropped the coveted title on him.

"What do you mean she's sick?" Every word was elongated, making the question more pronounced.

I blinked. "You don't know? She told me you knew." She'd hoodwinked me!

"How sick?" he demanded.

I took a half step back. Lamont Booker intimidated me by just being *Lamont Booker*. This brooding, towering version made me want to hide behind the pantry door until he turned back into the swoony version I was used to seeing. But I wasn't one to cower, so I tilted my chin up. "She said it's just a stomach bug, but her blinds are closed, and she's lying in bed, obviously in pain."

He flew out of the kitchen, his footfalls pounding against the steps. I winced, then looked at the messy countertops. I found a dishrag and wiped up the pasta, then found a broom to take care of the pieces that had landed on the hardwood floor.

A few minutes later, he stalked back into the kitchen. I froze midsweep.

He stopped in front of the farmhouse sink and ran a hand over his bald head. "I'm sorry for startling you earlier."

"No problem. I was in my own world anyway." Dreaming of owning a place so luxurious. Wouldn't that show my parents that Nevaeh Richards wasn't *just* a stylist? They thought my career beneath me and the education they'd provided. Newsflash: I loved what I did. Even if it didn't live up to their standards or pay enough to get me a kitchen like Lamont Booker's.

"I appreciate you taking care of her. She said you've been checking in on her since you arrived."

"Of course." I dumped the food into the stainless-steel trash can, then put the broom back in the supply closet I'd rummaged through and rinsed out the rag I'd found to clean with.

"I added the noodles, so the soup will be ready in about five minutes. After that, you can pour her a bowl."

He opened his wallet, but I held up a hand. "I didn't do her hair, so you don't owe me anything."

"But you cooked. Cleaned too." He pointed to the gleaming countertops to emphasize his point.

"I don't charge people for helping them. That's just wrong." I blew out a breath. "Besides, the whole point of helping is doing without expecting something in return." I slid my hands into my pockets, wishing Lamont Booker had come home a little later—so late I could've given Ms. Rosie her soup and left unnoticed.

Other than the day he'd hired me and the time we spoke to discuss my fees, our conversations weren't the lengthy types. A greeting here or there. A nod in passing if he looked busy. We didn't normally just stand in his gorgeous kitchen and chat about his mother's health, unless it was hair-care related.

Now he stood before me in a white tee and gray joggers, and I wanted to swoon. Well, just a little. Okay, maybe enough to have a fangirl moment and ask if he'd sign something. Though what I didn't know. It's not like I carried paper around for such a thing. Although, living near Hollywood certainly afforded me opportunities for star sightings. But if I wanted to be taken seriously in this business, I couldn't go up to a celebrity and act uncouth.

"Then thank you very much for taking time to look after her." He smiled.

"Anytime." I walked out of the kitchen before I lost my composure. Surely, I had some kind of paper in my styling case that had space for a Lamont Booker signature.

"Oh, I saw your case upstairs. Let me grab that for you."

Right. I nodded. As soon as he was out of sight, I internalized a scream and fanned my face. Thank the Lord I didn't have to talk to that man on a regular basis. I was better than this. I saw A-list actors and celebrities all the time. Just the other day, I was behind one at a stop sign. I probably wouldn't have even realized it if it hadn't been for the vanity plate on his BMW.

The sound of pattering steps greeted my ears, and I blew out a breath. "Thanks for grabbing that." Time to exit stage left while my inner fan's mouth remained sealed with duct tape.

"Sure. I'll walk you out."

I barely kept my brow from rising. Since when did he walk me out? Was this when he'd lean in close and tell me never to step foot in his kitchen again? To leave his glorious gas range stove to him?

Instead, we walked in silence until he opened the front door. "Thanks again, Nevaeh."

"Of course. I hope Ms. Rosie feels better." Would it be impertinent for me to ask him to text me an update on her?

"Me too." For a moment, his mouth drew down and deep groves appeared, and my earlier thoughts on cancer returned, flooding my brain.

"She'll be okay, right?" I asked softly.

His gaze met mine, and he nodded. "She will."

I gulped and turned away. My foot slipped off the step that had existed since the house was built, but apparently my brain had forgotten, despite the many times I'd stepped down before. My mouth opened to let out a panicked squeal, only a strong arm swooped around my stomach and tugged me close.

"You okay?" he murmured.

"Yeah," I breathed, heart hammering against my overalls.

He let me go, and my face heated as he lowered the suitcase. Obviously if I couldn't see a step, I couldn't drag a rolling suitcase behind me. Instead of thanking him for keeping my face from kissing the pavement, I pulled the handle up and walked away in embarrassment.

No wonder he was the Sexiest Man Alive. Even my pulse had reacted on instinct, and my stomach felt branded by his touch. Once again, I thanked God that I didn't have to see him on a daily basis. I'd be an absolute wreck.

Two

Lamont rested his forehead against the pantry door. His mom was sick.

He straightened, gaze going up the stairs as if he had X-ray vision and could see if she lay perfectly still in her bed. He hadn't been prepared to see her ill, even though Nevaeh had tried to warn him. His panic had been instantaneous, and the urge to diagnose his mom's need for care swift.

Only he *wasn't* a doctor, despite what IMDb credits might mention. He'd played one for a season on a Hulu show, and that had been as a pediatrician, not an oncologist. Still, he knew enough terminology thanks to his mother's bout with breast cancer. He slipped his cell out of his back pocket and pressed the speed dial for her doctor.

"Doctor Langley's office. How may I help you?"

"Hi, this is Lamont Booker calling on behalf of my mother, Rosie Booker." He started pacing around the kitchen island.

"Give me a moment to see if the doctor is available for your call, Mr. Booker."

"Thank you." Sometimes it paid to be famous in Beverly Hills. Instead of waiting for a doctor to call him back, he often jumped the queue and was automatically connected to the doctor's private line.

"Mr. Booker, Dr. Langley is on another call but assures me he'll get right back to you. Same number?"

"Same number."

"Then have a great day."

His mouth flattened. *Great*. Now he'd have to wait, which meant plenty of time for his mind to conjure up possibilities that would end with his mom severely ill and him pacing hospital hallways. Maybe if he ladled some of the soup Nevaeh had made for his mother into a bowl it would keep his mind from spiraling.

He shook his head. He still couldn't believe the hair stylist had taken the time to make soup from scratch. Before he'd made his presence known, he had taken a couple of seconds to try to recall if he'd ever given her leave to make herself at home. She'd made quite the picture in his kitchen. As she'd stirred the pot, her eyes had danced with delight. And once he'd confirmed his mom was indeed sick, the thoughtfulness of Nevaeh Richards had reminded him there was good in the world.

Before she'd left, concern for *his* mom had etched itself on every feature of her face. Since his eyes were fixed there, he'd realized for the first time she had dimples. Not that dimples were so unusual—plenty of women had them in Hollywood. He'd just never realized the hair stylist had two perfect divots in her cheeks. Unlike other women in the business, she didn't have the physique of someone one step away from checking into a "resort," which everyone in town knew meant a rehab for drugs or eating disorders. Or even recovery after plastic surgery.

He ladled up two scoops of the soup, and his stomach rumbled. Okay, so he'd fix himself a bowl as well. His current role as a horse trainer was whipping him into shape. Six months into filming, and he still didn't know how his friend Tucker Hale did it. He'd met Tuck a year ago to get advice on the horse trainer role since the man actually performed the job in real life.

They'd easily formed a friendship, so Lamont had also introduced Tuck to his other consultant friend, Christian Gamble. Chris had helped Lamont with a wildlife conservationist role a couple of years back. Now Lamont regularly kept in contact with the guys—mostly through texts. He pulled out his cell and typed up a quick text, asking for prayer for his mom.

Lamont placed the bowls of soup on a tray, then climbed the stairs. Balancing the wooden platter on his forearm, he twisted the knob gently with his other hand. "Mom?"

"Hmm?" She shifted in bed.

"How are you feeling?"

"I think that tea helped some." Her voice sounded feeble.

He forced a neutral expression. "You throw up again?"

She shook her head, placing a palm to her forehead.

"Fever?"

"No. I'm a little clammy though."

"Want me to open the balcony door?" Each bedroom on the second floor had its own private balcony. Maybe she just needed some fresh air.

"No, thanks, baby."

"I brought you a bowl of soup that Nevaeh made."

"She's such a sweet girl."

"Hmm." Hopefully that noise was enough to keep her talking. Her voice sounded stronger already, and he didn't feel so tense with worry as long as she kept talking. "Soup?"

"Help me sit."

Lamont reached for her forearm, gently lifting her as he fluffed the pillows behind her. "Room spinning?"

"A little." She looked at the tray. "You going to eat with me?"

"If that's okay."

"Of course."

Phew. If she wanted company, surely she wasn't at death's door. He pulled the nearest chair toward her bed, then sat with his bowl. "Want me to say grace?"

"Yes, please."

After he prayed, they ate in silence. Or rather, Mom did as he watched her carefully. He blew on a single spoonful while she took three bites. After her fourth, he finally ate. *Wow. This is pretty good.*

"Make sure you send Nevaeh flowers or something as a thank-you."

"Yes, ma'am." Or maybe he'd just send her the usual payment. Though she'd been adamant about not being paid for helping. Isn't that how she'd put it?

His phone rang, breaking the silence. "Hello?"

"Mr. Booker, this is Dr. Langley returning your call."

Thank You, Lord! "Yes, my mom's been pretty sick today. Vomiting earlier and dizzy. I just wanted to check with you on if this could be a simple bug or . . . or something else." His voice trailed off.

Though his mom had been given a clean bill of health six months ago, Lamont hadn't been able to relax just yet. He watched over her as if he were the parent and she the child.

"Can you bring her in for some tests, or is she pretty weak still?"

Lamont glanced at her, ignoring the exasperated expression drawing her lips into a pinched scowl. "I think it's too soon for that. I'm trying to see if she'll keep some soup down."

"All right, then. Shall I make a house call this evening?"

"Please." Relief flooded him at the offer.

"Then I'll see you at seven. How's that sound?"

Lamont glanced at the clock on his mother's nightstand. Three more hours of waiting? Would his sanity survive until then? *Do I have a choice?* "That'll work, Doc." He hung up.

"Really, Lamont? You called Dr. Langley?" His mom raised an eyebrow.

"What else am I supposed to do?"

"Let me puke like everyone else who gets a stomach bug. Supply me with electrolytes and call it a day."

His cheeks heated under her scrutiny. "I just wanted to make sure it was a one-day virus versus . . ."

"Versus what? Cancer? Is that what you're tiptoeing around?"

He sighed, rubbing the back of his head. She was so touchy about his concern these days.

"I'm not going to die anytime soon, son."

"Yet every time someone says that in the movies, they're dead in the next few minutes."

She rolled her eyes. "Life's not a movie set. Or even a reality TV show."

Point for her . . . "But people die every day. No one makes it out alive." One thing this past year had shown him was that waking up wasn't guaranteed. Life was precarious, and he knew the Lord could take her home whether Lamont was ready for it or not.

Her lips twitched in humor. "I think being around me has made you morbid."

"Or served me a heavy dose of realism. You know nothing else in this town has."

"I think you need a vacation."

He snorted and took another bite. He wasn't going down this road again. His mother thought he worked too hard. Sure, days like today when he'd been on set at four in the morning getting hair and makeup done before filming for eight hours were a bit much. But he also had the rest of the day off. Since he had no evening commitments, he could go to bed right now if he wanted. Not that he would. He'd probably work out until the doctor arrived. Unfortunately, tomorrow morning came with another four o'clock start *with* an event to attend in Hollywood at sunset.

Running the itinerary in his mind had him forcing back a yawn. "Maybe I'll take a vacation after this movie is done filming."

"You said that the last time."

He said it every time, but no use mentioning that. "I think I took a week off."

"If doing various interviews instead of acting ten to twelve hours a day is relaxing, then sure."

Lamont drained his soup, making a show of enjoying the chicken noodle creation.

"Are you ignoring me?"

"Choosing not to argue. I can't win."

She grinned, the first smile since he'd walked into her room. "You really can't."

"Mom, acting is my dream job. How many people get to say that?" He studied her, willing her to understand.

"Not many."

"Exactly, so why should I rest?"

"God commands it. Don't forget that." She shook a finger at him.

"I take at least one day off a week. It's even written in my contract."

"Yet you still do other things. I mean a true rest, son." She laid a hand on his. "One where you're floating on a boat somewhere in the middle of the Pacific Ocean, and your cell phone has no reception. You won't be able to receive any Google notifications of any articles or social media posts with you in them. Where your agent won't call and rope you into another movie or show before you've relaxed from the last one. Where even your own mother—though she is the best—can't reach you. A *true* vacation."

Lamont couldn't argue. She was merely stating facts, but if he responded with the "I'll rest when I'm dead" comment floating around his mind, his mom would Gibbs-slap him—he'd be forever grateful for *NCIS* adding that reference to his brain—and reprimand him for having a smart mouth. Just because he was thirty-one years old didn't mean his mom didn't deserve his respect, so he stood and grabbed his bowl and hers, though it was still half-full.

"One day, Mom." He kissed her forehead and straightened. "That food settle okay?"

"Yeah. I'll get another catnap in. Wake me when the doctor arrives."

"I will."

He headed back down the stairs and set the bowls in the dishwasher. What was he going to do if Dr. Langley told him the cancer was back and had spread? That could be the reason for her upset stomach, right? He tapped on the internet browser on his phone and typed *stomach cancer symptoms* into the search bar.

Hmm. He should have asked her if she'd vomited blood. Was her poor appetite a checkmark for another symptom or the result of throwing up earlier? And why couldn't he make the doctor get here any faster? What good was money if people didn't bow to the demands of it?

Lamont groaned, rubbing his face. *Sorry, Lord. That was extremely entitled and obviously a mark against my faith and trusting in You. I promise I know You heal.* After all, his mom had been healed from breast cancer.

I'm just worried. Please let it only be a stomach bug.

There was nothing he could do until the doctor showed

up. So he could work out, swim in his pool, or maybe hang out in the sauna. Yeah, that sounded like the better idea. He grabbed the duffel bag he'd left near the front entry and headed upstairs to his room.

The primary bedroom was separate from all the other rooms. It even had a separate entry to the rooftop deck that gave him a bird's-eye view of Beverly Hills and the LA skyline. The deck was his favorite place to sit and read his Bible. Something he hadn't done this morning due to the early on-set time. Maybe instead of some time in the sauna, he'd spend some time with the Lord. Because he seriously needed God to eradicate the fear that gripped him the moment Nevaeh had said his mother was ill.

His phone buzzed.

Tuck
Praying for Ms. Rosie.

Chris
Same. Is it serious?

Lamont
She claims it's a stomach bug.

Chris
Maybe it is.

Tuck
They do go around.

Lamont
Yeah. I'm about to sit down and pray that's all it is.

Tuck
I'll echo your prayer.

Chris
Likewise, man.

Lamont
Thanks, fellas.

Three

"Nevaeh!" my roommate shouted.

I shot up in bed, head swiveling faster than my mind could catch up. Had the noise been part of my dream?

"Nevaeh, get in here now!"

So not a dream. I flung my bedspread back and trotted from my doorway to the living room.

"You're on TV." Nora gestured frantically to the small flat-screen on the entertainment center.

"What are you talking about?" I hid a yawn behind my hand but grimaced as morning breath slapped me in the face.

She grabbed my arm and pulled me onto the threadbare couch next to her, then took a bite of beef jerky. Nora was in the middle of some fad high-protein diet, hoping to bulk up and get the role of a superhero I couldn't even remember the name of.

"You're on *StarGazer.*"

I rubbed the sleep from my eyes, trying to focus on what the talking heads were gossiping about. "That's not possible." I wasn't a celebrity.

"They're talking about you and Lamont Booker." She looked over at me, her eyes wide in her olive-tone face. "They have a picture of the two of you."

"What?" I whispered, voice trailing as said photo popped on-screen. I gasped. "Turn up the volume."

Nora pressed the button on the remote as the picture of me and Lamont Booker fell from the screen and the host, LJ Watt, resumed speaking. "No one knows who the mysterious woman in the photo is, but it's obvious she's more than acquainted with *People*'s 'Sexiest Man Alive,' Lamont Booker. Don't believe me? Sources confirm this photo was taken"—he leaned toward the camera as if spilling the tea on the latest scandal—"at his house."

"No, no, no." I dropped my head into my hands at Watt's insinuation.

Instead of a broad-view picture of me about to tumble down the stairs and Lamont Booker saving me from breaking a bone, some paparazzo had framed us close together with his arm around my waist while he whispered something in my ear. Only from whatever angle that photographer must have been at—I was guessing trees, and yes, I'd put nothing past these folks—it looked like I was reluctant to leave the warmth of Mr. SMA's arms. Somehow, they'd managed to make it appear he felt the exact same way.

"Kill me now." My arms fell at my sides as I tried to rasp the enormity of the situation. Was this something that would blow over by noon, or would it wreak havoc for a few days?

"Girl, you're famous. Let's see you get that key stylist spot now." Nora grinned, rubbing her hands gleefully.

"It's not what it looks like," I snapped.

"Who cares?" She flipped her long brown hair over her shoulders. "I'd capitalize on it if I were you."

I didn't bother responding and instead listened closer as LJ Watt went on to speculate more about our supposed relationship.

"You know, one really has to wonder what they were up to there all cozy-like in his home. America, I'm not sure if you remember Lamont spilling his newfound celibacy status when asked about his faith conversion by Oprah a few years back. *Nothing* about this picture screams a monk going to church on Sunday mornings," LJ said.

"You've got that right." Camille, the cohost, giggled as she fanned herself with exaggerated movements.

"Everyone in Hollywood knows about Lamont's transformation from bad boy to staunch Christian," LJ continued. "We haven't seen him date since his split with *the* Diva Jones. Instead, his current lifestyle only seemed to prove his claim to celibacy. But I have to say yet again, nothing in this picture shows that. In fact, I may go as far as to say it shows the exact opposite."

"He caught me from falling down the stairs!" I shouted at the TV.

"Sure, Nevaeh." Nora smirked.

I blinked. Why was her face made up at—a glance at the cable box showed *7:00 a.m.*—such an early hour? "Where are you going?"

She unfolded her long legs and stood from the couch, wearing an olive-green romper that made her skin glow all the more. "Audition. It's at nine."

"Do you need me to do your hair?" Usually she gave me ample warning, so maybe she'd be using her own tresses. Though they looked a little limp and lacking that Hollywood shine.

"Yes, please."

"Then let's turn that off and get to it." I couldn't stomach any more. Despite the thought, my brain itched to grab my cell and see if this was trending on Twitter. If so, I needed to panic further instead of halting my spiraling thoughts.

"Great," Nora said, interrupting my thoughts. "The appointment's in Studio City, so I should still look good by the time I get to it."

Nora and I lived in Studio City, home to hundreds of film production companies. The better to get me a job as a film stylist—*Hello, Lord! Still waiting for that top billet of key stylist*—and Nora a lead actress role. So far, neither one of us had landed that lead position we were desperately working toward. Thanks to Nora's good looks, she never had problems getting auditions. It was the callbacks that were harder for her to land.

Apparently, the part Nora would be auditioning for today called for a woman with curly hair. "You should have woken me earlier or told me last night. I could have had you looking cuter than Shirley Temple."

"Yeah, that's so old." She rolled her eyes. "Just give me a wig. Maybe one that makes me look like Blake Lively did when she premiered *The Age of Adaline*."

I knew the exact look she was talking about. "Are you supposed to be blond and blue-eyed?"

"No, I just want those type of curls."

They'd been more voluminous waves than anything, but I wouldn't argue with Nora. Plus, I had a wig that style in a rich sable color. I went to my wig station—an armoire I'd found at IKEA and made over—and reached for the correct one.

"How's this?" I held up the hair in question.

"Perfect."

Before long, I had the hairpiece situated perfectly, and Nora preened in the mirror.

"I look fantastic. Hopefully casting knows what they're doing." She turned from side to side, peering at the floor-length mirror.

"Break a leg."

"And don't forget to call a reporter and get your fifteen minutes of fame."

My nose wrinkled at the suggestion.

She shook her head. "See you later." She sauntered out of my room.

As soon as I heard the front door close, I pulled out my cell and typed Lamont Booker's name into the search bar of the internet browser and clicked on the first article I saw. *The Cheese* also speculated on my supposed relationship with Mr. SMA and whether he remained chaste or if I was the siren that had called him too far out into deep waters, drowning him in a sea of lust. My face heated as I read some of the comments.

How did she land him?
        SMAfan

Oh my word! You hypocrite! They should take away your endorsements for flaunting your floozy.
        JesusIsTheReason

Please, like Christians aren't having sex.
        GetaLifeSoon

If they're fornicating outside of marriage, then they'll burn for their transgressions.
        JesusIsTheReason

Just goes to show that Christians are hypocrites.
        ReligionIzACrutch

Okay, so yeah, I didn't go to church—you try finding a good fit in metro LA—but I was still a believer. Still prayed to God and occasionally took a look at my Bible. I was *not* a floozy.

"Ugh." I tossed my phone onto the bed. I couldn't read any more comments from the troll patrol. Had Lamont Booker seen this? Should I call him? Surely his publicist would be on the ball.

I bit my lip, staring at my phone in the middle of my comforter. Anyone who knew me could call one of these tabloids and release my name in a hot second. Would I have to wear one of those big floppy beach hats with oversized glasses that hid half a person's face in case there were paparazzi waiting outside my front door? I shook my head. Nora had left with no problem, so I should be fine.

The phone rang, interrupting my contemplation of my future on tabloids. I picked it up from where I'd thrown it and looked at the screen. Lamont Booker's name flashed on my caller ID, and relief poured out of the tightness that was my chest.

"Hello?" My voice warbled.

"Nevaeh, good, you answered." He sighed, the weighted sound reminding me of an anvil sinking to the bottom of the ocean. "I don't know how to ask this, but—"

"I saw." No need for him to explain the awkward situation.

"Can you come over for damage control?"

"Yes!" I winced. "Yes," I repeated more calmly. "I'm assuming time is of the essence, so if you can keep my name out of the tabloids, I'll do the next three sessions with Ms. Rosie free of charge."

He snorted. "I'm not going to let you work for free. We'll talk more when you get here. Oh, and my agent is here to help us brainstorm ideas on how to get the media to drop the story."

"Why not your publicist?" Then again, maybe he and his

agent were close. Would they be able to keep my name out of the gossips' mouths?

"He's both. See you soon."

I raced to my closet, staring at the various tops and bottoms littering it. Should I go in disguise or wear my usual style? Just in case reporters loitered outside of Lamont Booker's mansion, I reached for the lilac-colored, empire-waist maxi dress. Next choice was a chunky beaded necklace in a darker tone that would match perfectly. I could hide behind the layers of the dress, and my sunglasses would provide anonymity.

Not that I *needed* to hide my curves, but showcasing their ample bends in the city of skinny wasn't my favorite. I just wanted to feel my most confident when stepping outside my apartment and into an unknown fray.

My breath caught. What if Lamont Booker had really called me over to fire me and that's why he didn't take my offer of free hair care for Ms. Rosie? *Oh no!* Ms. Rosie. What must she think of me? Did she think I was some hussy that led her son into sin like a Jezebel? I shuddered remembering a keyboard bully's comment.

I groaned, banging my head against the doorframe. This was awful.

Pull it together. Fall apart later.

After dressing and grabbing my bag, I locked up.

"Hey, Nevaeh."

I glanced over my shoulder. My neighbor, Lenora Hazelton, sat on her front stoop. "Hey, Mrs. Hazelton. How are you?" *Please don't watch the news, please don't watch the news, please—*

"Wonderful, child. Every day above ground—"

"Is a good day," we finished together.

I smiled, letting some tension out. "Thanks for the reminder,

Mrs. Hazelton." Judging from the lack of cameras, I remained unknown, and my home was still a safe place.

"Anytime. You got fun plans today?"

"Time will tell." I waved across the small courtyard, then headed for the street parking, where my MINI sat.

The whole drive from Studio City to Beverly Hills had my guts bubbling with nerves. My hands were clammy as I tried to grip the steering wheel and cast my cares before the Lord. But after repeating the same pleas of *help me* over and over, I went silent. The Lord got the picture—I was one step from panic and had already passed Go on the way to anxiety.

I pressed the callbox to the security system, fingers tapping out a frantic rhythm.

"Ms. Richards, come on in."

My brows rose at Kyle's cold tone of voice. Was he mad? At *me*? Had he also believed what apparently the whole world was saying about me? I wanted to ask, but the need to know what Lamont Booker had planned had me following instructions to park in the private garage. When Kyle opened the door to the house, I took in the hard features on his tan face and wilted.

"It's not what it looks like. I promise." Not that I owed him anything. He'd flirted, I'd joked back, and we were friendly acquaintances. Still, it did something to my insides when others were upset with me.

"It's not that." His Adam's apple bobbed. "I'm just sorry that I didn't spot the paparazzo. If I'd done my job properly, none of this would be happening."

A breath of air whooshed from my lips. "It's not your fault. You know how they get." I studied his brown eyes. "Is he upset with you?"

Kyle shook his head.

"Then it'll be okay, right?"

"Yeah, but maybe not so much for Mr. Booker."

I glanced down the hall, then back at Kyle. "Why? What's going on?"

"Other than this hitting every channel, including actual news stations?"

My stomach sank to my toes. "What *news* shows?"

"CNN, Fox, you know, the mainstream ones. *Good Morning America* picked it up too."

"I saw it on *StarGazer*." They were a step above tabloids—TV version—but barely.

"They were the first to break the story, from my understanding. Mr. Booker's phone has been ringing nonstop ever since."

I groaned. "Do you think the media will start camping out in front of his place?" I slapped a hand over my mouth.

"Now, why did you go and say something like that?" Kyle's shoulders fell. "I'm going to go check the camera feeds again. He's in the living room, by the way."

"Thanks."

I wiped my hands against my thighs, then headed down the green mile. As soon as I passed the kitchen and rounded the gleaming pillar, making myself visible to the men seated in the living room, they stopped talking. Lamont Booker and an older gentleman stood as I stepped down into the sunken living room.

"Wow, a standing ovation for a paparazzi picture?" I tried to make a joke to lighten the mood, but my heart still pounded.

The agent laughed, but Lamont Booker looked none too pleased.

"Bryan Wilkinson." He stretched out his hand. "I'm Lamont's agent."

"Nevaeh Richards, Ms. Rosie's hair stylist."

"Have a seat."

I stared at the cream-colored sectional. *Lord, please*

don't let me be nervous sweating! My hands nestled into my lap as I gripped my fingers to hide the tension coursing through me.

"So, Nevaeh, I'm sure you've seen the news," Bryan started. "But let me give you an update on where we're at currently."

I nodded, glancing at the man who kept rubbing his hands over his head as if life couldn't get any worse. How did I manage to ruin my favorite actor's life?

"*StarGazer* broke the story and the photo, which was quickly picked up by various tabloids and entertainment stations. Twenty minutes ago, the moral and legal department at the production studio where Lamont is under contract called to find out if something inappropriate was going on and if we needed to revisit the terms of his contract."

Oh no. My mouth ran dry. How could one little picture do so much damage? "Is a morality clause a real thing?" I thought that was something only found in rom-coms and cheesy movies.

"It is. #MeToo struck fear into studio companies, so most contracts these days have them included."

This time my gaze flicked to Lamont Booker's in sympathy.

"Did you tell them I was only here to do his mom's hair?" Suddenly my thoughts turned toward my own dreams. Would film companies think I led their star astray and blacklist me from working as a key stylist?

"Their lawyers might be willing to take us at our word. However, perception is ninety percent law in Hollywood, and that photo says something more than just an employee doing the job she was hired for." Bryan shrugged as if to say, *"What can you do?"*

I wanted to drop my head in my hands just like the SMA. "This can't be real."

"So what should we do, Bry?" Lamont Booker finally spoke

up. "I can't have the fans thinking I've been lying about my faith and convictions for years. I stand by my word."

"Why not go on some talk shows and just tell the truth?" I suggested. Wouldn't that be the easiest thing?

Bryan snorted. "Yeah, tell America the hair stylist that *he* pays to work for *his* mother fell, and he caught her." He threw me a look that practically screamed, *"You poor delusional fool."* "If they don't accuse him of leveraging his fame for something sinister, they'll accuse you of being a gold digger and capitalizing on fifteen minutes of fame."

Nora's words from this morning echoed in my head. "So that's out, then?"

"What if Nevaeh agrees to come with me and explains that it's not what it looks like?" Lamont asked.

Now Bryan gave his client a *poor fool* look. "Yeah, again, perception is law in Hollywood. The public will probably believe she's been pressured to make a comment like that in order to keep her job. Honestly, her being employed here makes the morality clause more of a concern. Besides, that picture says you two are intimate—*not* coworkers."

"But we're not. I barely talk to her." Lamont Booker grimaced, meeting my gaze. "No offense."

"None taken. I'm hired to help your mom, not you. You don't owe me anything." But my brain screamed for me to find a way to make this all work out.

"This is a moment to tell your truth," Bryan said, a gleam entering his eyes.

"You just said I couldn't, Bry."

"No, *your* truth. The one we'll tell the media." Bryan clasped his hands, leaning his elbows on his thighs. "Tell them you and Ms. Richards fell in love over the months she's been styling your mother's hair since her battle with cancer. What the paparazzo managed to shoot was Ms. Richards and you maintaining boundaries already set in your relationship. This shows you're not a monk but not a hypocrite either. The Christians will applaud you for maintaining purity, and everyone else will believe you're a Christian who actually puts his money where his mouth is."

Bryan sat back, crossed his ankle over his opposite knee, and folded his arms behind his head. "And that is what will save both of your reputations."

Houston, we have a problem.

Four

This could *not* be happening.

Lamont stared at Bryan in disbelief.

"Say what now?" Nevaeh stood, gaping at his agent as if the man had grown another head.

Not that Lamont imagined the expression on his own face was any different. "That's not the truth though."

"It is if you don't want to be canceled by your adoring fans who believe you uphold Christian values." Bryan raised an eyebrow.

"Of course not! Ever since I rededicated my life to Christ, I've done my utmost to make sure I don't sin." Didn't Bryan know how difficult that was in Hollywood? Women threw themselves at Lamont all the time.

"Not possible," Nevaeh countered.

"What?" Lamont stared at her, trying to keep up with the conversation.

"We sin. We're human. The point is not to go out looking for ways to sin and act like you have a *get out of hell free* card."

Bryan laughed. "Are you a Christian too?"

"Yes, but I'm also a realist." She stared hard at Bryan. "I'm not perfect, I'm not Jesus. I'm going to sin. It's just a matter of when."

"Well, let that when be now," Bryan encouraged. "If you're game to stretch the truth and save Lamont's reputation, I'm sure we can make it worth your while."

Nevaeh's mouth dropped again.

Apparently, despite her realistic attitude, Bryan still shocked her. And why was he offering Lamont's pocketbook for his schemes? "I'm not even sure I'm on board. I'm not comfortable telling a lie, even for the sake of my reputation." The thought had his stomach all in knots.

"What hurts worse?" Bryan asked. "A lie you can ask forgiveness for later or endorsers ending their contracts? Two have already let me know they're watching the news and are prepared to end contracts if the backlash gathers steam. Not to mention one production company has already removed their request to enter into a future contract with you. Believe me, Ms. Richards, my client doesn't want to be blacklisted from working in the industry again. What kind of platform or message would he have then?"

Lamont squeezed the bridge of his nose, still having trouble fathoming people he'd built relationships with being ready to push the cancel button on the public's say-so. *This can't be happening, Lord. You know, You know I'm not doing anything untoward. I promised to honor You and glorify You. How can a lie ever be that?*

"Maybe we just need to take a moment and think of another way?" Nevaeh suggested. "Surely we haven't exhausted all avenues. Maybe you can charge the photographer with trespassing and deflect attention onto him?"

"Only if Kyle can find security footage with the guy on my property." Lamont met her gaze. "If the paparazzo took the photo from a public place, then no." He sighed. "I'm sorry for all of this."

She shook her head. "I'm the one who tripped. And believe me, my face thanks you for the rescue."

His lips twitched. He'd lost the ability to joke when his mother told him they were on the news, but he could appreciate Nevaeh's dry wit at a time like this.

"If we can't press charges, then what? Could Ms. Rosie validate our stories?" She studied Bryan, waiting for his response.

"Yeah, because everyone believes someone's mom coming to the rescue."

There went Bryan, raining joy on everyone.

Nevaeh gave his agent the side-eye. "Maybe you should leave so Lamont Booker and I can talk in private."

"You two do that." Bryan stood, pointing a finger at Nevaeh. "Make sure to tell him to follow my plan and pay you handsomely for your troubles, then teach yourself to call him by his first name. The way you use his full name is a dead giveaway that you two aren't in a real relationship." He hooked his thumb behind him. "I'll be out back."

Bryan headed for the sliding doors, and the room plunged into silence.

Lamont swallowed as his thoughts churned through the day's events. Unfortunately, Bryan had a point. The public would believe whatever yarn the media spun. If he and Nevaeh could somehow turn the story to their favor, they'd both be saved.

But a lie, Lord? I just . . .

"What do you think of his idea?" Nevaeh asked softly.

"I can't wrap my head around lying to save my own skin."

"What if we went out on a date before Bryan leaks his spin of the story? Then we could accurately say we're dating.

A loophole, but technically not lying . . . right?" Her face scrunched up in thought.

"Except he doesn't want us to just date. We're supposed to be madly in love." Lamont hadn't been in a relationship since the Lord pulled him from the last one—a toxic mess of epic proportions. He didn't relish jumping into one, even if it was fake.

"Then let's omit that part. We don't really know each other that well, even though I've been working here once a week for the past year."

He winced. Was that a barb at him? Was she implying that he was standoffish or merely stating facts? "I'm sorry. I'm usually pretty busy. It's hard for me to develop a relationship with everyone who comes through the front door." He bit back a groan. Yep, that was a privileged answer.

Nevaeh waved a hand in the air. "Not my point. I just meant we don't really know each other. If we do this, we have to make sure we can both live with ourselves at the end of the day and that we don't think God would find us out of line."

"I'm not sure one date is the definition of *dating*. It still feels like a lie." He ran a hand over his head.

She tilted her head to the side. "Rahab lied."

He chuckled. "So now we're saving God's chosen people with our deception?"

"I'm not saying that at all. Just . . ." She threw her hands up in the air. "Okay, I was totally grasping for straws. I say we pray on it. If we think Bryan's plan of fake dating could legitimately save both of our reputations and jobs without causing harm to our witness, then we commit to playing those parts. Take me out to some low-key places and then maybe a few more visible outings once Bryan releases a statement or whatever you celebrities do."

"What's in it for you? Why would you go along with this?"

Lamont tried to keep the skepticism from showing in his expression, but he didn't think he was too successful.

"If people think I've sullied Hollywood's golden child, I'll never get another position as a film hair stylist, much less the key stylist position I desperately want. Furthermore, I need my regular clients to continue paying me so I don't get kicked out by my roommate."

Lamont studied her. *Really* studied her. Her black hair hung straight past her shoulders, stopping at the top of her chest. Her curves were modestly covered by a dress that fell to the floor and gave peeks at her painted toenails through her open-toe sandals. Could he play along? He could only imagine the questions from the public since she didn't have Hollywood's ideal physique. Would they truly believe he'd fallen in love with her, or would more vitriol follow because she didn't match their standards?

Lamont didn't want to go down the drama-filled road again. *Once burned, twice shy* was an apt expression for a reason. His ex had ensured chaos followed them, and Lamont had no idea if the public would be kind toward Nevaeh. Still, if she was willing to help keep him from becoming a stumbling block to the world or being canceled for something that wasn't true, shouldn't he give the proposal the consideration and prayer it deserved?

"I'll pray about it." Though he was half-ready to agree. But was that just fear and the need to cover his own rear making yes seem easier to say?

Nevaeh nodded. "I will too." She bit her lip. "Was Ms. Rosie upset?"

His heart softened. "Not at all. She said I couldn't do any better. But she was irate that paparazzi were snooping around our house. Even mentioned looking for her own place so she could leave that nonsense behind."

Fear had gripped him then. How could he watch over her, make sure his mom was healthy and okay, if she moved away? He was still thankful the doctor had confirmed she had a simple bug and cancer wasn't something to worry about again. Fortunately, she had perked back up today.

"I can just imagine her sitting them down and telling them why they had no business pointing their lens at that doorway."

Lamont nodded as he pushed his thoughts back to focus on the current conversation. "She's a fighter."

"Is she feeling better?"

"Yeah, just a stomach bug."

"Thank goodness," Nevaeh breathed.

He studied Nevaeh. "Thank you. You've been good for her."

She smiled, and once more his gaze transfixed on her dimples. Why did those grooves draw him in?

He blinked. "So I'll give you a call tomorrow. See what our next steps are, if we're on the same page." Sleeping on the breaking-news story wouldn't cause more harm, would it?

She stood. "Okay." For a moment, she looked unsure, staring at her interlaced fingers. "What if the media figures out my identity before we come up with a better plan or put this one in place?"

"They won't." He slid his hands into his pockets as he rose.

"All right." She squared her shoulders. "Until tomorrow."

Lamont sent a text to Kyle. "I'll walk you out."

"Oh no." Nevaeh held up a hand. "I promise to watch where I'm going."

His lips twitched, but he just dipped his head in acknowledgment. "Bye, Nevaeh."

"Bye, Lamont Booker."

This time, his smile came out. Bryan was right. If—and

that was a *big* if—they decided to become a couple for the media's viewing pleasure, she'd have to call him Lamont. Though part of him liked the full name.

Was she a fan of his work?

Does it really matter, man? Pull it together. What. Are. You. Going. To. Do?

Pray. That was the only thing he could do right now. Because if he committed to Bryan's scheme, he had a feeling life was about to take a turn he wasn't ready for. Maybe the guys could offer some advice? Then again, no better expert than God for wisdom. Didn't the Bible say somewhere that He'd fight our battles? Did that include fixing reputations?

Lamont sighed and opened the text thread with his friends. His brows rose at the texts awaiting him.

Chris
My man, *what* is going on?

Tuck
Yeah, that news even hit Kentucky.

Lamont
It's all just a huge misunderstanding.

Chris
In what way? Who's the woman, btw?

Lamont
She's my mom's hair stylist.

Tuck
When did y'all start dating?

Lamont
We're not.

Chris

Tuck
Um, you might want to look at the photo one more time. There are some serious vibes going on.

45

> **Lamont**
> Are you two honestly saying you don't believe me?

> **Chris**
> Of course I believe you! I just had to give you a hard time.

> **Tuck**
> We know you're practically a monk.

> **Lamont**
> I'm not. I simply made a promise to God.

> **Chris**
> Hey, I can't even remember the last time I dated, so take my messages as a sign that men don't grow up after forty.

> **Tuck**
> Obviously, I can't talk either. Though I think my last date was in this century, unlike Chris.

> **Chris**
> Ha!

"Did she leave?" Bryan asked, strolling into the living room with an individual-size Perrier in his hands. He must have plucked it from the outdoor refrigerator.

> **Lamont**
> Agent's here. I'll text later.

> **Chris**
> Praying

> **Tuck**
> Same

"She did." Lamont set the phone on the coffee table. "We're going to pray about it and regroup tomorrow."

"Hope that's early tomorrow." Bryan took a swig of water. "I'm telling you, this will work. Plenty of relationships have been manufactured in Hollywood. Let's do this for good instead of just bolstering your brand and getting your name out there."

"By pretending to be in love?" Lamont shook his head. "Nevaeh suggested we pretend to date and drop the love act."

Bryan rolled his eyes. "If that gets you to agree. Fine. Pretending is no different than standing on set and doing the same thing. This time, your set is the public stage. All you need to do is pick a tabloid or entertainment news reporter to break the story to. Then go out and show the world you're in love—*dating*—and are no longer keeping the relationship private. Snap some pictures for social media. Heck, go to church and talk about it. I don't care as long as your career remains intact."

"What if the truth comes out?" Lamont swallowed.

Bryan snorted. "People always speculate over celebrity relationships. Your adoring fans will ship you, and if a hint of a rumor comes out that it's false, we'll defend you until their own relationships fall apart."

"When did you get so cynical?"

"Eh." Bryan shrugged. "I'm like Nevaeh, a realist. This is what happens in this town. You just gotta make sure the script says what you want it to say." Bryan raised his bottle in a toast, then chugged the rest. "Call me tomorrow. I'll type up a statement tonight in case you agree. And another one in case you decide to fall on your sword."

His agent walked away and left Lamont reeling with indecision. *Now what, Lord?*

Five

'd worked on dozens of sets in my short Hollywood career. Being behind the scenes brought me comfort, and I thrived on making over an actor into the role they played. But I had never appeared in front of the camera, which was exactly what Lamont Booker's agent was asking me to do.

How did I even comprehend the full magnitude of the many ways this could disrupt my life? Sure, I could turn on a rom-com like *The Proposal* or *Just Go with It* to see how the actors fared in their fake romance, but this was real life. *My* life. There was no how-to-fake-a-relationship book.

Honestly, I'm pretty sure half the words that had flown out of my mouth earlier due to shock weren't sitting right with the Lord. My flesh kept bringing up instances when someone in the Bible had lied to save another. But no matter what, it was a lie. *Lying lips were an abomination* and all that. No matter what I'd said to Lamont about dating beforehand, it was all just to make myself more comfortable with the charade, right?

I'm so sorry, Lord. How could I have inserted my foot and left You shaking Your head at my shenanigans once more? I'm sorry for speaking before thinking. For insinuating a lie would sit right with You. I just don't know what to do in this situation.

A knock sounded on the door, so I left the couch and looked through the peephole. Mrs. Hazelton stood on my front stoop, her horribly dyed red hair captivating my attention. Had she used Kool-Aid to get that look?

I opened the door. "Hey, Mrs. Hazelton."

"Nevaeh, dear, please tell me you have some sugar before I have to contend with sugarless cookies." She held up a measuring cup.

I laughed. "Nora is not a fan of sugar." I ran a hand down my hip. "But never fear, I didn't get these curves messing with Stevia."

Mrs. Hazelton chuckled as she shuffled into my apartment.

I headed for the kitchen. "How much do you need?"

"Just two cups. Is that okay?" Her red, painted-on eyebrows rose. "Do you have enough?"

"Mrs. Hazelton, I never run out of sugar."

"Good. Makes life a little sweeter to deal with."

That's a motto I could get behind. "What kind of cookies are you making?" I reached for the bag and tipped it over, the crystals slowly falling into her measuring cup.

"Sugar cookies. I add almond and orange extracts, and voilà." She smacked her fingers, then spread them out. "Guaranteed to elevate your blood sugar and make you feel alive."

I laughed.

"You're welcome to come over and have a few. I've got some sun tea going on my stoop."

Tea and cookies instead of thinking about the conundrum I'd ended up in? Sounded great to me.

"Maybe you can also tell me about you and Mr. Sexiest Man Alive."

I groaned. "I thought for sure you didn't watch TV."

She snorted. "I'm old. What else do old people do but pop up before God's awake and watch the news? I knew it was hot stuff when it interrupted CNN's normal drab talk. The newscasters were in a tizzy. I whooped and hollered and told them I knew you." She shuffled forward and squished my cheeks. "I knew you'd snag a good one."

"We're not together," I started out slowly. "In fact, that picture's story doesn't match what was shown on TV."

"I see." Her rheumy eyes regarded me. "Yes, come, let's have some cookies and tea and sort out your life's problems, Nevaeh."

"Yes, ma'am." I reverted back to the manners I'd learned in grade school.

While Mrs. Hazelton started her shuffle across the manicured courtyard, I locked up. The green grass shined brightly in the midday sun. Fortunately, the heat wasn't oppressive, and a light breeze swept through the yard between the four cottages that had long since been turned into apartments. I liked to imagine the stories the walls could tell of former residents. Or I could simply ask Mrs. Hazelton. She'd been here forever and was always up for a conversation.

She motioned toward a stool in the corner of her kitchen as I walked in. "Grab that and come chat with me in the kitchen."

I did as told, discreetly taking in the plastic-covered living room set from my position. "How long have you owned the sofa?"

"Since I married Mr. Hazelton. Who would have thought it would outlast him?" She shook her head. "Unfortunately, you can't go wrapping people in plastic. Oh, there are those who will quickly become so in hopes of stopping the marks of time, but let me tell you, nothing can do that but death."

She placed a hand on her hip, liver spots showing on her aged hands. "My Harold died at seventy. Twenty-two years have gone by without him around. And still, I age." She held up her hands. "These are not the hands that he first placed my wedding ring on. Yet they are." She sighed.

"How long were you two married?" I had never met her husband, but she talked of him often. Sometimes she'd show a picture of him, young and wearing a military uniform. Mrs. Hazelton had been a Vietnam War bride and proclaimed it the best decision she'd ever made.

"Forty years. What a way to start a new millennium and century—alone. But I tell you one thing, Nevaeh, the solitude has taught me what really matters."

"And what's that?" I leaned forward, eager to hear what she had to say.

"Time. Not in the way you may be thinking. But in how you use it. We often act like we have an abundance of it. Like it can't be wasted." She placed a cookie sheet into the oven. "But we don't. We just have no idea when we've used ours up. Not being able to see something often makes us take life for granted."

She had a point. Who knew how much time I'd wasted doing things that didn't matter? Wasn't that the problem with hindsight? You didn't know until the moment passed.

"Enough talk of living a widowed life. Tell me about Mr. Booker." She tilted her head. "You know I cried when I saw *Troubled*. The depth he brought to that role left me breathless." She laid her hands on her chest. "I adore his movies."

"He's done some great ones." Who was I kidding? He was my favorite actor. It seemed there wasn't a role he couldn't perform.

Does that include as your fake boyfriend? I gulped.

"So what's the real deal behind the photo?"

I told her of taking care of Ms. Rosie's hair—leaving out the cancer bit—and my almost face-plant yesterday.

She pursed her lips. "Guess the news really did make it more interesting."

I laughed. "Sorry to shatter your dreams."

"Now what? There's been lots of talk about his faith and how sincere he is about being celibate. Do you think the media will brand him a hypocrite?"

Wasn't that why I was in this conundrum in the first place? "His agent thinks we should fake a relationship. Spin a tale of being so in love, but keeping boundaries, hence the longing looks in the photo." I rolled my eyes.

"He's good. Been in Hollywood a long time, huh?"

I shrugged. I knew nothing about agents. Key stylists didn't need them.

"What do you think of his idea?" Mrs. Hazelton held out a cookie.

"I'm torn. I don't want to lie or suggest a falsehood." I bit into the sugary confection and almost groaned as flavor danced across my taste buds. Mrs. Hazelton was the best cook and baker in Studio City.

"But isn't that what you young folk do nowadays? With your social media filters and always posing in perfect fashion for the world to see. How much of what you show people is genuine?"

Hmm. Did she have a point? "But enhancing a photo isn't a lie." Was it?

"Then how can you object to enhancing a relationship? I'm sure he'll take you out, wine and dine you for the paparazzi watching. Isn't that dating? Would that be a lie?"

All this thinking was making my brain hurt. "The reason behind it all would be. We're trying to save his career and prevent him from being canceled. That's actually a concern these days." I thought back to some of the other online debacles I'd witnessed where people ended up closing their social media accounts to survive the onslaught of hatred from people who perceived they'd wronged another—whether true or not.

Now that I thought about it, how many of those instances had been the full story? When the public started using #canceling, employers and endorsers soon caved to demands and pulled their backing. I'd even seen syndicated episodes prevented from airing any longer.

"Then agreeing to this relationship will keep his reputation spotless?"

"Yes?"

Her rheumy eyes twinkled. "What will it do for you?"

"Keep me from being seen with a scarlet letter," I quipped.

"Psshah. In Hollywood? Half the starlets have worn the brand a time or two, some of the men as well. Does that really matter?"

"It could." My head bobbed up and down. "Lamont stands for something good. If people believe I'm the reason he's a hypocrite . . . I don't want to be the woman who caused the downfall of a Hollywood golden boy. I don't want this to be a distraction in every job interview I go to from now on."

"Two reputations and a lie? Sounds like a seedy novel."

I laughed and ate another cookie. "What do you think I should do, Mrs. Hazelton?"

"Sweetie, that's something only you can answer. But I will say, if you want to be real, want to be authentic, then you need to draw lines in the sand and stand firm. Those lines don't have to be straight, because nothing in life is ever that simple, but you do have to determine what you're comfortable with. If you believe this will save your reputation, do so. If you think it'll cause moral damage to your soul, accept the earthly consequences of the media storm. Either way, there will be drama to follow."

Ugh. I hated how right she was. I wanted a simple fix. Maybe even a Time-Turner to go back and keep from tripping over my own two feet. You'd think my body would be used to them by now. I wasn't an adolescent anymore—hello, twenty-eight—but I hadn't yet figured out how to keep from tripping over air, let alone steps.

"Thanks for the cookies, Mrs. Hazelton." I stood and wrapped my arm around her shoulder, giving a light squeeze.

"Anytime, dear." She patted my hand. "I'll say a prayer for you two. Maybe an angel will visit and tell you what to do."

"If only."

I waved and left her tiny apartment—the one she'd lived in by herself for the past twenty years. I needed to do better and check on her more often. Something more than the occasional greeting when I saw her outside sitting in her rocking chair.

Once back in my room, I opened my favorite social app and searched the hashtag for Lamont Booker. Only now there was another one attached to his name: #christianornot.

I shook my head. How could one photo make people question his values? Everything I'd seen about him appeared to be sincere. I'd never seen a parade of women in his house, and Ms. Rosie certainly didn't complain about supposed playboy ways. If anything, she mentioned how she wanted him to settle down with the right girl.

Plus, Ms. Rosie shared how he liked to read his Bible and go to church, and I'd read once that he had a clause in every contract that he got a day of rest. That didn't sound like a hypocrite with a ploy to gain more fans by being someone he wasn't. I believed his conversion was real. But more than that, who was I to judge whether he was Christian enough?

I bit my lip. I wasn't a big deal like Lamont Booker. No one cared about my values, but he was a light in a dark place. All kinds of sleazy things went on in this industry. It would be great to have one more person contributing to the goodness of it. Show another side.

As I read comment after comment, I knew in my heart exactly what I'd choose to do.

Six

Fellas, is it ridiculous to think a fake relationship will solve all my problems?

Tuck

What? Start from the top.

Chris

For real. Fake relationship with who? The nonexistent hair on your head?

Lamont

Ha! You know I can grow hair on my head, but I look better bald. That's what landed me in People magazine.

Tuck

Vain much?

Chris

He is an actor.

Lamont

Focus. I'm going to fake a relationship with Nevaeh.

Tuck

Are you joking?

Chris

Say what?

Lamont

How about I FaceTime?

Tuck

Gotta head to the barn. Give me two minutes.

Lamont checked his watch to see how much time had passed, then called his friends.

"What's this about a fake relationship?" Chris rubbed his beard-covered chin. His eyes looked a little weary. Was he still waking up? Or was that just an over-forty look?

"And with who?" Tuck asked, tipping back his cowboy hat. He too wore a beard, though he hadn't yet hit thirty. His skin was a little weathered, but he held a tan well for a white guy. Something Lamont and Chris liked to tease him about.

"Nevaeh. Bryan came up with the idea so that we could spin the story in a better direction."

"She's the hairdresser?" Tuck asked. "I mean hair stylist." He waved a hand. "Whatever y'all call them out there."

His Kentucky accent almost threw Lamont for a loop. It certainly wasn't an accent a person heard in LA, unless an actor was trying to land a role. "Yes, she works in film and at a salon, I believe, and goes to women's homes."

"Including your home," Chris added.

"I pay her, but my mom is her client, not me."

"So you're going to tell the world she's your girlfriend even though she's not?" Chris asked. "How's that fit with your brand or conscience?"

"That's what has me chewing antacids. I hate the thought of lying just to save my reputation. Seems so self-serving."

He wasn't that guy. *Am I?* He'd always thought he did a good job remaining humble in the face of the blessings God rained on him. But maybe he'd been fooling himself. After all, he was contemplating a fake relationship to save himself. If that wasn't self-serving . . .

"Why do you want to fake a relationship? Let's get to the heart of the matter, then go from there," Tuck said. He was always straightforward and ready to tell Lamont the hard things.

"I don't want people to think all Christians are hypocrites. I want people to look at my life, look at what I'm willing to do for my faith, and truly seek God as a result. If they think I'm sleeping with my mother's hair stylist, what is that going to do to God's message?"

"What will lying to the world do to your soul?" Chris asked. "I get the point you're trying to make. This is really blurring the lines though. Are you justifying lying to help God, and if so, you have to know that's not how our faith works. If you're justifying to save yourself, then be honest, and we'll help you brainstorm alternate solutions."

Lamont sighed, dropping his head for a moment. Why did they have to be so convicting? *Isn't that why you called them in the first place? Wise counsel and all that?*

He leaned against the balcony railing, holding tightly to his cell. "Of course I want to save my own skin. I don't want to lose supporters or the way of life I've built for me and my mom. I truly don't want to muddy my witness for Christ either. Especially considering I really have been celibate all these years."

How did one go about proving something like that? The world had seen him attend events with beautiful women on his arm, but he hadn't been in a serious relationship since he turned his life back to God and walked in the way his mother had raised him in. Diva no longer had him in her clutches. She'd moved on to the next poor fool.

"Fellas, what do I do? I was so sure that Bryan's plan was the way to go. Now I'm not."

Tuck grimaced. "You're in a hard spot. I can't say what I'd do in your shoes. Life in Kentucky can be pretty quiet. Sure, we have the Derby and the publicity that surrounds that, but working with animals and being outside kinda distances you from the life of social media and the world wondering what your workout routine is."

Lamont grinned. That reel still continued to get views. Last count had been over ten million. "People like to work out."

Chris snorted. "No, people like to look good. If they think the Sexiest Man Alive has a secret to better their appearance, they'll watch whatever video you put out."

"Hey, don't hate on me. You've got your own YouTube followers." Lamont smirked at the embarrassed expression on Chris's face.

"Conservation efforts require every gimmick—including YouTube videos."

"You do look excited when you speak though," Tuck added. "You never look like anyone forced you to do the videos."

Chris shook his head. "We're getting off track. This isn't about my measly following. It's about Lamont and what he represents."

"A light in a dark place," Tuck said.

"That's what I want to be. A witness for Christ." Lamont blew out a silent breath.

"What does your gut say?" Chris asked.

"It's churning more acid than an acid factory." He rubbed his stomach. Maybe it was time for some more antacids, or perhaps a ginger ale would help.

"Just talk it out for us." Chris circled his hand in a speak-up motion.

"I keep thinking that if Nevaeh and I fake a relationship, the world would see I wasn't preying on her or going against my word about being celibate. Though some people may question if one can abstain from intimacy when you're in a relationship, if she's willing to back me, then we can show the world it's possible. Not only that, but she stipulated that we go out before we drop the news so that we're not being entirely untruthful."

"Sounds like you're calling a lie a white lie, but it's still a lie." Chris frowned. "But maybe I'm being judgmental or in the role of devil's advocate."

"I wouldn't have messaged you guys if I didn't believe you had wisdom to share."

"Ol' man Chris has plenty to spare." Tuck smirked. "But I'm actually on the fence for this one. If you tell the world this story, it could indeed help you. But if you don't, what's gonna happen? Will the internet trolls continue to trash your reputation enough you end up being canceled and never work again?" Tuck tipped his hat back to scratch his head. "My heart goes out to you, man. There's no easy next step. Just whatever you do, be prepared for the consequences. That's about all I have as far as wisdom goes."

"I appreciate you guys. The producer has already made noise about the morality clause in my contract. Unfortunately some endorsers are also getting antsy. I woke up to see #cancelSMA trending on Twitter. I'm afraid of what will happen if I don't do something to change the narrative."

Chris nodded. "I can't imagine being in that position. If you choose to go through with this, please know I'll continue to pray for you. Just because I don't approve, doesn't mean I won't still have your back."

Chris's remarks hit his heart like lead, but Lamont wanted the honesty. "'Preciate that."

"Likewise," Tuck said. "I'll be praying too."

"What does your mom say?" Chris asked.

Lamont's mouth dried. "I didn't ask her opinion."

Tuck whistled, and Chris shook his head.

"Guess that's the next person I should talk to?"

"And the last," Chris said.

"Agreed. Find out what your mom thinks, then finish the convo with Nevaeh," Tuck said. He peered over his shoulder, then turned back to the phone. "Gotta go."

Chris seconded the sentiment, and Lamont placed his phone in his pocket after ending the call. A glance at his watch told him his mom was probably finishing up her yoga session with the instructor who came by twice a week. He headed downstairs to his in-home gym.

What would his mom think? And why couldn't he shake the apprehension?

He opened the glass door and grinned. His mom sat cross-legged on the yoga mat, a peaceful smile on her face.

"You know it's creepy to just watch a person, right?" She opened one eye in a squint.

"Says the woman who watched me sleeping hundreds of times over the years."

"A mother's prerogative." She opened both eyes and raised a hand toward him. "Help me up, please."

"Sure." He pulled her up, thankful she didn't feel as light as when she'd gone through chemo last year. "How was your session?"

"Fantastic as always. One day I need to follow yoga with a massage."

"Let me know, and I'll arrange it."

She patted his cheek. "I know you would. You take great care of me. Sometimes I think you do too much."

"You gave me life. I could never do enough to repay you." It had been him and his mom forever.

"I didn't do it to be paid."

"I know, Mom."

She eyed him. "Do you?"

"Not why I came down here." He grinned.

"Why did you? Is everything okay? Something else about the photo?" Her brow furrowed with concern.

"Sort of." He swallowed. "Bryan suggested that Nevaeh and I fake a relationship. I got Chris and Tuck's opinion on it all, and now I'm asking for yours."

Her perfectly arched eyebrows raised. "Fake how?"

"Tell the world we've been dating but abstaining from the sexual side of a relationship until we get to the altar." He shrugged. "Something to that effect. I'm sure Bryan's statement will be more eloquent if we both agree to it."

"So Nevaeh is considering this?" She studied him.

"Yes, ma'am."

"Hmm." She placed her hands on her hips, a faraway look coasting into her brown eyes.

Lamont studied his mother. She was petite, about the same height as Nevaeh, and had a skin tone that reminded him of some pottery they owned. But other than the color of her skin and the shape of her ears and nose, Lamont couldn't see much similarity between his mom's looks and his own. His forehead was broader, his mouth fuller and wider, his eyes darker. Family always said he was the spitting image of his dad, but perhaps because he died so young, people wanted to immortalize Robert Booker in Lamont's features.

He blinked, focusing back on the issue at hand. "Mom?"

She turned to face him, a serious expression on her face. "I think you should do it."

"Really?" Not at all what he'd thought she'd say. "Why?"

"Do you know how rare it is for someone in Hollywood to share your same beliefs? Values? Morals, even?"

"Yeah." He rubbed the back of his neck.

"Then you can understand how important it is for you to be a role model to those watching."

He rocked back on his heels. "Yeah, but lying to go about it? I don't know. It seems selfish, not to mention asking a lot of Nevaeh."

"It may be all of that. After all, we're viewing this from our lens, our perspective. But maybe some good can come from this."

"Like what?" he asked skeptically.

A soft smile curved her lips. "I have a few ideas."

Chill bumps broke across his arms. "I don't like that look. Maybe this isn't a good idea."

Mom grabbed his face, pulling him down to stare right into his eyes. "Trust your mom, but only do what Nevaeh agrees to and continue to espouse your beliefs. You hear me?"

"Yes, ma'am."

"Good." She patted his cheek. "I'm off to have a girls' day with Claire. Let me know how your meeting with Nevaeh goes."

"Have a good time."

"Thanks, baby. I'll be praying."

Wasn't everyone? He sighed. Now to pray that he and Nevaeh could agree on the terms of their arrangement.

Seven

had full armor on. Yes, the spiritual armor, but more specifically, my glamour armor—full makeup, maxi dress, painted nails, and accessories. If I was going to pose as the superstar's girlfriend, then I needed to step up my fashion game. Usually, I went for comfort, hence the maxi dress, but if Lamont Booker accepted my proposal, then the newly added shapewear would become a lasting staple in my wardrobe.

Not that I had a problem with my shape, but Hollywood and all the keyboard crusaders who followed our story sure would. I'd already seen the comments. Speaking of which, I turned off the radio talk show that was currently speculating on my identity. Couldn't some other actor put their foot in their mouth and take the spotlight off us? Then again, there was nothing entertainment news liked to do more than exhaust a subject until people willingly went out to create the next breaking news.

I knocked on the door leading from the garage to the house, thankful Kyle had directed me to park right inside the garage in case reporters were staking out the property. I'd assumed the rest of the vultures would be perched in the trees like the first one. Then again, maybe they weren't pack animals.

Kyle led me into the home, and I made my way through the main floor and found Lamont standing in the living room, gazing out the windows. Was he fixated on the LA skyline, or were his thoughts tossing at the possibilities before us? Not that I could fault him the skyline viewing. The skyscrapers rising in the distance made a pretty picture.

I cleared my throat, and he swung around.

"Oh, good, you're here."

"Yep." My lips smacked as more words tried to form. Anxiety had ratcheted up to DEFCON levels, and I could literally feel my body shaking.

"Have a seat."

I nodded. *Lord, please help.*

"Have you come to a decision?" he asked softly.

"I have. Do you still want me to pretend to be your girlfriend?" Because if he didn't, my decision could remain a secret.

He blew out a breath, rubbing a hand over his head. "I've been giving that a lot of thought."

"And?" I bit down on my lip. Did that mean he wasn't for it?

"I don't want to lie. I'd like to do as little of that as possible."

"Agreed." Suddenly my shapewear didn't feel so constrictive.

He gazed straight into my eyes, his dark eyes twin pools of uncertainty. "I would like to take you out on a date. And another one and another one, until all of this dies down, and we amicably part ways."

Wow. Though I had come here to commit to the role of fake girlfriend, there was something earthshaking about hearing him say he wanted to date me.

"Well, isn't that what pretending is all about?"

He shook his head. "No. I'm saying, if at all possible, I don't want to pretend. I genuinely want to get to know you. When people ask me questions, I want to be able to truthfully say we're dating. We're taking things slowly. We'll see what happens." His knee started bouncing. "The parting ways amicably is if we feel there's nothing there."

My stomach tensed. *Wait. What?* My mouth dropped open as I struggled for a response. "So . . . you want to date for *real*, so we won't be lying?"

"Yes. Are you comfortable with that?"

Was he serious? Did he think I was going to turn down Mr. Hollywood asking me—Nevaeh Richards, regular ol' hair stylist—to be his actual girlfriend? I was not that saved.

"I'm good with that." Two mental claps on the back for sounding calm and collected because my inner self was squealing like a '90s preteen at a Backstreet Boys concert or a Gen Xer at a New Kids on the Block Mixtape Tour show.

Relief coursed over Lamont's face. "Great. I'm still willing to help you. I can ensure you get a key hair stylist position on a movie set, or if you need some money . . ." His voice trailed.

If he did that, wouldn't that taint our agreement to date for real?

But don't you want to be key hair stylist?

Don't sell yourself and lose your soul, Nevaeh.

Darn my two selves. But the better half of me was right. "No, you don't have to do that."

"Are you sure?" His brows rose.

"Yes. Let's just . . . get to know each other better." My pulse beat an erratic rhythm in my neck.

A half smile tilted his lips, and I remembered how he'd earned his spot on the cover of *People* magazine.

"Great. You free right now? Want to go out to brunch?"

"Yes. That works." I'd skipped breakfast knowing I would

see him. Who could eat when your stomach tossed more than Willow Smith whipping her hair back and forth?

"Perfect. I'll just call Bryan real quick and let him know what's going on, and we can make sure we agree with his statement."

I nodded, too stunned by the turn of events. I was about to go out with Lamont Booker. Legitimately date one of the most famous men in Hollywood. How was this my life? How was I going to tell my parents? Nora? And what did Ms. Rosie think of the whole situation? We didn't have an appointment for a few more days, and I'd been avoiding her presence. I didn't want her ashamed to know me.

"Yeah, we've agreed to start a relationship. . . . No, for real. . . . Mm-hmm."

I listened as Lamont Booker—no, *Lamont*—made noises here and there. Finally, he turned and motioned me closer.

He hit a button on his phone, then placed it on the coffee table. "Hey, Bry, you're on speaker."

"Hey, Nevaeh."

"Hi."

"Lamont wants me to read the statement I've put together to make sure you're good with it."

"Bring it on." Time to see if Mr. Agent Man was worth his money.

He chuckled. "I'll have a heading on here that it's a statement approved by you two, put out by me."

"Got it."

"All right. Here goes." He cleared his throat. "Since Lamont Booker rededicated his life to Christ, he has lived his life upholding the values that glorify God. A certain picture was recently sold to the press, and questions around it have circulated. Some people have speculated Lamont is no longer adhering to his belief of saving sexual intimacy until marriage."

Lamont grimaced but continued to listen while I had to make sure not to lose my composure at the deeply personal nature of the statement. Was this what I was signing up for? Relinquishing my privacy?

Oh, Lord, what have I done?

"He would like people to know that the woman in the photo is his girlfriend, also a Christian, and the photo in question was illegally gained. It in no way declares a step away from his beliefs. The couple has mutually put boundaries in place to ensure they do not cross any lines regarding intimacy. A more in-depth interview will be coming in the near future." Bryan paused. "Sound good?"

"You didn't mention my name," I said.

"The moment you two sit down with our interviewer of choice, your anonymity will vanish. Lamont thought it best to give you time to adjust."

Thank you, I mouthed.

Lamont nodded.

"I appreciate that, Bryan," I said.

"Great. I'll get it posted to your socials, Lamont. I'll also send the statement to a couple of entertainment news stations."

"Thanks, Bry."

"Nevaeh, I'll also send you a nondisclosure agreement to sign. We don't want this ever getting out."

I reared back. They didn't trust me?

"Bry, is that necessary?" Lamont asked. He furrowed his brow, a look of discomfort crossing his face. Goodness. His brooding look was too fine for words.

"It's just to protect you, that's all."

"Fine."

"Great. I'll fax it over." Bryan paused. "So where's the happy couple going out to eat?" His voice held a full-on smirk, even if I couldn't see him to verify what my ears heard.

"Le Feu."

I stifled a gasp. Did Lamont have a reservation already, or was he so famous he could just walk in any time he felt like it? Le Feu had to be *the* trendiest spot for brunch in LA. A quick glance at my outfit reassured me I wouldn't be considered an outsider—at least, not because of what I wore. However, people would know I wasn't someone famous the moment I walked in there.

My palms dampened. What if I couldn't do this? Yes, Lamont said I didn't have to play a part, but could I be his real girlfriend? The world would expect some glamorous woman to be on the arm of an A-lister. All I could be was Nevaeh Richards from Inglewood.

I shook out my arms as Lamont ended the call and slid his cell into his slacks pocket. The room fell silent for a couple of beats. I inhaled, drawing in a shaky breath. "Shall we do this?"

His jet-black eyes met mine. "Let's." He held out a hand, and I placed mine into his.

Tingles erupted as if my hand had been sleeping up until this moment. "Do we hold hands on the first date?" I asked, trying to cover my nerves as we headed toward the garage.

"For this one, yes. Even though Le Feu is paparazzi-free, you never know who'll be watching the place."

True. My head bobbed up and down as I thought through his statement. "What if I'm opposed to hand-holding?"

He dropped my hand faster than a running back fumbling the ball. "I'm sorry. I should've asked."

I laughed and took his hand in mine once more. "It was a question. We didn't really talk about boundaries, though Bryan's statement says we have."

"Oh." His grip relaxed. "I won't go past any line you draw. I'll ask permission for everything." He raised our hands. "Sorry for that misstep."

"It's okay. I wouldn't have put my hand in yours if I'd truly been uncomfortable." Plus, I had wanted to know what it would feel like.

Lamont opened the car door, and I slipped into the passenger seat. I ran my hands along the leather interior. Everything gleamed and shined as if the vehicle were fresh off the lot. As we drove, the silence began to prick at me.

"Should we be talking? Getting to know each other?" I asked, studying his profile.

He glanced at me. "Sorry. I'm a bit nervous. It's been a while since I've dated."

"How long's a while?" I knew he got saved about five years ago. That was the last time his name had been linked with a woman and the term *serious relationship*.

"Since Diva."

I still couldn't believe someone chose that as their celebrity name. She was born with a stereotypical name—Jane? Sarah? I couldn't remember—but chose to go by Diva Jones.

"Have you seen her since?" Did he have any hidden skeletons regarding his ex?

"You can't help it in this corner of the world. I do make it a point to avoid her when possible. Nothing about her is good." He winced. "Sorry, I shouldn't have said that."

"Well, since we're dating, I think telling your current girlfriend"—I shivered—"about your old one makes sense."

"Right." He rubbed his chin. "How about you? When's the last time you were in a relationship?"

My cheeks heated. "Um, two years ago."

"What happened? If you don't mind me asking?"

I did. Only hadn't I just told him honesty was warranted? But he was a celebrity, and I was not. My story sounded infinitely more pathetic. "Uh, well, it's a common tale. We dated for a year, he found someone better, and I decided to take a break from dating."

Lamont grinned and winked at me. "Now you've upgraded."

I laughed. "Oh my word, are you vain? Is that something new I'm going to learn about you?"

He barked out a laugh. "Actually, my friends tease me about it, but I never thought of myself like that."

"How can you not, Mr. SMA? I'm not sure I wouldn't be strutting around town if I'd been marked with a female equivalent of the title."

Wait, was there an equivalent? Maybe America's Sweetheart was as close as celebrity women got with the title. Or Diva, though now Ms. Jones had ruined that connotation for the rest of us.

Lamont laughed again. "So you're funny? Is that the new thing I'm learning?"

"I'm not. I promise." I shrug. "It's a defense mechanism. My nerves spike and jokes spill out of my mouth as if I have no filter." Like talking too much. I really wanted to know what age filters kicked in at. Though I did know plenty of older women who walked around without them. Maybe it wasn't an age thing but personality?

"Better than being scripted. I have to have a writer feed me jokes before I can get a genuine laugh."

I stared at him. "You don't joke at all?"

"It's not that I don't, it's that they're terrible. Worse than dad jokes."

"So like bad puns?" I asked, trying to come to grips with Lamont Booker being bad at something.

"Sure, we'll leave it at that."

71

"This should be interesting to see." I rubbed my hands.

He groaned. "Trust me, it's not." He slowed down, then stopped at the light.

I looked around and noticed we were near the restaurant. The anxiety that had died down in shared laughter came roaring back. "We're almost there," I whispered.

Lamont reached out his hand and laced his fingers between mine. "We've got this."

"You're an actor. You have experience playing a part. I'm the novice here."

Lamont squeezed my hand. "Just be yourself, and I won't let you fall."

I stared into his dark eyes. "Don't make promises you can't keep."

* * *

Tuck
What happened with Nevaeh?

Chris
I've been wondering the same thing. Been praying for you, man.

Tuck
Likewise

5 min later

Tuck
Lamont, you there?

Chris
Should he be on set right now?

Tuck
Maybe he's avoiding us because he thinks we won't like his answer.

Chris

I already said I'd support him regardless, didn't I? 🥴

Tuck

Maybe they went on a date, and he wants to tell us about it later.

Chris

I'll do an internet search.

2 min later

Chris

They've been spotted eating at Le Feu. Social media is going crazy. Some of these comments are downright hostile. 🙁

Tuck

Guess we need to ramp up our prayers. That poor girl is being thrown to the wolves.

Chris

We're praying for both of you, Lamont.

Tuck

Amen and amen. I'll even ask my folks and Piper to pray.

Chris

Show-off. You know I don't have an army of folks to pray.

Tuck

That's okay. Your prayers will be added to ours, and it'll be a spiritual army of prayer. Hey, gotta run. Talk later.

Chris

Same. And Lamont, we want a text or FaceTime to know everything is okay when you get a chance.

Eight

veryone's staring.

You'd think he'd be used to the spotlight, but knowing it was because of Nevaeh made the attention different. Lamont couldn't remember the last time he'd walked into Le Feu with a woman on his arm, which might have contributed to some of the rubbernecking. Fortunately, the place had a reputation for being a spot celebrities could relax and enjoy their meal sans paparazzi.

Now here he was with Nevaeh Richards, his mother's personal hair stylist.

He winced inwardly. Lamont had always thought he'd remained humble in the face of the overwhelming opulence of Hollywood. Only now that this whole ordeal had blown up in his face, he was beginning to think snobbery and an elitist attitude had snuck in after all. *I'm sorry, Lord. I'm trying to keep my eyes on You.*

The maître d' stopped at a round table for two and pulled a chair out for Lamont's new girlfriend. She smiled, thanking him. Lamont scanned the room as he sat down. There were some faces he recognized and ones he should probably say hello to once he and Nevaeh finished their meal.

"I've never been here before," she murmured, picking up her menu.

"You'll love it. The chef is top-notch."

"He should be with these prices," she groused.

Lamont held back a chuckle. "Well, it is a two-star Michelin restaurant."

She stared at him. "And that means?"

"Uh"—his face heated—"it means it's a very prestigious restaurant. Three stars is the best, but that's rare. They don't hand those out like boxes of candy."

"If you know of a place handing out free candy, by all means share." She placed the menu down. "I have no idea what I'm supposed to order. Why does everything have separate prices?"

Her words were snarky, but Lamont could detect the underlying fear and nerves. He reached a hand across the table, covering hers with his palm. "Breathe," he spoke quietly. "I'm paying, and I assure you, I can afford the prices."

Her dark brown eyes studied him.

"I promise." He didn't know why he felt the need to reiterate, but he did. "I'll pay for everything. You'll never have to worry about that."

"I'm not a gold digger," she stated. She slid her hand from underneath his. "I'd never want you to think that."

"I *know* that." He'd known her over a year, and she'd never raised her rates for his mother nor asked him for money to fund a start-up or whatever else people asked rich people for. He'd had plenty of those conversations with relatives crawling out of the woodwork. "Believe me. Those types are easy to spot in this town, and I know you don't fall in that category."

She nodded. "Thank you."

Lamont picked up his menu, staring unseeingly at the words. "Was that our first fight?"

Nevaeh laughed. "No. But that was definitely something." She placed her chin in her hand. "What should I order? Or should I be old-fashioned and let you order for me?"

He grinned at her. "Are you feeling daring?"

"I am now." She winked. "Bring it on, Mr. SMA."

He laughed outright. "Are you going to call me that the whole time we're together?"

"I think I should." Something flitted through her eyes. "We'll consider it a pet name."

"Does that mean I should have a term of endearment for you?"

She shrugged a shoulder. "I don't know. Do you like pet names?"

"Sometimes they're weird. Like *honey*—honey's a real thing. Why would I call you something I drizzle on my post-workout snack?"

Nevaeh leaned forward. "What kind of healthy snack uses honey?"

"One that involves bananas, nut butter, and a rice cake."

She faked a shudder. "Does that mean you don't enjoy Ben & Jerry's or Häagen-Dazs?"

"Not when I'm filming. When I'm not, I usually get a Coolhaus ice cream sandwich."

"Yum." Nevaeh sat back in her seat as the server came to take their order. She gave Lamont a nod, so he ordered two avocado toasts to start, a shrimp appetizer, and the Le Feu brunch waffles, which came with an amazing side of berries with maple-flavored cream.

When the server walked away, Nevaeh spoke. "Should we order a meat dish too?"

Lamont rested his steepled hands on the table. "We can wait and see how full you are. Sometimes their portions are a bit much."

She snorted. "At a fancy restaurant? I can't see myself getting full." She froze, eyes widening a fraction. "Not that I necessarily eat a lot. I have curves because I have curves."

He held up his hands. "No judgment."

"But you'll get some. I've seen the comments on social media already."

His jaw tightened. He had a bad feeling they'd only ramp up. "You know the media is toxic, right? Don't read the comments. They're never helpful." There were far more trolls spewing hate than there were encouragers spreading cheer.

"Right." A stiff smile replaced the open expression that had been there only moments before.

Lamont wanted to groan in frustration. Seriously, the media *was* toxic. They would dehumanize anyone, given the chance. He didn't know exactly what Nevaeh wanted him to say.

"Help me out here." He went out on a limb. "This is new to me. It's been a while since I had a girlfriend, and she wasn't exactly a very good one." He rubbed the back of his neck. "I don't want to say the wrong thing, but I've got a feeling I already did."

Nevaeh studied him a moment before speaking. "This is going to be awkward until it's not. I don't know if you *can* say the right thing in this situation. I don't have the Hollywood figure, and there will be people who'll speak on that ad nauseam. I guess when it comes down to it . . ." She bit her lip. "I just want to know you'll have my back. Even if you agree with them."

His eyes bugged out. "I don't agree with them. You look great." She was pretty, especially with those eye-catching dimples, just not his usual type.

Granted, his type usually landed him some vapid women who only wanted to launch their careers to new levels or take from him in some other way. All the women he'd dated in the past had the same hairstyle, fashion sense, and knack for making him run to vices that had led him away from the Lord. So to say he needed to change his type was an understatement. Only now, Lamont simply wanted what the Lord wanted. But how did that translate into physical attraction?

"Do you know how long it took to look like this?" She arched a brow.

If she stood and put her hands on her curvy hips, Lamont would have no choice but to laugh. Not that he was laughing *at* her, but she was kind of cute when irritated. "No, ma'am. I'm assuming dressing for a date is different than the time it takes to get through hair and makeup on a set."

Besides, he really didn't care to try to understand fashion. That's why he employed a personal stylist for himself. He only had so much brain storage, and none of it was devoted to fashion trends.

Nevaeh's lips twitched. "Let's just say, shapewear and makeup are part of my arsenal."

"I've seen you without makeup; you don't need it. And I'm assuming shapewear is like compression clothing or something?"

She nodded.

"Do you wear it when you do my mom's hair?"

"No."

"Then you don't need that either."

She ducked her head, peeking up at him. Lamont never counted Nevaeh for shy. Were the sarcasm and sass a cover-up for that as well?

"We good?" he asked.

Slowly, she lifted her chin. "We're good."

He grinned. "Fantastic. Food is here." He pointed with his head. "Let's pray, then eat."

After Lamont said a short prayer, he pointed toward the

line of shrimp on the appetizer tray. "This is a spicy appetizer with sauces going from lowest heat to hottest." He gestured from the right to left. "We can halve them and make it a challenge."

Nevaeh's eyes sparkled with amusement. "What do I win if I can withstand the heat?"

"A bottle of Tums."

She laughed. "Fair enough. What about if I lose?"

"The kitchen has milk."

"Okay." She nodded. "Let's do this."

He cut the first shrimp in half. Nevaeh grabbed a piece, popping it into her mouth without qualm.

"That's definitely low heat. I wouldn't even qualify that as spicy."

"That's how they lure you in." He ate his half while she cut up the next shrimp.

Before they could say anything else, a shadow fell over their table. Lamont looked up to see Blake Smythe. He rose to his feet, shaking the Emmy award–winning actor's hand.

"Hey, good to see you." Lamont gestured to Nevaeh. "This is my girlfriend, Nevaeh. Nevaeh, this is Blake."

"Nice to meet you." She gave a dimpled grin.

"Nice to meet you as well. I didn't realize you were here with someone special." Blake squinted, scrutinizing Lamont.

He wanted to roll his eyes. They were obviously on a date. Blake would've had to be living under a rock not to see the media storm over him and Nevaeh, and since the Hollywood legend stayed in the news more than Lamont, that was highly unlikely.

"No worries. We were just challenging each other to the heat test."

Blake laughed. "I do that with my wife. Hey, are you going to the charity event in a couple of weeks?"

Actually, Lamont hadn't planned on attending it. So many of the celebrities showed up to get the crowd's approval. Lamont preferred to keep his charitable donations anonymous. However, that might be a good place to help Nevaeh get used to the limelight. "When was the RSVP due?"

"Today, actually. So if you haven't made a decision, now's your chance." He punched Lamont in the shoulder.

Even though it was light, Lamont didn't appreciate the breach of his personal bubble. "Thanks for the reminder."

"No problem." Blake slapped Lamont on the back. "See you around." He turned to Nevaeh. "And nice to meet you."

"You as well."

Lamont took his seat, glad he didn't have to worry about being touched again.

As soon as Blake was far away, Nevaeh leaned forward. "That was Blake Smythe."

"You a fan?"

Her mouth dropped. "He was on SNL. Not to mention every soap opera known to man before moving on to prime time. And he has an extensive filmography."

"So you *are* a fan." He smirked.

She rolled her eyes. "No. I haven't seen every movie, and I don't rush to see a new one either. But I can recognize a legend."

Now it was time for Lamont to lean forward and whisper. "I think I can keep you as a girlfriend now. I can't stand that man."

She chuckled. "Don't like getting hit while a person talks?"

"Not at all. In what way is that fun?"

"Eh." She shrugged. "People who hit for emphasis are their own breed."

"Agreed."

"What charity event was he talking about?"

"You know *Sands of Time*?" The longtime soap opera was an iconic part of television history.

Nevaeh nodded.

"Well, they throw a charity event each year. It's the who's who of daytime TV. I've gotten an invitation every year since I appeared on an episode a few years ago. This year they're widening their scope to include other industry professionals because they're also celebrating fifty years running with no cancelation in sight."

"What organization do they support?"

Lamont tried to recall what it said on the invitation. "I can't remember." He grabbed his cell. "Let me look at the Evite."

"No paper invitation?"

"They send two. Paper and email."

She nodded.

"Donations go to a foundation intent on getting food to school-age kids in need."

"How can you *not* donate?"

"I usually do. They give that option instead of attending." He paused. "However, this year it might be good to make an appearance. Give you a chance to get used to being around a lot of celebrities."

"You do know I work on movie sets." She arched a brow.

"Of course I do. But doing their hair is different than rubbing elbows and letting paparazzi take a ridiculous number of photos."

"Good point." She gulped. "Okay. RSVP for two. Then tell me how I should dress."

"Uh, maybe we should ask my mom or stylist. I have no idea."

She shook her head, but her lips curved into a full smile. "You're helpless."

"No. I just recognize when I need help. I'll ask my mom if

she can take you shopping. She's on some of my accounts, which means I can pay for the dress."

Nevaeh's mouth dropped. "Lamont . . ."

He held up a hand. "Remember my promise from earlier."

"Maybe." Her nose wrinkled.

"You do. It's fine."

She blew out a breath. "Fine. But I'm going to figure out a way to do something nice for you."

"Deal."

The rest of their brunch was spent getting to know each other. For the first time in a long time, Lamont relaxed a little. If their relationship didn't naturally progress to more, maybe Lamont could walk away with another friend, something he had few of under the Hollywood sign.

Unfortunately, Tuck and Chris were in other parts of the country. The chances of them flying out for any premiere or event Lamont was part of were pretty slim. Tuck was married to the horses he trained, and Chris couldn't stop talking about conservation efforts long enough to think of anything else.

Or maybe Lamont was being harsh. They were all workaholics. Even this time with Nevaeh felt like a business meeting. Not that he'd tell her that. No, the best he could hope for was turning his temporary girlfriend into a friend. True love just wasn't in the cards for actors. Experience had taught him that.

Learning that Diva hadn't wanted to date him for him had bruised his ego. Learning the lengths to which she'd gone to orchestrate their meeting in the first place soured him on dating in Hollywood. Her other actions—the ones he liked to stuff into the farthest recesses of his mind—had almost ruined his belief that good women existed. Nevaeh not wanting to be compensated for their new relationship had him part thankful and part wary. Was it a trick? Would she flip the script on him? He could only pray that she was the real deal.

Nine

I leaned back against my bedroom door, eyes squeezed shut as my brain tried to catch up on the morning I'd experienced.

Had I really sat at a table for two with the famous Lamont Booker while legend Blake Smythe came to our table to remind my new boyfriend of a charity event we'd *both* be attending? Since said event was in a couple of weeks—where I'd publicly appear on Lamont's arm as his girlfriend—that gave me time to acclimate to this whole change. Until then . . .

Pinch me!

Mrs. Hazelton had cheered with a loud whoop when I walked up to my front stoop. She'd been sitting on hers when I came home. Apparently, Bryan's PR statement was already circulating, and people were now trying to place me. She'd shown me how people were guessing I was some sort of secret heiress while others assumed I'd been in the latest streaming show.

Oh, and I'm sorry, but not all Black people look alike. They'd tried to name me as some other Black celebrities. I could only hope Black Twitter would rake them over the coals for their barely concealed racist behavior.

I pushed off the door and raised my maxi dress, reaching under the hem. It was time to get rid of Maxine the Shapewear. She'd done her job, and I could no longer inhale a full breath. I shimmied, looking like a backup dancer in Beyoncé's latest music video, trying to release my body from the prison of women's fashion. I exhaled a sigh of relief as the body shaper fell to the ground. I barely stepped out of it before I catapulted myself onto my queen-size bed. The lilac bedspread with gray flowers cushioned my fall as I rolled onto my back to stare up at the ceiling.

Lord, how was this morning real?

Lamont said he wanted to really date, but part of me couldn't help but think he was merely presenting a role. Maybe he was a method actor, and in order not to lie, he'd convinced himself he wanted a relationship with me. Because—get real—the man had barely spared me two glances before our picture was splashed all over every single media outlet known to man. I think it even reached newscasters' desks in Asia.

My cell phone rang, and I squeezed my eyes shut. If my name had been leaked already, I was in deep.

My hand slid around the covers, searching for the mobile playing Dante Bowe's "Joyful." I grinned in triumph when my fingers connected with the cold case keeping my phone safe.

"Hello?" Why hadn't I looked at caller ID before accepting the call?

"Nevaeh, hey, it's Monica. Do you have a moment?"

A ragged exhale escaped me. "Sure. What's up?"

"Danica got food poisoning. Can you come in? I know it's short notice and all, but I need another girl for the load of clients coming in this afternoon."

Ugh. Danica was always finding some way to get out of working. Why did Monica still employ her? And why was

Danica paying a rental fee for her chair at the salon if she was never there?

"All right. Give me an hour." I needed to change into something more salon suited than *I just had brunch with my Hollywood A-list boyfriend*. Or maybe I should still think of this as a fake relationship so my feelings wouldn't get hurt when he revealed it had all been a ruse to keep from lying.

I shook my head. Even my thoughts confused me.

"That's fantastic. I appreciate it so much, Nevaeh." Monica rushed out a good-bye, then hung up.

Good thing I'd already pulled out a black T-shirt and cropped leggings from my dresser drawer. The apron Monica required us to wear in her salon would keep my clothes from getting stained. I took time to grab some gray snakeskin hoops and a wide matching headband, twisting my black hair and securing the rounded bun with a hair tie. Just because I dressed down didn't mean I couldn't accessorize. Plus, what if salon clients recognized me? Wouldn't they expect me to look my best?

I winced, imagining the fishbowl that was slowly encasing me.

I set my purse from earlier onto the bed, then slid the mirrored closet door to the side and rummaged through the shelves for my backpack purse. It was my work accessory of choice. It had almost made it into the trash can from a set I'd been working on two summers ago. The costume designer thought the bag too awful for anyone to own. Since I didn't see a thing wrong with it—other than the fluorescent green color begging for me to put on a pair of sunglasses—I asked if I could keep it. With a wave of her hand and a *good riddance* curl of her lips, the designer made me the proud owner and future trendsetter of said bag.

No lie, fluorescent color accessories were the new *it* thing.

My mom grumbled about the '80s making a comeback, but secretly, I think she longed to throw on some slouch socks, a scrunchie, and a rock band T-shirt. Or maybe even a New Edition boy band shirt.

I took the 405 to the 2 to get to Beverly Hills, where The Mane Do was situated. Monica had decorated the shop in an Old Hollywood style. Black walls, silver mirrors, and stenciled words here and there to finish out the décor. She only played songs about California or performed by California natives. I snuck into the shop via the back entrance and went to the stylist room. Gray lockers covered one wall. I opened mine, stuffing my backpack into the metal container and switching it out for the black apron that hung on the inside hook. A silver outline of a Black woman sporting a huge afro was centered on the bib with *The Mane Do* stenciled under the figure. I slipped my cell into the pocket lined into my leggings, then secured my locker.

A Snoop Dogg song filtered through the speakers as I entered the styling area. I chuckled to myself as various ladies cheered, dancing as best they could while sitting under the hair dryer. I walked up to Monica and smiled.

"Afternoon. I made it."

She glanced at the clock, then focused on the curling iron in her hand. "Great. Tell Jewel you're here and available to take the next client."

"Any client or only Danica's?"

Monica paused, manipulating the curling iron to leave a fresh ringlet in the customer's hair. Then her brown eyes snapped to mine. "I already told her you'll take Danica's if they don't want to reschedule with her. However, we're also starting to get backlogged, so any customer who doesn't want to wait, you get."

Yay! That meant more tips for me. "Got it. I'll let her know."

Monica said nothing, her focus already on the woman sitting in her chair. Judging from the number of ringlets in her hair, I guessed a bridesmaid or the bride herself.

I walked across the black-tiled floor to the front, where women sat on tufted benches, waiting their turns. Jewel stood behind the counter, purple braids situated in a beehive atop her head.

"Hey, Jewel."

Her head popped up from the magazine in front of her. I relayed everything Monica had informed me of. Instead of Jewel agreeing, she squinted.

"What?" I asked. I resisted the urge to turn and see if anyone had walked up behind me. Surely that scrutiny wasn't for me.

"I only see you in an apron and dark clothing," she said.

"Work uniform." There wasn't an official uniform, per se, but no stylist walked into The Mane Do without a dark shirt and equally dark bottoms. I just chose leggings. If I had to stand on my feet for hours, I might as well be comfortable.

"I know. But I imagine you'd look different in something else."

I laughed. "I imagine you would too." Even though Jewel was a receptionist and not a stylist, she still wore a black blouse and black jeans.

"What do you look like with your hair down?" Jewel asked.

"Okay." I leaned my forearm on the counter. "What's with all the weird questions?"

"It's just you look an awful lot like Lamont Booker's new main squeeze."

My breath hitched as spots danced before my eyes. Jewel didn't know how to keep a secret. How could I expect her to keep this revelation under wraps? I swallowed, wishing I had gum instead of the dry desert my mouth had just become. "What are the odds?"

Jewel arched a perfectly thick eyebrow. "Probably better than winning the lottery, which is one in forty-two million."

My mouth dropped. "Considering the metro area has about eighteen million people, yeah, I guess the odds are better."

Jewel rolled her eyes as if my sarcasm was as annoying as the prying questions she was throwing my way. "Crystal needs a trim." Jewel pointed to a thin woman perusing her phone.

"Thanks." I pivoted and walked up to the woman, pulling for my most professional tone of voice. "Good afternoon, I'm Nevaeh, and I'll be your stylist today."

Crystal looked up from her phone, scanned my figure from head to toe, then stood. "All I need is a trim." She flipped her weave over her shoulder. "I told the last woman that I didn't want this too long."

"It suits your face."

She paused, then tilted her head. "So you don't think I should trim it?"

I slid a lock of her hair through my fingers, pausing to examine the ends. This wasn't the best weave I'd seen. In fact, the ends were downright shaggy. "No, I think a trim will only enhance your look." I dropped the lock. "Maybe take two inches off to make it really shine."

Relief filled Crystal's eyes. "Sounds perfect."

I motioned for her to follow me to my booth and threw a cape around her neck once she sat. I reached for a brush. "I'm assuming we're keeping your current part?"

She froze. "What's wrong with it?"

"Nothing. Sometimes people come in and change it up. I was simply trying to gauge your preference."

Air went out of her like a flat tire. "Yes. This same part. Just the two inches off."

I nodded. My mind drifted from brunch to Lamont. What

was he doing now? Earlier he'd said today was an off day for set as was tomorrow. Tomorrow we were supposed to get together again.

Seriously, how was this my life? Me, Nevaeh Richards, planning an outing with one of Hollywood's most recognizable actors. I'd pinch myself if my hands weren't already occupied cutting hair. *Focus on Crystal.*

I blew out a breath and did just that. She seemed very nervous, eyes widening with each snip of the scissors. What she couldn't yet see was how the weave was coming to life.

"Just wait," I murmured. "You'll look fabulous when I'm done."

"Are you sure?" Crystal asked hesitantly.

"Positive."

Finished, I spun her around, allowing Crystal to take in her reflection. My heart picked up speed as she looked into the mirror. Did she like it? I gave her a handheld mirror, then spun her around so she could see the back. She looked stunning if I did say so myself.

"Oh my word," she whispered.

I tensed. "Is that not what you were envisioning?" Had I done something wrong?

"No." She shook her head, watching as the hair slid right back into place like a hair commercial. "This is so much better."

Relief poured through me, and I grinned. Another satisfied client.

Clients moved in and out of my chair with a swiftness, but each one left delighted with their style. My mind went on autopilot as time clicked by. Soon, I looked up from the leaving customer to see I had about another hour before quitting time.

What would I do about dinner? There were a few food

trucks that parked near my neighborhood. One of them would win the eenie meenie miney moe festivities and provide me with dinner. Until then, the little Dove chocolates I stored on my counter would have to power me through. I balled up the purple wrapper and tossed it into the trash, making a swoosh sound.

"Nevaeh, you have another client," Jewel said.

I turned away from the trash can with a ready smile on my lips. "Good evening."

The young woman's eyes widened. "No way!" she screeched.

My head jerked back, and my finger raised automatically to rub the ear that was still ringing.

"You're Lamont Booker's girlfriend, aren't you?" she cried.

Lord, sound the trumpet. Only Jesus didn't call me, and a black hole didn't swallow me up, so I switched the subject. "How can I fix your hair for you today?"

She pointed to my empty chair, to me, then dropped her hands. "This is the coolest thing that's ever happened to me. I *told* Shanice that you were just a regular person. I recognized those overalls, and they didn't come from a shop on Rodeo. Only she didn't believe me. She said Lamont Booker *had* to be dating a celebrity. Swore she saw you on Hulu's *Love and Lost*, but I've seen every episode and knew you weren't a cast member." The teen shut her mouth.

Too late. The damage was done. Heads swiveled in the shop, and an evil gleam—okay, so maybe not evil, but definitely predatory—entered Jewel's eyes.

"I said the same thing earlier." She nodded to the teen. "You almost can't tell because of all the black and her hair in an updo." Jewel mimed a bun.

"Oh, you can tell," the teen prattled on. "She's got the prettiest dimples ever. Even when she's not smiling, like now." She gestured toward my face.

I could only imagine it was stuck on stupefied. Something inside snapped, and my spine straightened. "Do you want your hair done or not?"

"By you? Of course!" She sat down. "I can't wait to tell Shanice. Can I take a picture with you?"

My stomach twisted. Nothing had prepared me for this. Had I thought that people would gawk? Of course. Did I think people would talk us up on their social platforms? Without a doubt. Had I ever considered someone wanting to take a picture with me? Nope. Never even crossed my mind.

Was taking a picture with her the right thing? I could only pray it would work to Lamont's favor and not hurt his cause or platform. *Lord, let this be the right thing.*

Ten

Lamont
First date at Le Feu. Think it was a success.

Tuck
What in the devil's den is Le Feu? Some inferno club?

Chris
😂 It's a Michelin star restaurant.

Lamont
Two stars

Tuck
I never understood why people took a tire company's opinion as gold for which restaurants are the best to eat at. I'd rather read Yelp reviews.

Lamont
I picked it because it's paparazzi-free. I didn't want to toss Nevaeh into the deep end.

Chris
Too late. They know who she is.

Lamont
What? How do you know that?!

Tuck

Bro, even I saw that. Some fan snapped a
picture where she works and shared it.

Lamont

Give me a sec, still searching.

Chris

http://thecheese.com/who-is-nevaeh-richards

There you go.

Tuck

That's the one I saw too.

Lamont

No, no, no! She's going to . . . Actually, I have no
idea how she'll react. The picture with the fan
doesn't look so bad.

Tuck

Not at all. The deer on my daddy's walls hold
the same expression.

Chris

Lamont

You need to exit the chat if all you're going to
do is laugh, ol' man.

Chris

That's fine. I've got an interview to do. Peace
out.

Tuck

I've gotta go too. Tell Nevaeh we're praying for
her.

Lamont exited the text thread and hit the speed dial for
Nevaeh's number as he paced out on his balcony. The smog
seemed heavy over the skyscrapers off in the distance. A
foreshadowing of what his girlfriend's—that was still weird
to think—mood would be? Bryan had promised to keep

Nevaeh's name out of the tabloids, which he had, but apparently that didn't help. Not even a full twenty-four hours had passed since the PR statement hit the media outlets, and already she'd been discovered.

"Hey," Nevaeh said, her voice sounding forlorn.

"I saw The Cheese. You okay?"

She scoffed. "I'm surprised you didn't see the breaking news segment on *StarGazer*."

He rubbed his forehead. "How did they discover your identity?"

"I'm guessing the enthusiastic customer at the shop sold it to them or they picked it up from The Cheese." She groaned. "How is this real life?"

Lamont stopped pacing, searching for words to help. "It's not, but it is."

"I hate that that makes sense."

"Me too." He resumed his prowl up and down the walkway. "I thought for sure it would be a few days, maybe even a week or two, before they figured out who you were."

"I certainly didn't think it would be the first day we had brunch." She gasped. "Do you think it was actually Blake Smythe who said something?"

"Why would he?" The actor had his own run-ins with the media. Lamont couldn't imagine him outing someone else.

"To take the heat off of himself. Didn't he just marry again for the fifth time to someone younger than his youngest daughter?"

Lamont grimaced. Blake's newest wife was twenty-six, four years younger than his daughter, actress Jeudi Smythe. "I don't think he's that type of guy."

Nevaeh snorted. "This is Hollywood. I wouldn't put it past him."

"I take it this means your fangirling moment is over."

"No," she drew out. "I'm just upset. Monica told me to leave early because I brought unwanted attention to the shop."

He froze. "She can't do that. Can she? I can have my lawyer look into it."

"No, please don't. It's not like she fired me."

"Well, if she does, let me know. We'll get it taken care of."

"Let's change the subject."

Lamont rubbed the top of his head and resumed his pacing. "If we must. But first, please let me know if you can't handle this—" He winced. He hadn't meant that to come out accusatory. "If this is all too much, then I understand. We can break up." Though did one date constitute the need to break up?

"No, I said I was in. Besides, your reputation isn't repaired yet, and we still haven't done any of the interviews Bryan planned."

Lamont ran a hand over his face. "Are you sure?" His tone dipped low.

"Yes."

How come her resolute answer didn't bring him immediate peace? Would she lie to calm him down? Despite them being in a "relationship," Lamont had no idea how to read Nevaeh.

"Are we still getting together tomorrow?" she asked.

"I want to." He sank into the lounge chair. "We can do breakfast."

"But brunch is so much better. Besides, tomorrow is Saturday, and everyone likes a good brunch in this area."

That was true. Lamont could barely keep the days straight sometimes. "All right. Do you have a specific place you'd like to eat at?"

"No, but let's make it low-key wherever we choose."

Hmm. "Is it okay if we eat in Beverly Hills?" He didn't

really want to venture out of his zip code on the weekend if he didn't have to. Unfortunately, that meant Nevaeh would have to. "I can have a car pick you up and take you to the restaurant, if that's okay with you."

"Uh, sure. Though we haven't picked a place yet."

"I'll figure it out. I'll send a car to get you at ten. Is that good?"

"Sounds great."

They hung up, and Lamont groaned. Being in a relationship was so much work. Trying to figure out what the other person was thinking and feeling made his mind work harder than pistons in an engine. He'd never been good at figuring out what his girlfriends needed from him in a relationship. Granted, he'd been full of himself and dabbling in other vices that meant he didn't have to care.

This time around, Lamont wanted to ensure he and Nevaeh walked away unscathed. Their origin story meant their relationship was already on shaky ground. Lamont couldn't help but think about all the manipulation Diva threw his way. Was he doing something similar? He shook his head. Nevaeh knew where he stood. Somehow, this had to work, had to be better than his past relationships. At least there was mutual respect.

He wiped his face and stood, glancing at his watch. His trainer would be over in about fifteen minutes to go through Lamont's current exercise regime. He had to be athletic for his current role, and Diego helped Lamont maintain that physique.

He slid the glass door open, latching the lock behind him. Lamont quickly changed into a workout tank and shorts and switched out his dress shoes for tennis shoes. While he waited for Diego to arrive, Lamont could warm up by jumping rope. He took the stairs two at a time, descending to the bottom floor.

The black-and-gray nylon cord hung from a hook near the mirrored wall in the gym. Lamont reached for the rope, then grabbed each wooden handle. He didn't bother counting or even timing himself. Lamont simply let the steady sound of the wind whooshing by his ears lull his mind into a blank space. He pushed out the worries about his reputation, worries about whether he was making a mistake dating Nevaeh, worries about his mother's health. All of it pushed to the side.

Diego walked into the room. "Already warmed up, I see." He slapped hands with Lamont, sliding his palm back, then snapping his fingers.

"Yeah. Needed time to clear my head." Now that he'd stopped jumping, the thoughts were back, clamoring for attention.

"Well, if you need a good workout, then you'll love today's routine." Diego rubbed his hands together.

Lamont bit back a groan. He didn't want to be worked so hard that he'd need to soak in a tub of ice water. At the same time, he needed peace from his thoughts. "Bring it on."

Diego led Lamont through every torturous exercise there was. Burpees, cherry pickers, mountain climbers, 180-degree jumps, lunges, squats. By the time their hour-long session was over, sweat dripped from Lamont onto the rubber mat that lined the gym floor.

He used the edge of his tank to dry his face. "Thanks, man. That was a great session."

His body felt like it had gone through a noodle press, but at least Lamont wouldn't give the production company reason to question his physique. So what if they were waiting to see if the news tide would change before deciding if Lamont would receive the proverbial pink slip.

Diego grabbed his duffel and headed up the stairs to exit.

Lamont trailed, wondering if he should shuffle to the elevator instead of willing his feet to lift up and land on the risers. That seemed like too much of an ordeal.

"Come on, Booker. You're not tired yet," Diego called over his shoulder.

Lamont huffed out a breath but followed. "Kindly show yourself out."

"You love it, or you wouldn't keep booking appointments." Diego laughed.

"Maybe I'm a glutton for punishment."

Diego smirked when they got to the main floor. "Nah. But you want to keep those leading roles coming." He lifted his chin. "I do couples sessions as well. If your girlfriend is interested."

Nevaeh working out? The thought made him want to laugh. She didn't have the workout vibe or even the outdoor vibe. Though maybe she would be willing to go hiking one weekend.

Lamont fixed a thoughtful expression on his face. "I'll ask her."

"You do that." Diego waved, then left.

Lamont guzzled the bottle of water in his hands. His phone rang before he could swallow the last drop. *Bryan Wilkinson* flashed on his screen.

"Why is Nevaeh's name in the press?" Lamont asked.

"Hello to you too."

He huffed. "Sorry. How are you? Why is Nevaeh's name in the press?"

"I've been better. My main client is leaving me voicemail after voicemail about something that can't be helped. Plus, he thinks he's my only client."

Lamont rubbed his face. "I apologize. Truly. I just feel bad. We promised her some breathing room."

"Hey, are they calling her phone?"

"No."

"Camping outside her place?"

"No."

"Then she's not being harassed, and we did what we could. You have your calendar up?"

"No, why?"

"I've got an interview tentatively scheduled for you and Nevaeh with Meredith Walsh at *Luminary*. She'll bring her photographer along so they can get photos for the front-page spread they're planning."

Lamont gulped. This was getting real. "Appreciate that, Bry. What day?"

"Monday."

"As in the twelfth?"

"Yep."

At least it was before the charity event. That could work. "When are they running it?"

"I forgot to get that info. I'll ask when I call to confirm the time."

"All right. Let me text Nevaeh. If she can do it, then pen us in."

"It's two in the afternoon. Text me back with a yay or nay."

"Got it." Lamont tapped on the text message icon and typed up a question for his new girlfriend.

Lamont
Can you interview in person at 2 p.m. Monday?
It's with Luminary.

Nevaeh
Does the 5 have traffic?

His lips twitched.

Lamont
Take that as a yes?

Nevaeh
An emphatic yes. Don't forget that. Maybe I
need exclamation points.

He laughed.

Lamont
I didn't know you liked being on the front page
of magazines that much.

Nevaeh
Oh my word. I need to tell my parents.

Lamont
What's wrong?

Nevaeh
They don't pay attention to entertainment
news, but my mom's one guilty pleasure is
her subscription to Luminary. She's been a
subscriber ever since I can remember. If I don't
tell them in person, they'll kill me.

Nevaeh
Figuratively speaking of course.

Lamont
Do you want me to go with you?

Ellipses appeared, disappeared, and appeared once more.
Lamont stared at his phone, waiting to see what decision
Nevaeh came to. Was meeting parents this early in the game
a no-no? She had met his mother. Granted, she had known
her for a year already. . . .

Nevaeh
Sure. I usually go to their house for Sunday
dinner. Will you be on set?

Lamont
Sunday is my guaranteed day off for this
current project.

Other contracts he hadn't been so lucky to get Sunday off, so when he did, it felt like extra freedom.

Nevaeh
Great. Would you like to come?

Lamont
Yes. Thank you.

Nevaeh
I'll pick you up. What should I wear Monday?

Lamont
I'll ask Bry. The interviewer may already have an idea of how she wants us to appear.

Nevaeh
Okay. Let me know.

He stuffed his phone back into his pocket, then ran up another flight of stairs to his room. A call to his personal stylist was necessary. Nevaeh needed some Hollywood-worthy wardrobe items, especially if she was going to appear on his arm at publicized events.

Maybe they could make a date of it, or was that lame?

Lord, why does this all feel awkward?

Maybe because it was. He hadn't *known* Nevaeh despite her presence in his mom's life the past year. Now they were forced to go around town as if they'd been dating the entire time. One date wasn't going to speed up his feelings no matter how much he wished to avoid lying. When they had their interview on Monday, Lamont was very much afraid it would appear a sham.

What do I do about that, Lord? Are You okay with this? Are we now outside Your will?

Because of the way his thoughts churned, Lamont had a feeling he was only fooling himself about his intentions.

Eleven

arranged the banana slices all over my plate, then dropped a dollop of Nutella on each face before sprinkling the confection with walnuts. Next, I grabbed the whipped cream, shaking the can until my arm got a good workout, then aerosoled cream over the plate. I added more nuts and finished with drizzled honey and strawberry syrup on top.

Obviously not the healthiest breakfast one could have, but I considered the concoction high in protein and a serving of fruit. If anyone wanted to argue with me, I dared them to—*after* they'd had a few bites. Besides, Lamont had changed our brunch plans. His production company needed to reshoot a scene, so he was working. Which meant I was going shopping with his personal assistant, or wait . . . *stylist*? Whatever the title, I'd be tortured by fitting room mirrors for the majority of my day. The least I could do was enjoy breakfast.

I moved to the living room since our kitchen was too small for a dining table, and we didn't have a dining room. Instead, we had TV tray stands that made sitting on the couch in front of the television reminiscent of the '50s. I grabbed one from behind the couch and set it up. Just as I took my first bite, Nora came stomping into the living room, her brown hair hidden by a satin scarf. She propped a hand on her hip and squinted at me.

"What?" I asked after swallowing my bite.

"You said it wasn't what it looked like."

"What wasn't?" Seriously, she always woke up in such a strange mood.

"The thing between you and Lamont Booker. I saw on the news yesterday that someone tagged you as his girlfriend. *And* I heard you had lunch with him at Le Feu."

My spine stiffened. "How did you hear that?" I *knew* Blake Smythe was a snitch.

Nora sniffed, pointing her petite nose in the air. "Hugo works there."

"Your brother works at Le Feu? How did I not know that? All the times we wanted to go, and he couldn't get us in?" I felt personally affronted, not to mention the need to stall for time. I couldn't say anything that would violate the NDA.

She rolled her eyes. "He's a server. They eat in the back, where celebrities can pretend they don't exist."

Telling her it had been our first date didn't seem like a good idea. *So what should I say?* "Lamont thought I'd like it."

"Oh, he's *Lamont* now, huh?"

Bryan would be proud I'd finally dropped his last name.

Was Nora mad? It's not like we were BFFs and regularly talked about our love lives—not that what I had with Lamont could constitute as that. Nora and I were college roommates by lottery pick of the school system. After freshman year, we chose to maintain the status quo after comparing notes and realizing half the people who went to our school were weirdos. Now we were housemates thanks to the unreasonably high housing prices in metro LA. But I had never thought of us as super close.

She flopped onto the pink armchair we'd taken off a student who'd moved out of the dorms the same weekend we had. "I thought you two weren't dating?" Her Latina accent was particularly thick this morning. A sure sign she was irritated.

"I distinctly remember saying it's not what it looks like." Which it hadn't been. We weren't lovers. I wrinkled my nose inwardly. That title conjured up such awful connotations. Even my thoughts wanted to be washed with soap.

"But obviously you *are* dating."

"We are." That was the truth. Though I'd be happier with more dates under my belt. This all still felt like treading the line of lying. My mom would panic, knowing her lessons on truth telling were being ignored right now. Not to mention how I wanted to avoid God's judgment on the whole matter.

"Why didn't you say something?"

If Lamont and I were serious, what would be the most logical answer? I shrugged. "Mostly because I wanted to stay out of the limelight."

"How did you two meet?"

I stared at Nora. "Is this an interview, or are you genuinely curious?"

"An interview?" She shook her head, throwing her hands up in the air. "You ask a few questions with someone you've known for almost ten years, and they treat you like a stranger."

"I'm sorry. It's just that with me on the news, I'm feeling unnerved." Not to mention the hostile DMs popping up in my social inboxes. I pressed a hand to my forehead. "I don't like being on display. There's a reason I picked cosmetology and not acting."

Nora's lips pursed in sympathy. "I can't imagine how you must feel. Still, you must know I'd keep your secret."

Did I? I distinctly remember her telling me to capitalize on the moment. "I do his mom's hair. That's how we met."

Nora's eyes widened. "Oh my goodness, please tell me it's like some Cinderella-type story?"

She wanted to believe that Prince Charming forgot what I looked like after hours of dancing and supposedly experienced love at first sight? *I don't think so.* "Not at all. We've gotten to know one another, he asked me out, and I said yes."

Because he's Lamont SMA Booker! I told my inner voice to pipe down and act nonchalant. I didn't want Nora sniffing out any weakness in my explanation. Plus, if she ever became a "source close to Nevaeh Richards," I didn't want the media having any ammunition.

"Then what's the story behind the picture?"

I smiled cheekily. "You'll have to read the exclusive with *Luminary* to find out." I took a bite of my food, thankful talking with one's mouth full was unladylike.

Nora was a stickler for appropriate behavior and wouldn't dare continue her line of questions if I kept shoveling food into my mouth like the Pontipee brothers before Milly got ahold of them in *Seven Brides for Seven Brothers.*

"Will you be on the front page?"

I nodded, a little stunned she was still talking.

She clapped her hands. "So exciting. I hope you'll let me pick out your outfit."

My food lodged in my throat, and I coughed, trying to figure out which movement would get me air again. Nora sat up and slapped me on the back. My half-masticated banana flew out of my mouth and landed in the center of my plate. Disgusted, I placed the dish on the tray and guzzled the glass of water I had.

"Sorry, didn't mean to startle you."

"It's okay. I'm not sure yet what I'm wearing, but apparently we'll have to coordinate outfits." Which made me want to panic.

People would be dissecting my outfit for years to come. They'd get their magnifying glass to determine the brand, the fit, and whether or not we looked good as a couple. How was I supposed to get through a photo shoot with my brand-new boyfriend when we hadn't even kissed or gazed longingly into each other's eyes? Also, how much shapewear would *Luminary* require me to squeeze into to be coverworthy?

"Does your boyfriend have personal shoppers?"

I nodded. "I'm meeting her today to get a dress to wear for the *Sands of Time* charity event."

Nora gasped, hand to her heart. "You're going to the event?" She sank into the couch's cushions. "I'm so jealous of you right now." She gave me a sweet grin. "You couldn't possibly get me a ticket, could you?"

I swallowed. "Um, maybe Lamont can get you a ticket."

"Really? I'd love that." She beamed, her teeth straight and white thanks to some cosmetic dentistry she'd invested in to help her career.

Why did the request twist my insides? "Well, no promises, but I'll ask him."

"You're the best, Nevaeh." Nora squealed, then came over and squeezed my hands. Then she flounced out of the room.

Was this going to be a reoccurrence? Would I have to figure out boundaries with Nora? Surely, I couldn't bring her along to every event we had. That was just absurd. *You're making a mountain. It was an ask to one event.*

I pulled out my cell and saw a text from Lamont—still a surreal moment.

Lamont
Meredith wants us to wear emerald green for the interview. Do you have anything in that color?

Nevaeh
I do. Should I take a pic, and you can determine if it's acceptable?

Lamont
Nah. Jody will know. My stylist will be your guru today. She'll also make sure you have enough wardrobe pieces for future events.

Did he think my clothing beneath him? My brain warred with being offended and accepting maybe he was right in this situation.

Nevaeh
You have more than one charity event lined up?

Lamont
I do have a movie premiere coming up.

I gulped. I could *not* walk the red carpet. I'd be blinded by the lights and overwhelmed by the attention. Not to mention my worries over entertainment media dissecting my gown and everything else about me.

You don't have a choice, girlfriend.

Nevaeh
Oh.

Lamont
Breathe. I promise it'll be fine.

It wouldn't. He was going to meet my parents tomorrow. We were beginning our plan to appear all over LA on each other's arms. The world was going to actually believe he was my boyfriend. I needed a paper bag or something to calm me down. My thoughts were spiraling faster than a spinning top. I placed a hand to my forehead as if that would stop the merry-go-round.

Another text chimed. This one from Jody.

> Nevaeh
> Jody will be here in a few. See you tomorrow?

> Lamont
> Yep. You going to church with your parents?

> Nevaeh
> No.

It was too old-fashioned for my taste. I think they were still solely preaching Old Testament fire-and-brimstone-type sermons. Not for me. Besides, you didn't have to attend church to be a believer. The Lord and I were great friends. Plus, I didn't want to drive all the way out there every Sunday, come back home, then drive back out for Sunday dinner.

> Lamont
> Then you're going to yours?

> Nevaeh
> Um, I haven't been in a few years.

Try ten, since I left home for college. At least that was when I'd been attending regularly.

> Lamont
> Then come with me? I'll pick you up at nine, service starts at ten. Then we can head to your parents' house. What do you say?

Go to church with him? Wasn't that something a girlfriend would do?

Okay.

Great. See you then.

I stared at my phone. How had my life already changed so much I didn't even recognize it anymore?

But that wasn't the most pressing thought. I couldn't help but think about the length of time that had passed since I'd stepped into a sanctuary. Some churches hadn't yet diversified the look of their congregation. And I needed to see a few of those faces in a congregation before I could feel comfortable. Being the only dark-skinned one in the pews kept me from singing along during worship and focusing on the sermon.

Weren't people from all the tribes on earth going to heaven? If that was so, the churches here were failing to resemble that. Finding a church that fit my beliefs and desires seemed an impossible task, and one I had honestly stopped trying to complete. I didn't believe that made me any less of a follower of Christ. I loved the Lord, and I didn't need a church building to affirm that. But I couldn't shake the unsettling feeling pricking my heart.

I shook my head. Jody was probably pulling up to the curb, and I needed to leave. I headed for the street, scanning the cars alongside the curb to see if any were idling. A woman with a red bob stepped out of a dark sedan and waved.

"Nevaeh?"

"That's me. I take it you're Jody?"

"Yep." She placed a hand on her chest. "I'm so excited to go shopping with you today."

"That makes one of us." I grimaced. "Sorry. Ignore that. Shopping's not my favorite."

"It's so hard to find clothes that make you feel like you, isn't it?"

She got me. Though her petite frame made me think that shopping should be a breeze. Still, I nodded and settled into the passenger seat, buckling in.

"Lamont gave me an idea of how many outfits to get you, where you'll be going, and even the *Luminary* color scheme."

"Oh, good." Yet my insides didn't feel so hot. They were whipping more butter than a dairy farm. Jody was about to see me stuff, shift, and lift my body into clothes that just weren't meant for me.

If they fit over my backside, then I might have too much material at the waist. If she tried to slap a belt around my waist, then I might end up looking like a sack of potatoes with a band around the middle. Maybe I should have brought Maxine with me.

"Uh, should I go back and grab my shapewear?"

Jody shook her head. "You'll be fine. We're going to a couple of places that were made for women with your great figure. Better an hourglass figure than a stick-of-chewing-gum shape like mine."

I snorted. "I bet you find all sorts of clothing in your size."

"Maybe in the kids' department, but no twenty-year-old wants to resort to pink animal print or have kid cartoon figures all over their clothing."

"Ouch. That's gotta be bad."

She grinned. "It's why fashion is my passion. I'm convinced there's something we can all wear, look good in, and not have to be subjected to society's ideals on impossible standards."

"I think I'm going to like you."

Which turned out to be true. Jody was a dream to shop with. She didn't make me feel embarrassed by the number on the tag or the constant try-ons because so many out-fits just weren't working for me. But the shoppers taking not-so-discreet photos of me or the staff whispering behind their hands were another story. I wouldn't be surprised if a reporter with *StarGazer* was waiting to ambush me the moment I stepped out of the store and onto LA proper—aka the sidewalk.

Pretty sure I would also be tagged in photos from the shoppers who were cataloging my difficulties with shopping. As much as I tried to ignore them, their stares followed me around the store and out onto the streets, where I attempted to breathe in calmness. I could only hope tomorrow would be better at church and my parents' house. Then again . . .

Twelve

Lamont
I need prayers. Going to meet Nevaeh's parents today.

Chris
You've got them.

Tuck
You'll need them.

Lamont
What's that supposed to mean?

Tuck
Parents don't like men who might just be playing with their daughter's heart. It's written in Dating 101.

Chris
Lol, he might be telling the truth.

Lamont
How would you know? You're dating your work.

Chris
I may have tried before. My singleness speaks for itself.

Tuck
Ouch. I'd offer you a cigar in commiseration, but I hear they cause cancer.

Lamont
Then I should be worried?

Chris
Yes

Tuck
Yes

Lamont
Thanks a lot. Now I'm nervous.

Tuck
The real question is, why weren't you nervous before?

Chris
Ego. Those Hollywood types are all the same. 😌

Lamont
Parents love me.

Tuck
Hollywood parents.

Lamont
Ugh, Nevaeh said the same thing.

Chris
Then listen to her but know we'll be praying. I'm sure it's not as bad as we're portraying it'll be.

Tuck
Here's praying it won't be worse.

Lamont
🙏

Lamont placed his cell on the hook on the dashboard, then programmed his GPS to take him to Nevaeh's house. Last night, pictures of her shopping had surfaced on social media. The comments had been pretty harsh. He'd said a prayer she wouldn't see them, and if she had, that the words wouldn't take root. Hollywood could be brutal to those they considered plus-size. Unfortunately, a woman size six or bigger could fit that category in this town.

Lamont had no idea Nevaeh's actual size, but he liked her figure. Where were the fans that were her size? Why had the only comments that hit the news sources complained about her weight and claimed she glorified obesity?

She didn't mention the comments when they went to church together this morning, and they had parted ways shortly after. He to have lunch with his mother, and Nevaeh to do a personal hair appointment with a client.

As he pulled up to her place, he breathed out a sigh of relief. No reporters, no neighbors out. He knocked on the door, which quickly opened. His mouth dropped as he took in the silk blouse and slacks she wore. What happened to those flowy dresses or even the overalls he normally saw her in?

"You're wearing dress pants." He only wore a blazer with his jeans.

"My mother likes me to wear presentable clothing. Her words, not mine." She locked up the door. "And this is an outfit she previously gifted me. I wear it often, so she knows I'm getting good mileage." She tilted her head. "No driver today?"

There was so much information to unpack, but he settled on her question. "Just me and my regular car."

She raised an eyebrow. "This I gotta see."

Lamont guided her back to his Mercedes, where she promptly snorted at the sight. "Regular car, huh?"

Heat filled his cheeks. "Is it excessive?"

She shook her head. "But it's not an average vehicle either."

He opened the door for her, closing it once she settled comfortably into the passenger seat. He rounded the front of the car. After programming her parents' address into his GPS, Lamont intermingled with LA traffic. His mind went back to the texts from Chris and Tuck. Would Nevaeh's parents like him?

"Why are you so quiet?" she asked.

Lamont gripped the steering wheel, taking a quick glance at her. "I'm nervous."

"So am I," she admitted.

"Same reasons as yesterday, or did something new creep into your mind?" He'd had some weird dreams that made him feel a tad bit desperate to make a good impression.

"This morning it dawned on me that I'm not sure they'll believe we're really dating."

"How come?"

Nevaeh sighed. "It's been years since I've invited a boyfriend home, and you're you."

He bit back a chuckle at her exasperated tone. "How many years are we talking, exactly?" His hands tightened, waiting for her answer.

"Um, five."

"But didn't you say you dated a couple of years ago?"

"He wasn't bring-home-worthy."

"Great." He forced a chuckle. "No pressure."

She reached over and squeezed his forearm. "Look, it'll be uncomfortable for a while, so we just have to persevere. Keep the story of how we met simple and go from there."

"Is there anything I should know before I meet them?" *Favorites? Why haven't we discussed favorites?*

"Right. A bio on the folks." She slid her hands against the dress slacks she wore. "Okay, so my mom is an English professor at Loyola Marymount University. She's been teaching for as long as I can remember. First at a high school, then she moved to the college level, where she seems to thrive."

"Impressive."

"She knows it."

Uh-oh. Something about Nevaeh's relationship with her mom cloaked her like a shroud. She wasn't as vibrant as usual. In fact, there was an air of dread around her. Lamont said a quick prayer that everything would go well.

Nevaeh continued. "My dad is a history professor at the same place. He's always worked there, and I think he's the reason my mom got a job there in the first place."

"Does working so closely together cause any tension?"

"No. Different departments. According to them, they rarely see one another unless it's planned lunch dates."

"How do they feel about you being a hair stylist?"

She scoffed. "They hate it. They don't think it's a real job that can give me security. They think I'm wasting my education."

He shook his head. His mom had always been encouraging in his endeavors. He couldn't imagine the hurt Nevaeh felt.

"I'm sorry."

"It is what it is."

Unfortunately. "Do you have other talents I need to know about? Secretly a good singer? Or maybe you have the next American novel sitting in a drawer in your room?" He winked, hoping to coax her into a good mood.

She rewarded his efforts with a melodic laugh. There was the woman he was starting to know.

"I can draw caricatures, but I never worked hard to develop the skill because I didn't have a passion for it. Making a person feel their very best, or in Hollywood's case, look their best for film, that's something that makes me practically vibrate with energy."

He believed her. The waves of excitement were present and strumming from her. "I feel the same about acting."

"You started at eighteen, right?"

"Sort of. I got discovered at sixteen via YouTube. Someone put up a theatrical performance from our high school in which I played the lead."

"Wait, wait, wait. You did theater in high school?"

Lamont nodded, making a turn at the GPS's prompting. "I joined drama club in middle school at my mom's encouragement. She said I was always putting on an act at home so I might as well get good use of it."

Nevaeh laughed. "So what happened with the YouTube video?"

"My agent saw it. Bryan."

"Bryan's been your agent since you were sixteen?" Her voice rose.

He nodded. "Said he knew a star when he saw one. I got my start on Broadway with secondary roles. Then one day, a film producer came to one of the shows, saw me, and thought I'd be perfect for the role in *Troubled*."

"My neighbor said she cried when she watched that."

"Did you?" He held his breath.

"*Maybe*," she drew out. She looked at him. "I've seen every single one of your movies."

Why did pleasure fill his chest at the thought? Were his feelings moving from the casual to genuinely interested? His mind flashed to Diva, all the times she feigned interest. He cleared his throat.

"Oh, there it is." Nevaeh pointed to the left. "That's their house."

The white-stucco home stood out in the sea of multicolored homes. It was also the only one with a red roof that reminded him of the hotel chain with the same name. "Does the gate open automatically?" The white iron gate looked older than the Hollywood sign.

"For my parents. Let me call and tell them we're here."
A few seconds later, she asked them to open the gate, then
hung up. "Just drive straight back. The garage is in the very
back, but their cars usually sit in front of it."

"No problem." Once the rickety gate stopped squeaking—
sounded like nails on a chalkboard—Lamont drove ahead
as ordered. He put the car in park, then looked at Nevaeh.
"Anything else I should know?"

"My mom will throw snooty barbs at me, but she loves
me. My dad is a big teddy bear but turns into a grizzly when
boys are around."

"'Scariest environment imaginable.' Thanks."

"Ha! One of my favorite quotes from *Armageddon*." She
sighed, then motioned to her door. "Better open it. Your
boyfriend grading starts now."

"Right." He cleared his throat and rounded the vehicle to
open her door. His palms were clammy, and his heart had
moved into the vicinity of his throat.

"We can use the back entrance." Nevaeh pointed to the
white screen door.

"You sure? Should I do the gentlemanly thing and come
to the front?"

"Nah, you're not picking me up for a date. You drove us
here, remember?"

"I do, but my deodorant doesn't."

Nevaeh nudged his side. "Hush. You'll be fine. We have
no choice but to make the best of it."

"You're fabulous at pep talks, anyone ever tell you that?"

"No."

"I wonder why," he said dryly.

Before she could comment, the door flew open, and an
older man filled the doorway. He stared at Lamont through
clear-framed eyeglasses. Despite hair that was more salt than

pepper, his brown eyes held no rheumy tinge. They were sharp and piercing. Guilt swamped Lamont. As much as he wanted to tell the world he and Nevaeh were the real deal, that just wasn't true today. How could he step foot in her father's house and imply such a thing?

Calm down. Just tell him you're dating, and let the conversation go from there.

"Daddy!" Nevaeh stepped up on the step and threw her arms around the man.

Mr. Richards never broke the hold he had on Lamont's gaze. Lamont could feel his Adam's apple moving up his throat and back down. He didn't dare take another breath until the man broke their visual Wild West standoff.

"I missed you," Nevaeh said.

Finally, the gruff man turned his full attention toward his daughter, swallowing her up in his arms.

"Daddy, I'd like you to meet Lamont Booker, my boyfriend." She bit her lip.

Lamont offered his hand. "Nice to meet you, sir."

Mr. Richards squeezed Lamont's hand briefly, then let him go. Somehow, that amount of grace didn't bring relief like Lamont imagined it would because the man was back to sizing him up.

"Should we go inside?" Nevaeh asked nervously.

"Yes. Your mother said dinner was ready five minutes ago. Let's hope she's not in a snit over it."

Lamont wanted to ask about that, but he kept his mouth shut, taking the moment to get a breather. The stare-down with Nevaeh's father had been intense. He could see what she meant by *grizzly*, though maybe *tiger* would be more apt. Lamont thought Mr. Richards would've gone for the jugular if Nevaeh hadn't reminded them of the pressing meal.

As her father led them through the living room to an arched

opening to the dining room, Lamont said a quick prayer that her parents would like him. Not because he thought the whole dating bit would be easier, but because he had an uneasy feeling in his middle whenever Nevaeh's mother was introduced into conversation.

Just then an older woman walked out of the kitchen. Her hair piled up in a beehive-style do looked regal, and the added touch of pearls with a cream-colored sweater on top of a black blouse with matching slacks completed the image. But the frost emitting from her was enough to make Lamont thankful his blazer provided an extra layer against the dipping temps.

"Mom, this is Lamont. Lamont, my mom, Maletha Richards."

Mrs. Richards dipped her head. "Let's be seated." Hopefully that clipped tone didn't set the mood for dinner.

Lamont contrasted Nevaeh's parents, how her mother was dressed in "proper attire," but her dad seemed more casual in a sweater and khakis. It actually made Lamont feel better about the jeans he'd donned this morning. Lamont and Nevaeh sat across from her parents. Mr. Richards said grace, then began passing food around.

Lord, please don't let me drop one of these dishes. The china looked dated, as did some of the other items in the home. Were they antiques or simply treasured items? Nothing about the home spoke of wealth, but maybe they weren't flashy and saved their funds for specialty items to pass on.

"So, Nevaeh, this is certainly a surprise." Her mother's high tone tensed Lamont's back.

Lamont took a bite of his meatloaf, trying to feign nonchalance as he waited for Nevaeh to speak.

"I told you I was bringing a guest."

"Yes, you did. You just failed to tell us he was your boy-friend and that you've been on the news lately."

Nevaeh froze next to him. He snuck his hand under the table, squeezing her fingers in solidarity. At least, he hoped she'd see it that way.

"Honestly, I didn't think you guys watched that kind of news."

"Oh, you were on CNN," Mr. Richards interjected. "The story came on right after the fires going on in the Midwest."

"I'm sorry," she stated quietly. "I thought it better to in-troduce him in person. So you could meet the real person versus whatever the news is saying."

"They're saying quite a lot." Her mom dabbed her lips. "Are you two sticking to your faith?" Mrs. Richards's search-ing stare landed on Lamont's face, as if the question was for him.

Was that an inquiry he should take at surface level or dive for deeper meaning? *Keep it simple.* "Yes, ma'am. We are." He cleared his throat. "In fact, Nevaeh attended church with me this morning. She's been great trying to coordinate our schedules so we can have time to spend together. Mine isn't the norm."

Her mother shook her head, tutting the whole time. "As if that child has a schedule to coordinate. It's not like her jobs offer her any kind of structure. A hair appointment here, salon work there, not to mention trying to always get on a movie set." She waved her hand in the air. "It's all a bit chaotic if you ask me."

"Which no one did, dear. But we thank you for sharing regardless." Mr. Richards's tone was kind and patient, which surprised Lamont. Mr. Richards took a sip of his water. "Have you met his family, Nevaeh?"

"I've known his mother for a year, Daddy."

"And my father passed away," Lamont offered.

"I'm sorry to hear that," Mrs. Richards said. She eyed him. "How is it our daughter has known your mother for a year, but this is the first time we're hearing about your relationship?" She rested her chin on her hand, all pretense of eating gone.

Lamont set his fork down. "I met Nevaeh on set. I heard her talking about the importance of hair care. At the time, my mom was going through chemo, and even though she was losing her hair faster than she'd anticipated, I still thought maybe Nevaeh could pamper her in some way. So I approached her to see if my mom could be a client."

Mrs. Richards's eyes widened. "Oh my. Is she okay now?"

"Yes, thank the Lord. She's in remission." Lamont would never stop praising God for that mercy. Now if he could only believe in her healing and stop watching her for signs of a relapse. "Nevaeh's been doing her hair ever since."

"Ms. Rosie is amazing. She's shown me such faith over the past year. I've learned a lot from her." Nevaeh looked at him, a soft smile on her lips and her dark eyes shining.

"She sounds like an amazing woman." Mrs. Richards pointed at them with her fork. "If you two are serious, we should plan a day to meet her."

"My mom would love that. Nevaeh is one of her favorite people." Lamont let out a breath. This was okay. Not fantastic, but not bad either.

"We're still waiting to hear how this developed from a business relationship into a real one," Mr. Richards added.

Because the paparazzi are cockroaches, and I need to save my skin. So far Lamont had yet to see any turn of the tide with their relationship news. Maybe the *Luminary* article would help change that.

He rubbed his hand on his jean-clad leg. "I started taking notice of her, and we started talking, and then I let her know how much I wanted to get to know her better." He shrugged his shoulders. "I was up-front about my unusual life and the desire to genuinely date her as much as we can in the spotlight."

"And you were okay with that, bean?" Mr. Richards studied Nevaeh for once.

Coolness enveloped Lamont's face. It was almost like he'd been under stage lights, but now that the gentleman had turned the spotlight on Nevaeh, Lamont could breathe.

"Yes. I admit part of the appeal of dating him was being a longtime fan."

"If that's what you call the T-shirts, posters, and DVD collection, then, yes, 'longtime fan' works." Her mother snorted.

Kind of cute to learn Nevaeh got her sarcastic snorts from her mom.

"I also can't lie about his looks."

"People may have exaggerated," Mr. Richards groused.

Lamont chuckled, stifling it when her father glared at him. Still, Lamont thought he saw a twitch of the older man's lips. Maybe Mr. Richards didn't want to admit how odd the situation was, but the repressed humor said otherwise.

"So what made you say yes?" her mother asked.

"I couldn't help but feel like it would be a missed opportunity if I didn't."

Good answer.

"And you two have been dating ever since?" Mr. Richards asked.

"Yes, sir," Nevaeh replied.

"Did you go right from high school to film?" Mrs. Richards asked. "What's your background? Surely your mother encouraged you to pursue a real career."

Lamont bit back a sigh, then Nevaeh's hand squeezed

his and his irritation dissipated. Maybe this was a way for him to help Nevaeh. He straightened in his seat. "Actually, my mom fully supported my acting career. She said I was destined to be in front of an audience, whether that was on stage or in front of a camera. However, I had other interests, so I pursued an education in between sets."

"Really?" A sudden gleam entered Mr. Richards's eyes. "What did you major in?"

"I got a bachelor's degree in education."

Mrs. Richards's mouth dropped open, and her husband sat back with a smile on his face. "Well, I'll be."

Thirteen

A degree in education?

It took every ounce of willpower to school my features as my new boyfriend won my parents over with a bachelor's degree. I didn't even know it was possible to see two unwilling-to-look-on-the-bright-side people change their minds. If I hadn't witnessed the transformation with my own two eyes, I wouldn't have believed it.

The next thing I knew, Mom was sharing her favorite of Lamont's movies. Even scolded him a time or two for the few villain roles he'd played. Then my dad offered him a glass of whiskey. The whiskey that he only pulled out for special occasions. Never having a full glass, just enough to coat the bottom of the tumbler.

What's happening here?

Finally, we finished dinner, and Lamont offered to clear dishes.

I stood. "I'll help too."

He winked, and I fought the urge to keep the blush from developing, but it was no use. Despite getting to know Lamont Booker away from the whole Hollywood heartthrob moniker, my cheeks still heated, and my mind still asked, *Why me?*

I mean, duh, the paparazzo photo. As much as I told myself that, the rapid heartbeat, clammy hands, and stars in my eyes had failed to dissipate. I didn't want to swoon over something as simple as him offering to clear the table. Besides, that's probably how Ms. Rosie raised him. Or maybe he was trying to win points from my parents.

Either way, I found myself wiping down the counters while Lamont loaded the dishwasher. Something perfectly domestic and surreal at the same time. How was this my life?

"Your parents are nice," he said after a few minutes of silence.

I barely repressed the scoff. "They're just impressed with your degree because they have the same one. Though they also have master's degrees."

"I'm surprised you don't have a bachelor's in education, considering how your parents are."

The snort flew free. "I *do* have one."

"Wait, what?" He paused, a plate in hand.

"In order for them to pay for college, I had to follow their same career path. I ended up paying for cosmetology school and a license a year later."

"I'm sorry they're not supportive of your career path." He took a step closer. "How do you handle their disapproval?"

Because I had no other choice. "They're my parents. I want them to understand me but . . ." I scrubbed hard at an imaginary spot. "Enough about me. Did you really want to work in education?" I kept him in my peripheral view.

"I always figured I'd end up teaching. The whole 'those who can't, teach' thing. I minored in history because I find the past interesting."

Ugh. Was he seriously telling me he was a combination of both my parents? What were the odds? I took the time to study him. He'd ditched the blazer and rolled up the sleeves of his periwinkle button-down, and his countenance appeared lighter than the public smiles I'd seen over the years.

"My parents are going to end up falling in love with you," I whined.

Lamont looked amused, straightening to his full height. "You'd have a problem with that?" He slid his hands into his pockets.

I shrugged a shoulder and dropped the sponge. No point scrubbing a clean counter. "It seems like it might make things difficult. That's all." *When you dump me, and I have to settle for a mere mortal.*

"Why?" He shut the dishwasher and came to stand before me.

"Lamont, what happens when all of this ends?" I asked, staring at my shoes. Knowing Mom's strict rules for dressing appropriately for Sunday dinner, I'd ditched my beloved sandals for boring two-inch heels. What *was* this color? Puce?

Lamont's finger came to rest under my chin, raising my eyes to peer into his. My breath hitched at the nearness. Had we ever been this close?

"Maybe it won't."

"Are you really saying you could find yourself falling for me?" That made no sense. I wasn't his type, and Lamont, well, he was everyone's type.

"I know I don't know everything I want to know about you yet. Not even close. And after Diva . . ." He shook his head. "I never imagined feeling this way, so that tells me there's a whole lot I still don't know," he murmured.

My mouth dried, eyes dropping to his lips. "What does that all mean?"

"It means I like you. I'm hoping that we can at least be friends if dating doesn't lead to friendlier feelings."

What if I already had friendlier feelings? Could that be the reason why these butterflies stalked me when he was around?

"Friendship's a good start." Saying that to my supposed boyfriend was a tad awkward, but the beautiful smile that curved his lips was worth the uncertainty filling me.

After that, the mood seemed to lighten, and I found myself genuinely enjoying his company. Not that I hadn't before, but then I'd felt the pressure to act like a girlfriend despite not knowing him too well. Now I could be me.

We said good-bye to my parents, then headed back to my place. I stared out the window, catching the orange-and-purple sky, wondering how the sunset looked at the beach. It amazed me how different it was every single day.

"You're awfully quiet over there. Are you thinking, or just feeling sleepy from the meal?" Lamont asked.

"Thinking. You know the interview's tomorrow." Would it do what Bryan hoped? Would Lamont's reputation be saved? Would the awful comments about me on social media stop? I was this close to shutting down my accounts just to avoid being tagged in the malicious posts people were writing.

"Yes. That."

"Are you nervous?" I stared at his strong profile. How was his jawline so defined? And what would it look like with a hint of stubble?

"Maybe. It's the first time I've done an interview as a couple."

"Really? You didn't do one with Diva Jones?" Why did that knowledge thrill me?

Lamont shook his head. "Do you call every celebrity by their first and last name?"

"Of course not. No one goes around saying Beyoncé Knowles or Adele Adkins."

"Yet you know both of their last names." Lamont glanced at me. "Tell the truth, you read gossip rags."

"Of course not." He didn't need to know I followed a few celebrities online and may have read as many articles—legitimate ones—as I could about them. That sounded a little stalkerish, and I was not that. Just a fan. Besides, if they put it online for me to read, didn't I owe it to them to follow suit?

Do you want everyone reading the articles about you and Lamont? Definitely not, just the Luminary *one.*

"Sure, Nevaeh."

My lips curved on their own accord. "Do you think the interviewer will see anything wrong in our story?" Meeting the parents and going on a few dates didn't constitute a long relationship or seal the deal on attraction.

Again, I was an average woman, and Lamont was a blessed unicorn. I swatted my mental self as she swooned.

"No." Lamont threaded his fingers through mine. "I'll have a driver pick you up."

"You know I can just drive to your house, right?"

"What kind of celebrity boyfriend would I be if I made my girl do that?" He spared me a glance.

"One who recognizes your *girlfriend* is independent."

"Yes, but using my driver allows me to ensure your safety and show off just a tad."

Okay, he had me there. I ran my other hand on top of his. "Do you think my safety is in question?"

"Not now, but we don't know if that will change."

"Fine," I murmured.

"Does that mean I win that point?"

"If we were keeping track, which we're not."

"Says you." He smirked.

I had to resist the urge to roll my eyes. They'd been taking too many orbits around my sockets thanks to his cheekiness. Still, I liked to think this was us settling into a good friendship.

The rest of the ride was silent as he drove back to my place. However, the closer we got to Studio City, the more nervous I became. Should I invite him inside? Did he think the modest two-bedroom apartment beneath him? I hadn't invited him in when he'd picked me up twice today, so maybe I should.

Yet maybe time apart would give us some time to truly prep for tomorrow's interview. I didn't want to manufacture loving feelings if he turned up his nose at my apartment. Not that Lamont had given me the impression that he would hold an elitist attitude toward me or my place. He'd been charmed by my parents' house in Inglewood, complimenting my mother on her decorating skills and the wonderful meal. She was probably planning our wedding by the time we left.

Not that I was upset my parents liked Lamont. Unfortunately, it made everything so much more real. How could I maintain a status quo when everyone around me was ready to succumb to Lamont's charm? If all the people in my life believed our relationship was genuine, where did that leave me? Was I the last to take him seriously? He was an actor after all. How could I determine if his friendship request was sincere?

Yet his declaration in the kitchen had seemed heartfelt and authentic. I *wanted* to believe him, but I also couldn't afford to. My heart would be obliterated when we broke up if I went ahead and gave in to my desire to be loved for who I was.

When you were dealing with a guy who drove a Mercedes because he'd already driven his other cars during the week, your self-esteem was bound to take a hit. I wasn't good enough for Lamont Booker. I was sure once my mother came to her senses, she'd concur. But I had agreed to play the part, and that's what I would do. My prayer: not to lose myself in the process.

I carefully removed my hand from Lamont's and placed it in my lap. The move did nothing to settle my heart, but my mind cleared. That was a win in my book.

Fourteen

Lamont viewed his reflection in the full-length mirror. The emerald green suit looked better than he'd thought it would. Originally, he'd wanted to pair a green shirt with a white suit, but Jody had convinced him this would be more eye-catching. Now seeing the final result, he couldn't agree more. He picked up his cell to check the time and saw a text from Tuck.

Tuck
Today's the day, right?

Lamont
Yep. All dressed and waiting on Nevaeh.

Tuck
Hitting the big times, huh?

Chris
Nothing but the best for Hollywood's favorite actor.

Lamont
I'm not the favorite, but thanks.

Tuck
I snorted so loud the horse startled.

Chris

Ha! Same effect here, but it was a 🐑.

Lamont

You two are a riot.

Chris

Nah, but I bet you and Nevaeh will cause one
with your interview.

Lamont

I hope not. I want the spotlight to dim a bit.

Tuck

Good luck with that. Are y'all going to wear
matching outfits?

Lamont

Maybe

Chris

Tuck

Lamont

Sometimes I don't like you two.

Chris

You love us.

Tuck

You'd be lost without us.

Lamont

Maybe

He shook his head, then jogged down the stairs. Meredith
at *Luminary* had asked that he and Nevaeh remain barefoot
for the photo-shoot portion. Apparently, the look would add
a touch of vulnerability and intimacy to the pictures. Only
that wasn't the reason his stomach acted like he'd downed a
bunch of jalapeño poppers. It was the expectation that came

with the shoot. He would have to appear to be infatuated with a woman he'd only been dating for four days.

When they'd sealed their friendship last night at her parents' house, Lamont had felt a twinge of something. Too soon to call it attraction, what with battling thoughts of Diva and seeing where Nevaeh differed. He didn't want to compare, but his mind wouldn't stop the process. Now the guilt of today's interview and how they would be portraying a lie had his mind riddled with land mines.

Am I in the wrong, Lord? Surely protecting our reputations can't be wrong. He rubbed his eyes, letting out a long exhale.

"You okay, son?"

He jumped around. Mom closed the sliding door, eyeing him with concern.

"Um, just a little nervous."

"*Luminary* interview, right?"

Lamont nodded, fiddling with the tie around his neck.

"Stop. You look wonderful." Her gaze skimmed his suit. "Jody did a wonderful job. I can't wait to see how Nevaeh looks."

"I'm sure she'll look just fine."

His mom placed her hands on her hips. "That does *not* sound like a man who's been dating awhile."

"I don't think I can do this." His Adam's apple bobbed. "This isn't going to work."

"Why?" She tilted her head. "Do you object to hanging out with Nevaeh? She's such a sweetheart."

"No. She makes me laugh, and I do relax more when I'm around her." *Huh*. He hadn't realized that until he said it.

"Then don't worry about the interview. You'll do fine."

Please let her be right, Lord. "Thanks, Mom."

She patted his cheek. "Of course, baby. I love you. I know

you're worried about how this looks and if it aligns with your beliefs, but I believe God can bring good in this."

"What if you're wrong?" He stared down into her light brown eyes. What was it about moms that was so comforting? There was a strength in them he just didn't understand, especially considering everything his own had gone through.

"Don't you know mothers are never wrong?"

A chuckle slipped free, loosening the bands squeezing his insides. "I'll remember that."

"You should." She grinned and headed for the kitchen. "I'll make a smoothie, then be out of your hair until the interview is over."

Lamont slid his hands into his pockets. "I have a question."

She laid out the ingredients, nodding for him to continue.

"Meredith is going to ask how Nevaeh and I met. Do you have a problem with the world knowing you had breast cancer?"

Her movements stilled, and she met his gaze. Lamont's stomach dipped in the wave of silence. Maybe asking was a mistake.

"Son, I never understood why you kept it quiet in the first place."

He gaped. "The world already has so much of me. How could I give them more? Besides, you're your own person and didn't sign up to be harassed by the snaparazzi."

"Then you have my permission."

His shoulders sagged, and he leaned against the wall. "Thank you," he murmured.

"Of course. Now go see Nevaeh. I think I heard the garage lift."

He straightened, eyes already transfixed on the door leading to the four-car space.

"Go," she said with more emphasis.

Lamont strolled toward the entrance right as the door opened. Logically, he knew that slow motion was only an effect seen in movies, yet that didn't stop his brain from entering a turtle's pace where his senses picked out every single detail. Nevaeh's normally straight hair had loose curls flowing in a breeze—seriously, had she brought a CGI crew to aid in her entrance? Her makeup was artfully applied and highlighted those adorable dimples while also drawing his gaze to her stunning eyes. At the sight of the wrapped dress hugging her middle, then flaring out, his mouth dried.

He blinked, and she stood before him, a quirk to her lips and humor in her eyes.

"Earth to Lamont Booker."

"You cannot call me that today," he snapped. He rubbed a hand over his bald head as he sighed. "Sorry."

"It's okay." She pulled his hand down, interlaced their fingers, and squeezed. "We'll be okay."

"How do you know that?"

"Because you're Mr. SMA and I'm . . ." She tilted her head, thinking.

"'Pretty hot and tempting'?"

"Ha." Her dimples bloomed. "Talk about old school. *Money Talks* is an underrated classic."

"I'm pretty sure a movie has to be older than twenty-five years to be considered a classic."

"Hmm. Give it a decade, and it'll pop up on Netflix."

Lamont laughed. "You wish."

"I really do." She beamed, staring up into his eyes. "Are you good now? Freak-out passed?"

"I think so." Had he thought only a smidgen of attraction existed? How wrong he'd been. She looked stunning. "Um, hey, my mom gave us permission to talk about her diagnosis and treatment and whatnot."

Nevaeh nodded.

"Also"—he looked into her eyes—"you look beautiful today."

The doorbell pealed through the house, and he jerked at the sound.

Nevaeh's soft laughter filled the room. "Yeah, maybe you're still a little unnerved."

"So I'm a little anxious. These things happen."

She tugged his hand as she strolled toward the front entrance. "Come on, Mr. SMA. We'll show *Luminary* how to fall in love the sanctified way."

"And how's that?" he asked.

Nevaeh looked over her shoulder, staring right into his soul. "With God leading, duh."

He chuckled, feeling a little touch of relief. Thank goodness she had such a good mood about her. *Seriously, Lord, thank You.*

Before Nevaeh could twist the knob, Lamont laid a hand over hers. "I've got this," he whispered.

She nodded, stepping back but keeping their fingers linked.

Lamont opened the door and smiled the practiced grin he used for public appearances. "Good morning, Ms. Walsh." He spread out his unencumbered arm. "Welcome."

"Thank you." She tossed her blond locks over her shoulder, then motioned toward a photographer behind her. "This is Gary. He'll be doing the photos."

Lamont shook his hand. "Nice to meet both of you." He dropped Nevaeh's hand and wrapped an arm around her. "This is Nevaeh."

The two women shook hands, exchanging greetings. Lamont took a moment to breathe before asking where they'd like to set up. "We could do the interview in the living room, or there's the terrace outside?" He gestured toward each space.

"Well, if you don't mind, Gary would like to tour the grounds and the main floor. From there, he'll determine the best spots for the shoot."

"Sounds good."

Meredith nodded to Gary, who gave a salute and walked away. She turned back toward Lamont. "I think the living room sounds perfect for the interview."

"Great, right this way." Lamont kept his arm around Nevaeh as they moved forward.

She placed a hand on his chest. "You okay?" she whispered softly.

He nodded.

Lamont gestured toward the sofa and waited for Nevaeh to sit before he did. He made sure to sit right next to her, hoping the move looked routine and not him winging it on a prayer. His new girlfriend immediately looped her arm through his.

"I must say you two look absolutely stunning in those colors."

"Doesn't he look handsome?" Nevaeh smiled at him. "I was floored when his stylist picked out the dress. It's a color I have severely underestimated."

"I agree. It should be in a lot more A-listers' wardrobes." Meredith flashed a toothpaste-commercial smile. "Maybe you two will get that trending."

Nevaeh laughed. "I'm not sure I'm the one to set trends."

Lamont arched an eyebrow. "Modest, aren't we? I saw your tutorial for perfecting beach waves on YouTube has more than a few likes."

Her mouth dropped open. Good, he wanted her to realize how much he took an interest in her life. Then again, it had started as an investigation—hey, it paid to know who was around you in this way of life—but it soon moved to interest.

Nevaeh had star power, and since she didn't seem to realize it, that made her all the more appealing.

"They only reached the thousands when my name became public knowledge."

"Oh, no. Lamont is correct," Meredith interjected. "I, too, looked at your channel. You have a charismatic personality."

"Wow. Thank you." She ducked her head.

Lamont squeezed her hand again.

Meredith opened up her portfolio that legit held a legal pad inside. "If it's okay with you two, I'll record the interview." She held up a device, looking at them expectantly.

"Of course," he said.

"Sure," Nevaeh echoed.

"Great." She set the device on the coffee table, then flipped her hair over her shoulder. "Let's get started. This is Meredith Walsh for *Luminary* recording the interview with Lamont Booker and Nevaeh Richards."

She perused her notes, then looked up. "I think what everyone in America wants to know is how on earth did you two meet?"

Nevaeh straightened, gripping his arm. "I would love to answer that."

"Please do."

"A year ago—"

"January twelfth to be exact," Lamont interjected. He wasn't sure why that date was imprinted on his mind, it just was.

Nevaeh bumped his shoulder. "Hush, I'm telling the story."

"Fine, I'll be quiet." He made a motion of zipping his lips, grateful that their interviewer was eating up their antics.

"Anyway, I met Lamont on the set of the Netflix series *The Brave*. Lamont here was eavesdropping on my conversation—"

"What? It wasn't a private conversation."

Nevaeh arched her brow, staring him down.

He heaved a sigh. "Tell the story."

"Good." She smiled and turned back to Meredith, who leaned forward. "He overheard me talking about the importance of hair care no matter what you are going through. He approached me and asked if I could help his mom, who was in the midst of chemo treatments."

Meredith placed a hand to her heart, gaze darting to Lamont's face. "I'm so sorry. That must have been a difficult time for you."

He nodded, hating how his face heated from her sympathy. "She's in remission and doing much better now."

"I'm so happy to hear that." Her gaze shifted. "So you ended up becoming his mom's hair stylist?"

"Yes, I come once a week. In fact, I'll be back tomorrow for our standard appointment." Nevaeh paused for a moment. "In the beginning, I'd often give her a scalp massage, but eventually, her hair grew back in, and my styling efforts lengthened."

"So you two just hit it off?" Meredith pointed between Lamont and Nevaeh.

"Nevaeh is very easy to be around." Lamont picked up the story. "Her personality was so engaging, I found myself relaxing and wanting to know more." Which was true. Only God and Nevaeh knew it took Lamont more than a year to figure that out.

Meredith wrote in her legal pad, then looked up. "I think another question the public has is where you two stand on intimacy in an unmarried relationship. Lamont, you've previously claimed to be living a celibate lifestyle. And that picture . . ." Her voice trailed.

Nevaeh shifted beside him, but this time there was no sign she wanted to answer. Guess that meant he had to speak up first this time.

"I'm happy to talk about that. I've never been quiet about my faith once I became saved. I've also never shied away from sharing the value of celibacy. Some people seem to believe you can't wait for physical intimacy until marriage in this day and age, but Nevaeh and I have no intention of crossing that line unless we're married. After our dates, we always go to our separate homes."

"But doesn't kissing one another make you want to cross the line?"

"Of course. I have a pulse, right?" Now his mind wondered what it would be like to kiss Nevaeh. He pushed the thought aside.

Meredith laughed, but Nevaeh was strangely quiet.

"What would you add, Nevaeh? Do you hold Lamont's same faith? Do you agree with his beliefs on saving intimacy until after the I dos?"

Nevaeh shifted. "I am a Christian and was raised by two parents who took me to church every Sunday. So, yes, we share the same faith, and I agree with his stance on intimacy. Considering that I would never want to do anything to hurt his new way of life or disappoint God or myself, maintaining boundaries is a blessing and not a hindrance."

"Again, I have to ask the same thing I asked Lamont. Don't you ever get carried away?" Meredith sat forward, a look of disbelief on her face.

"I haven't yet."

Lamont stiffened. Was Nevaeh saying she was still a virgin? He wanted to stare into her eyes and ask all sorts of questions, but he couldn't. Because as her boyfriend, he should already know that answer. He thought about all he'd shared with her and the public display of his relationship with Diva. What must she think of him?

People make mistakes. You made mistakes. Just because

Nevaeh didn't in this area doesn't mean you aren't both sinners saved by grace.

He blew out a breath.

"I'm sorry." Meredith's voice interrupted the silence. "Are you saying you're a virgin?" Incredulity had the question ending in a high octave.

"Excuse me, is that important to the interview?" Lamont didn't like the idea of the world finding out something so personal. Nevaeh didn't sign up for that level of invasion of privacy.

She rubbed his arm as if to say *I'm okay.* "I am." Nevaeh's dimples became more pronounced as she dipped her head.

"How *old* are you?"

"Again, does that matter?" Lamont asked. He didn't need Ms. Walsh making Nevaeh feel bad about her choice.

"Of course it does. People will be shocked that she's a virgin at . . . ?"

"Twenty-eight," Nevaeh supplied.

Meredith's jaw dropped. "How? How is that even possible?"

"When you have convictions and believe in a Source greater than yourself, you make every effort to uphold them."

Lamont couldn't have said it any better.

Fifteen

did it. I survived my first major interview with Meredith Walsh of *Luminary* magazine. Nausea had been my companion the entire time. I was still kicking myself for admitting my virgin status. Did the world really need to know that? That info should have stayed between me and my boyfriend. He'd even interjected, but acting like it didn't affect me had seemed the smarter tactic at the time.

But knowing Lamont knew upped the nausea seas of discomfort and had me wishing I'd taken a motion sickness pill. Telling journalists the personal details of your life was a ride I needed to hop off stat. But once Meredith had finished the interrogation—I mean *interview*—her photographer had taken so many pictures of us that I was seeing more lights when I blinked than those that shone in the LA skyline at night.

All I wanted to do was go home, get rid of the new body shaper I'd bought specifically for this interview, and eat a pint of Halo Top ice cream. The lower calorie count would take the judgment off when I finished the pint before whatever streaming show I binged came to an end.

Lamont closed the door behind *Luminary*'s representatives, leaned against it, then a small smile appeared on his full lips. My mouth dried as I took in the perfect picture he made. It really was a shame that he was so fine. How could I be myself in our relationship when I had to constantly worry about how I looked compared to him?

My thoughts turned toward social media. I had closed my YouTube account this morning thanks to the haters spamming my videos with dislikes and vile comments. I had almost closed my Twitter account, but then my alarm went off, reminding me it was time to get ready for the interview.

"Want to hang out?" Lamont asked.

And let more people gawk? *No, thanks.* "I have something to do." *Get rid of these clothes!* Cinderella would gladly be taking off all this finery and trading in the teardrop earrings and wrap dress for a nightshirt. It was never too early to wear pj's.

Lamont poked his bottom lip out. "Come on. How about dinner?"

"Don't you have another engagement? A night scene to film?" Didn't he have yesterday off too?

"There was an issue with the set this morning, but I got a text an hour ago that we're good for tomorrow."

"So when will I see you again?" Not that I'd go through withdrawals or anything. Our relationship wouldn't actually last.

Yeah, keep telling yourself that.

It was actually easy to convince myself when we hadn't kissed or anything. Surely I could keep my emotions intact when my lips weren't involved in an intimate connection. God willing, the *Luminary* interview would take the heat off us, and we could slowly part with a friendship intact and the world none the wiser.

"Well, I did just propose dinner." He straightened from the doorway and sauntered over to me, stopping a breath apart. "We could do something casual, or should we do something fancy since we're all dressed up?"

Why did he have to use that low voice that made him famous? My skin couldn't handle that amount of goosebumps.

I gulped. "How 'bout casual? I've had enough of glitz and glam." I gestured to my outfit. Plus, I needed to draw a complete breath as soon as possible. Maybe I should take off the shapewear before driving home.

"Casual is good. Should I grab takeout and come by your place?"

All the blood drained from my face and headed toward my toes. "Um, I don't know if my roommate will be home this evening." We didn't exactly keep each other abreast of our individual schedules. I also couldn't forget Nora's request to go to the charity event.

"Is it a problem if she is? Will she want to hang out or something?"

Or something. Who knew what Nora was up to? "She's trying to be an actress. I'm not sure if her home training will kick in enough for her to exhibit some manners instead of trying to strengthen her degree of separation to you."

Lamont laughed. "So she doesn't know—"

I shook my head. "I signed an NDA, remember?" Still couldn't believe Bryan had that at the ready, but whatever.

"Right." He paused. "All right. I'll go incognito and pick you up. We'll hit a food truck."

"Really?" I allowed myself to relax. "I can't wait to see your concealed look."

"It's great."

"See you later?" I asked, turning toward the garage.

Lamont reached for my arm, heat burning my skin on contact. "Why are you in a rush? Is it this personal thing you've got?"

I threw my hands up in the air. "Lamont Booker, your girlfriend can't breathe because I squished my love handles into an hourglass shape and my diaphragm objects. So unless you want me to pass out, let me go home and be free."

He stepped back, hands in the air and mouth twitching uncontrollably.

"If you start laughing"—I pointed a finger in his face—"the Holy Spirit better intervene."

"I was going to offer one of the many bathrooms here to rid yourself of your constraints. You can even borrow some scissors if it's going to be a major issue." His eyes twinkled.

I would've breathed out a sigh of relief, but this shapewear wouldn't even allow that much. "Thank you," I mumbled.

"Mm-hmm. There's a half bath behind the kitchen."

"I might need more room than that. Taking off shapewear is worse than removing a sports bra after an hour of doing Zumba."

"You can dance?" he asked.

I snapped my fingers. "You're getting off topic."

"You're getting a little hangry, too, huh? Should I make you a snack before you go, or should I change, too, so we can head straight to the food trucks?"

I huffed and walked past him. "I'll use the bathroom near Ms. Rosie's room. It's the one I usually use. And you, you can do whatever."

Lamont chuckled. "Now I understand why that bathroom always smells like you."

I whirled around, and his hands flew up once more.

"*Not* in a bad way. You smell like sunshine."

My mouth dropped, and I tried to think of something to say, but my brain had been wiped clean. Knowing the award-winning actor thought I smelled like sunshine had me floating into the bathroom, or that could have been the shapewear

146

turning me into a helium balloon. I hung my dress on the hook on the back of the door, then examined the monstrosity around my waist stopping under my chest.

"The things we do for beauty," I muttered.

I began unhooking the triple hooks that were worse than the ones found on triple-lettered bras. With each pop of a hook, oxygen inflated my lungs and the light-headedness that had hung around all afternoon started to vanish. Soon my diaphragm inflated properly, and gravity righted my curves to their usual location. I slipped the dress back on, ignoring the outline that hinted at my stomach size. There were no cameras so no need to feel self-conscious.

Yet all the comments I'd seen online, not to mention the commentary that attached to the newly released photos of my shopping adventure, had begun chipping at my self-esteem. I was an overweight hair stylist in a league of beauty pageant–worthy celebrities. I'd even been accused of dimming Lamont's light with my mediocre features. Would the *Luminary* article help or only put the nail in the coffin of what everyone was thinking: How did a woman who looked like me land a man who looked like Mr. SMA?

Logically, I knew I wasn't ugly. Hello, I had dimples. But not having the "right" body shape in this part of the world put a target on my back, or at least made me ignorable. Working behind the scenes had been my coping mechanism. Clients didn't care what size I was as long as I made them look good. Seeing the joy that bloomed on their faces cemented that I was doing the right thing. Stepping into the spotlight to help Lamont almost made me feel like a troll myself, inspecting my reflection more than usual to assess my worth.

I turned my back on the high-priced mirror hanging in the bathroom and made my way back downstairs.

Remember, be yourself. Lamont said you didn't need makeup or shapewear. Just because you're attracted and want him to be as well doesn't mean you change yourself. Besides, the attraction was probably one-sided.

As long as I could remember that, I should be fine.

The sight in the kitchen froze my feet. Lamont had ditched his jacket, vest, and tie. His green shirt had been rolled to his elbows and his top button undone. He looked completely at ease in the kitchen as he placed mashed avocados on slices of bread. Then he took some smoked salmon and placed it artfully on top, sprinkling it with cracked pepper and sesame seeds.

Seeing a man make avocado toast shouldn't be so attractive. Even though it was a simple recipe, knowing he'd made the small meal for me changed my outlook on the snack. This small act was no longer about fuel for my body but fuel for my soul.

A lump formed in my throat as Lamont slid the two plates across the island in front of the stools tucked underneath the counter.

"Hey, you're done." He ducked, grabbing a grocery bag from the bottom cabinet. "In case you're modest and want to hide the boa constrictor."

A chuckle left my lips before I could check myself. I took the reusable bag and discreetly dropped the offensive shapewear inside. "Thanks, Lamont."

"No Mr. SMA?"

"Somehow I don't think he cooks."

"But Lamont does?" He arched a brow.

I nodded, then took a bite, barely holding back a moan. Why was smoked salmon so good?

"What time do you want to meet up for dinner?"

"Give me three hours." I needed to decompress. I stood,

placing my plate in the sink. "Thanks for the snack and the use of your bathroom."

"Anytime, girlfriend."

My body flushed. I wished he wouldn't use that term so loosely. My mind and heart were going to get used to it and expect other things that went along with that title. Instead, I just smiled. "See you later."

"See you in three hours." He dabbed at his mouth. "I'll pick you up."

"Don't pick me up in the Mercedes. That won't help any with the disguise."

He smirked. "Don't worry about me, girlfriend."

As if. This man could handle his own. As obvious as his use of that antiquated word. He was trying to get under my skin. I just didn't know why. Or maybe he was still in interview mode. *That has to be it.*

I waved a hand in the air and walked toward the garage, where I'd parked. Time to surround myself with the creature comforts of my old MINI Cooper. The leather seats that had started to crack, and the cloth ceiling that sagged in the middle.

This Beverly Hills life was *not* my life. This temporary rubbing elbows with my celebrity boyfriend would end soon, and Studio City would be my permanent residence. Hustling for another set stylist position was my end goal, not whatever fairy tale Lamont and I had manufactured.

Sixteen

R aise your arms," Zane said.

Lamont did as instructed and tried to ignore the set costumer so he could run lines in his head for today's scene while Zane ensured Lamont looked his best.

"All right, Booker, you're all set." Zane stepped back, a scrutinizing expression on his normally stoic face.

"Thanks."

Lamont pushed the trailer door open and stepped outside. The lot had been transformed into a countryside with a round pen, where Dalton's ladylove would meet him. Lamont shook his arms, getting into character.

"Lamont!"

He groaned, turning around. The director's assistant pushed his black square frames back against his nose. "Brad wants to speak to you."

"Okay. Where is he?" Lamont tried not to let dread pull his stomach, but knowing the *Luminary* article had probably hit the newsstand made him tense.

Bryan had warned Lamont that the article would be published as soon as possible. Considering it had only been a few days, he couldn't imagine it had already been printed. Surely his agent would have warned him if it released.

"Brad's in his trailer."

Lamont nodded and headed for the director's trailer. He went up the cinder block steps and knocked.

"Yeah, come in."

He ducked, eyes adjusting to the dim light. "Your assistant said you wanted to see me."

Brad turned from his seat at a table and waved him forward. He mumbled into the cell plastered to his ear. "Gotcha. We'll make sure everything is good. . . . All right." Brad set the phone down. "Have a seat."

This wasn't good. Lamont pulled out a chair. "Everything okay?"

"That's why I called you in here."

"What's going on?"

"The *Luminary* article was sent out to all their online subscribers. You're trending."

Lamont's mouth dried. "In a good way or . . . ?"

Brad leaned back, placing his interlaced fingers behind his head. "In a good way."

A whoosh of air fell from Lamont's mouth.

"That was the producer. He said people are shipping you and the hair stylist—"

"Nevaeh." Lamont raised an eyebrow.

"Right. Her. Anyway, people are favorable toward you. There's even been pushback on the trolls who have been spamming her account."

Lamont's brow furrowed. "What do you mean?"

"You don't know?" Brad cocked his head. "Your girlfriend has closed at least two of her social accounts thanks to the amount of hate speech filling her feed. I assumed you had advised her to close them."

If Lamont had known, he would've. "I didn't know."

Brad tutted. "You understand how to ignore the press, but someone like her doesn't."

"What do you mean?"

"Your girl is green. She doesn't know the ways of Hollywood or how to avoid the news rags. I'd advise her before she has to shut down all of her accounts and start walking around with a bodyguard."

Great, now Lamont needed to down some antacids. "Thanks for the advice."

"Keep up the favorable press, and the producers will continue fulfilling their side of the contract."

"Understood."

"See you on set." Brad flicked a hand toward the door.

Lamont stood and left the trailer. He blew out a breath, rubbing the back of his head. Should he call Nevaeh? He'd check the time, but a watch didn't come with his outfit. Apparently, Dalton didn't wear one. Plus, he probably needed to head to the set before he missed the call and other cast members thought he was fashionably late on purpose. His long strides ate up the ground.

As much as he wanted to think about Nevaeh having to close her social accounts, Lamont really needed to get into character. The quicker he did that, the faster he'd be able to recite the lines in the way Dalton was known to do. He'd just have to talk to his girlfriend after this scene was filmed.

He scanned the set, thankful to see the leading lady had yet to make an appearance. Good. He didn't want to be the last one ready. He took his place, mentally viewing the script. His assistant would be behind the scenes somewhere in case Lamont needed anything. Would it be weird to ask Greg to check on Nevaeh? Maybe Lamont could get him to text her while he was on set.

"Places, everyone."

Lamont moved to the round pen entrance, placed a foot on the fence, and rested an arm on the top rail. He put a faraway expression on his face and waited for the director to call action. Although he hadn't seen Alyssa, the director would only call for places if everyone was accounted for.

"Action!"

Dalton imagined the breeze blowing through the countryside, then stiffened, as if sensing Lena behind him. He turned slowly and let his gaze roam the figure of the lead actress. "Lena," he whispered hoarsely.

"Dalton." She took a step forward as if shy.

But at this point in the story, they were done with hiding their attraction. Today's scene called for their first on-screen kiss. Considering they had already filmed the ending a few weeks ago, it was a little strange to film the kiss today. But filming was rarely sequential.

"I'd hoped," he murmured, closing the gap between them and placing her hands on his chest.

"Couldn't you tell?"

"I thought." He shrugged. "I just didn't want it to be my imagination."

"It's not." She slid a hand on the back of his head.

He dipped lower, pausing a breath away. He waited a moment to make sure the director wouldn't call cut, then placed his lips against his costar's.

On-screen kissing was about as romantic as eating a vat of onions before your first date and expecting the woman to swoon. Oh, her head would drop back, but from disgust and not a desire to kiss.

Lamont waited for the cut, but it wasn't coming. How long did the director want them to hold this position? Was it a fade-away scene, and he'd forgotten?

"Cut!"

"Finally," Alyssa muttered as she stepped back.

Someone from the hair-and-makeup team rushed to reapply Alyssa's lipstick while another rushed to Lamont's side to remove the lipstick stain on his mouth.

"Thanks."

The woman nodded and walked back off set. Lamont turned to see what the next direction was, but Brad was talking to the screenwriter.

Lamont placed his hands on his hips.

"Antsy to get out of here and back to your ladylove?" Alyssa smirked.

"Just want to do the best job today."

She rolled her eyes. "You say that every day."

"I mean it every day."

She folded her arms and closed the gap between them. "Is it real?"

"What?"

"This holier-than-thou act?"

"Have I given you that impression?" Lamont never wanted to appear like he had it altogether. Far from it. If it weren't for God's daily grace, Lamont would be wallowing in failure.

"Well, no. But you say hello to everyone. You don't swear on set like half the other leading men I've come across. You never proposition me." She huffed. "So, like, is your faith legit? I saw that article with your girlfriend. And I admit I'm having a hard time believing she's a virgin and neither of you have 'crossed a line.'" She mimed air quotes, her mouth twisted with snark.

Lord, please give me the words. He slid his hand in his loose pocket. "What have I done to make you think my faith is fake?"

Alyssa's mouth dropped, then shut. She looked up as if

thinking of the answer. Finally, she met his gaze. "Well, nothing really."

"Then you're just wondering how we could save intimacy for marriage?"

"Of course. No one does that. *No one.*"

"I do. I don't want to go back to the place I was." The path where he used people, and they used people, and it was all a mess that had him checking into a "retreat" to find himself. Fortunately, he'd found God instead of replacing one vice with another.

"Then that's it? You don't want to be bad, so you decided to be good?"

"I don't think it's as black-and-white as that. It's more like I was in such a state that once God opened my eyes to Him, I couldn't help but choose the things that would only glorify Him. It's no longer about me."

Alyssa snorted. "When is it not about us?"

"When you have someone ask you about your faith, and you can see they're hurting."

Her gaze locked onto his. "What do you mean?" she whispered.

"I'm guessing you're asking questions because something inside of you recognizes God could be the answer. Sometimes that comes from a place of mere curiosity, and other times we're searching for meaning when we feel empty."

Her eyes welled up, and she stepped back.

"Alyssa—"

She held up a hand. "I'm okay."

"I didn't offend you, did I?"

"No, but you certainly gave me something to think about."

He could only pray that God would continue to open her eyes. "If you ever have any more questions, please ask."

She nodded.

"Places, people! Let's take it from the top. We've got two more scenes to shoot after this."

Lamont sighed and went back to the fence. But before he set his arm back on the rail, he glanced at Alyssa off set, waiting for her entrance. This. This was why he'd been willing to enter into a relationship with Nevaeh. People needed to see the goodness of God, and if the media had its way, he'd be canceled right now, his career over. He still wasn't one-hundred-percent sure he'd done the right thing, but Alyssa's questions made him believe what his mom had been saying all along. Something good could come of all of this.

Seventeen

fluffed the bottom of Ms. Rosie's curls and grinned at her reflection in the mirror. "There. You look beautiful."

She smiled, tilting her head left, then right. "I certainly feel it. You do wonders with my hair." She bunted the bottom like I had done. "I still can't get over how soft my hair is now."

"That seems to be a common side effect from chemo." I had done so much research to make sure I encouraged her hair to grow back in a healthy way, including ensuring all of her hair-styling products remained chemical-free. Ms. Rosie had had enough of that to last a lifetime.

I hoped.

"That's what a lot of ladies in my support group said." She got out of the chair and opened her arms for a hug.

I lightly squeezed her petite frame. Ms. Rosie gave the best hugs, and the comfort almost made me want to spill my guts. Only how could I tell my sort-of-fake boyfriend's mom that this was all too much? People were giving me double glances when I went out, and thanks to the *Luminary* article hitting a few days ago, I had more people following my Instagram account than I could handle. The DMs ranged from sweet solidarity comments from other Christians who were waiting for their future husbands to judgmental Bible thumpers telling me not to be unequally yoked with Lamont. They doubted his salvation and cautioned me against dating him. But the ones that shocked me the most were supposed celebrities asking me out. Surely those were spam accounts, though one had a blue checkmark, which meant it was verified. *Right?*

I stepped out of Ms. Rosie's embrace and started putting my supplies away.

"What do you have planned for the rest of your day?" Ms. Rosie asked.

"I've got a shift at The Mane Do I'm headed to."

"Any news on your applications for film hair stylists?"

I turned back toward her. "I did get an email from one production company letting me know they filled the position and to apply if a new spot opened in the future."

She frowned. "You'll get one. Just wait. I know good things are coming."

"I hope you're right."

I closed up my case and grabbed the handle to drag it to the elevator. "I'll see you next week?"

"Maybe sooner." She smiled. "What do you think of getting together for lunch one day?"

I stopped, stunned. "Really?" Why would she want to hang out with me?

Ms. Rosie nodded. "I know you only came here to be my hair stylist, but don't you think we should start spending more time together? After all, you're dating my son now."

Right. Of course Ms. Rosie would be on board with helping Lamont's image. My stomach clenched. Had I really believed she wanted to hang out with me for me? "Sure. We can do that one day." I forced my lips into a curve.

"Great. Text me your schedule so we can figure out a time."

"Okay." I waved and left.

All the way to the salon, I kept thinking of Ms. Rosie's offer. It was really unfortunate dating a celebrity. How was I supposed to know who was sincere in their attention toward me? I couldn't even trust Lamont when he said he was interested in getting to know me more.

Wasn't he just trying to appease his conscience and force feelings that weren't there? At least on his end. I couldn't help but think of the reasons my admiration for him continued to grow. He was doing so much good in the world—not just with charities but also in choosing movie roles that fans could watch without worrying if scenes would dip into rated-R territory—and the way he treated his mom with such affection was endearing. However, that didn't mean I had to fall for his charm. I couldn't! Friends didn't fall for friends. Not sure where I heard that, but it sounded like a movie quote.

I parked in the back alley behind The Mane Do and hustled inside. After storing my things in my locker, I grabbed my apron and tied it around my waist. My Ankara-print headband was still in place and added color to the boring black I wore.

Nineties R&B music drummed through the sound system, and the low murmur of voices reached my ears as I walked up to my booth. Suddenly the music seemed louder. I turned to see if someone had turned up the volume and found all eyes on me. Since the mirror in my locker had proved I looked presentable, obviously there was nothing horrifying hanging off my face. Which could only mean that the stares were due to my recent status in the news.

I tilted my chin and ignored the many looks. No need to spend time dissecting them. I had clients to attend to and professionalism to uphold. So what if the moment I stepped through the doorway, the hum of voices stopped. I didn't care what they thought of me . . . much.

"Your client is here." Jewel gave a nod toward a woman sitting on the sofa.

"Thanks."

She nodded and crossed off an item on her clipboard.

"Come on back, Kace."

The woman eyed me, and my stomach clenched. Kace was a new client, and I could only pray she was here for an actual appointment and not some fact-finding mission.

"How are you today?" I asked.

"Good. I just need a wash and press."

"Of course. Do you want the same look?" I pointed toward her hair, which hung in soft waves.

Her nose wrinkled in disgust. "No, this look is tired. I want to look like a star."

"Oh, do you have an audition?" I motioned for her to sit before the sink bowl and draped a hand towel around her neck, followed by a smock around her person.

"No." She snorted. "I don't want to do all of that work. But if I could snag a celebrity, then I'd be set." Her black eyes roamed up and down my figure. "How did *you* do it?"

I flinched inwardly. But outwardly, I gave my most saccharine smile. "It was my winning personality."

I wish I could say Kace was a one-off, but client after client made comments about me and Lamont. Some were subtle, and some were outright. The current person in my chair was working my every last nerve.

"I mean, do you know how hard it is to make it as an actress?" Mercedes asked.

"I have an idea." Nora was upset she hadn't gotten a callback on her latest audition. She'd been reminding me of the charity event and how she *still* didn't have a ticket. But how could I ask Lamont for something I didn't even want Nora to show up to?

"Really? Is that why you're dating Lamont Booker? You want to be an actress?"

I stifled a sigh. "No. I actually like him as a person. I'm not with him so he can do something for me." *Actually, it's the other way around. Wouldn't that shock you?*

Nevertheless, I kept mute as I ran the hot comb through Mercedes's edges.

"No one in Hollywood likes someone just to like them." Her gaze met mine, reflected in the station mirror before us. "You're, like, gonna start your own business or *something*, right? You two aren't dating just to"—she shrugged—"fall in love?" Her voice rose in question.

"Actually, Mercedes, that's exactly our plan."

"Where is she?" a voice shrieked.

I tensed at the noise, immediately holding the hot comb as if it were a weapon. I could probably knock someone over the head or burn them with the hot tool, but it would be pointless if that shriek belonged to a person with a gun.

"Miss, you can't go in there!" Jewel shouted.

A wide-eyed woman stood in the doorway, her chest heaving as she scanned the room. Her entire countenance shifted as she spotted me. "You!" She pointed. "How dare you date Lamont Booker?"

What in the world? My feet rooted to the floor, and my hand clenched the hot comb. "Can I help you?" I asked cautiously.

"There's no way that fine, beautiful man is dating someone like you. Not when I could make him happy." Her voice took on a hysterical tinge.

I backed up, gaze darting to Jewel. She was on the phone. God willing, she was calling the police.

"I'm sure you don't want to come between a couple." No, I wasn't. I just needed some sort of wisdom to come out of my mouth and calm her down.

"Why shouldn't I?" She gestured toward her body. "I would know how to make him happy. Something a virgin like you wouldn't know about."

These comments were becoming increasingly irritating, but now wasn't the moment to ignore the Holy Spirit and let my flesh speak for me. This woman was unhinged with a capital *U*.

Before I could speak, cops filled the salon and hustled the screaming woman out onto the sidewalk. I blew out a breath and dropped the tool into the mini furnace.

"You're all done." I unwrapped the smock from Mercedes.

She looked at me with pity. "Is love really worth *that*?" She hooked a thumb over her shoulder.

My lips flattened. "You can pay at the front desk."

The police took statements from a few of us before deciding no harm had been done. Only they couldn't see the woman inside of me who wanted to shrink inside of herself. Wasn't the *Luminary* article supposed to show people we were the real deal? That nothing untoward had happened? Yet I was still being maligned by entertainment news and the zealots who believed everything they stated. Somehow my curves and the lack of blockbuster hits behind my name made me less-than.

For the first time since this started, I was actually worried about my safety. I didn't have security at my apartment or a driver to ensure no one could get at me in a vehicle. Not to mention the world knew where I was thanks to social media posts. Who knew where the next fanatic fan would pop up?

Lord, I'm starting to have doubts. About myself, this relationship, all of it. Help me, please!

Eighteen

Lamont wanted nothing more than to take a hot shower and wash the stench away. The smell of horses seemed to have permeated his skin after being on the *Kentucky Tracks* film set all day, but tonight, he needed to look and *smell* his best. He and Nevaeh would be attending the *Sands of Time* charity event this evening as their first couple event. This would be another opportunity to solidify their relationship in the public's eyes. Give them better news than some irate fan showing up at Nevaeh's work.

A simple text reading *Guess I'm really famous now* had been all she'd said on the subject. Even though she said her humor was a sign of nervousness, this time Lamont sensed her joke was covering up more. Finding out from someone else—and not his girlfriend—that she'd closed some social media accounts had worried him. What was going on in that beautiful head of hers?

This morning, he'd spent time praying that the charity event would go smoothly. That security would ensure the safety of the celebrities, but more specifically, for Nevaeh. Lamont had even prayed Nevaeh would be able to handle the absurd number of camera flashes that would come their way. Surely this publicity coupled with the *Luminary* article would take the heat off her and show the world they were a united front.

Lamont trudged up the stairs toward his bedroom. Before he walked fully onto the second floor, his mother's door flew open.

She stalked up to him, fisted her small hands on her hips, and squinted at him.

"What did I do?" He took a step back, heart racing. He'd seen the same censure on her face countless times growing up right before receiving a tongue lashing.

"If you hurt that girl, I'll move out."

His stomach heaved. "What are you talking about? And why would you move out? Haven't I taken good care of you?" He'd gotten her access to the best doctors and ensured she had access to health and fitness gurus to keep her in tip-top shape.

Lamont would do everything in his power to make sure she never had to battle cancer again.

With a sigh, Mom's irate expression faded to one of love. "You're the best son I could ever have. God blessed me with you, Lamont, but you have to know I can't live in your house forever."

"Why not? Do you need a bigger room?" He could switch suites with her. Or even hire a contractor and knock down a wall somewhere. Maybe even renovate the pool house to be an in-law suite.

"No, son. I'm just a grown woman who's used to living in my own space. I only agreed to move in because I knew how much chemo would wreck me." She held up her arms. "Look at me now." She flexed her biceps and winked.

He nodded. "You look good, Mom." She really did. Why should she stress herself with keeping up her own place when he had everything covered? "You know there's plenty of room here, right? I don't want you to feel like you have to move. You can stay forever." *Please, so I know you're okay.*

"Maybe not forever, but I will move into a hotel if I find out you've done anything to hurt that girl." She shook a finger in his face.

"Who?" he cried. This conversation was giving him whiplash.

"Nevaeh, boy! Who do you think I'm harping about?"

"Mom, you just said 'her.' That could be anyone." He resisted the urge to throw his hands in the air.

"Please." She rolled her eyes. "Like there isn't only one woman that's got you trying to look your best lately."

"Are you saying I don't normally look this handsome?"

Her nose wrinkled. "You might need a shower and an extra hint of cologne."

"I thought of that already. But thanks for lowering my self-esteem and pointing it out."

She shoved his shoulder. "Please."

"What prompted this feminine solidarity?"

"I read the article. I've been meaning to talk to you about it, but you've been on set."

"Was it bad? Bryan said it looked good." He couldn't bring himself to read it. See his own words declaring himself in a relationship where intimacy was respected. More like nonexistent.

Mom smirked. "He's probably rolling around on his proverbial bed of riches. Nevaeh boosted your respectability, no doubt about it. But don't forget she also has a reputation to guard. Now that the world has been told she's a virgin, scrutiny will be on both of you. Some will be waiting to see you fail. I'm sure the critics will share any photo that looks like you two compromised your morals."

Mom shook her head. "Such a double standard in this world."

Lamont worried about Nevaeh. He had never imagined she'd say something so personal in their interview. The pressure to make sure she came out unscathed increased daily. "I'll do my best."

"You better ask for some holy intervention. I mean it. I don't want her hurt by this."

"I get it, Mom."

"You better." She reached up and pinched his cheeks. "You're my son, but she definitely earned a spot in my heart this past year."

"What about me? What if she hurts me?" His question was half in jest and half curiosity.

"I'll give her a similar talk when we meet up for lunch."

"Lunch?"

She grinned and stepped back. "I have to get to know the lady in your life." She waved. "Have fun at the charity event."

"That's all you're going to say?" He turned, trying to keep her in view as she headed down the flight of stairs.

"Yep. Love you!"

Lamont wanted to argue, but their conversation had altered his timetable. His driver would pick him up in twenty minutes before going to Nevaeh's. The *Sands of Time* production company had rented out the Griffith Observatory, so they'd have a nice commute up the Hills.

He rushed through a shower, lathering twice for good measure, and adding an extra dab of cologne per his mom's suggestion. His black suit had already been pressed and readied by the dry cleaners. Last, he added moisturizer to his bald head, thankful for the clean shave he'd gotten yesterday.

By the time he stepped downstairs, Kyle's voice over the intercom alerted him to the driver's arrival.

"Have a good time," his mom said from her spot on the couch.

"Thanks."

"Don't forget to stop and get her some flowers."

Lamont smiled and leaned over to kiss her on the cheek. "I already got her something."

"What?"

He started whistling and walked away, just as she'd done to him earlier.

"What, Lamont!"

"Love you."

"Oh, you!" She chuckled.

Lee greeted him outside the garage, the back door to the sedan already opened.

"Thanks, man."

Lamont settled into his seat, his thoughts replaying his mother's warning. Did she really think he'd intentionally hurt Nevaeh? He was doing everything he could to avoid that. He'd been burned before and had no intention of doing that to someone else.

It's why he continued to take her on dates as well as chat daily either by text or by phone. Now he looked forward to seeing her dressed up and ready to dance the night away, so to speak. Did she feel like this was a real relationship, or was she merely posing for pictures?

He shook his head. Nevaeh wasn't like that. She wasn't Diva. Still, the thought of actively trying to fall in love sounded like a risk he couldn't afford. What if he *actually* fell for Nevaeh Richards—someone he was only dating because he'd kept her from face-planting? Then she'd have the power to hurt him, to affect his future in ways he couldn't predict. How could he trust she was the right person to be vulnerable with?

Because she hasn't asked one thing of you. There were so many ways she could try to take advantage of dating a movie star, and she hadn't tried a single one. He'd even overheard her telling her roommate she wouldn't ask him for another ticket to the charity event. When he'd questioned her about the conversation, Nevaeh had confessed she suspected Nora of trying to use the situation. He had been willing to invite the roommate along, but Nevaeh had stood firm.

Maybe his heart would truly be safe with her, and he could stop trying to hold back the affection that rose inside every time he saw her. The one that had wanted to kiss her at her parents' house and instead agreed to be friends at the least.

Only the idea of a fake-dating beginning kind of made things awkward. Made him question her motives. He should've never let Bryan run with that suggestion. Then again, she had signed an NDA. He never would have thought to ask for one in the first place, so maybe that meant he'd trusted her on some level in the beginning. Surely that trust had increased. Right?

Though he'd lost a couple of endorsements, others had doubled down and backed him and what he stood for. Good things were happening, and that had been the whole point of the arrangement. He'd also made a promise to truly try with Nevaeh. Lamont couldn't do that if he was too busy protecting his heart.

He shouldn't act like he was waiting for the proverbial shoe to drop with her. She wasn't his ex. He could see that clearly. So maybe now it was time to treat her like a real girlfriend and not just a friend. He would make tonight different. *Please, help me show her how much I'm beginning to care, Lord.*

The car slowed, and the partition lowered. "Do you want to wait in the car, sir? I can get Ms. Richards."

"No, I've got it." If he was going to pick his girlfriend

up—even if he had a driver—then he'd knock on the door like a gentleman. Plus, he wanted to be the first to see her in her dress.

He still couldn't get the vision she made for the *Luminary* article out of his head. Surely tonight would be even better. He walked down the sidewalk to the charming white-stucco apartments. As he rounded the corner, a whistle rent the air.

Lamont froze, scanning the area. His eyes stopped on an elderly woman sitting on her front stoop.

"Evening, ma'am."

"Well, good evening to you, Mr. Booker. Your darling girl is right in that building." She pointed to the apartment across from her. "You two out for a date?"

Before he could respond, Nevaeh's door opened, and she walked out. Her one-shoulder gown flowed out from a high waist in dark pink wisps, somehow emphasizing her curves yet remaining modest at the same time. A contorted updo and gold hoop earrings completed her look to perfection.

Nevaeh's eyes darted from the neighbor to Lamont and back to the neighbor. "Are you behaving, Mrs. Hazelton?"

"Just complimenting your man on his finery. I also asked if you two were going on a date, but judging by your beautiful dress, I'll take that as a yes."

Beautiful wasn't the right word for the picture Nevaeh made. Lamont unconsciously stepped forward. "You look . . ." He shook his head. "Wow."

Her lips curved, and those dimples grabbed his attention. "So do you." She lowered her voice. "Do you mind meeting my neighbor before we go?"

"Sure." He offered an arm, and she slipped her hand into the crook of his elbow, then he guided them across the grassy knoll.

"Mrs. Hazelton, this is Lamont Booker. Lamont, this is my neighbor Lenora Hazelton, my baking buddy."

Mrs. Hazelton laughed, the sound similar to an emphysema patient's cough. "I bake, she samples."

"Everyone knows taste tester is the best job in the kitchen," Lamont quipped.

"No wonder she likes you. You come back during the day, and I'll make sure to have something for you to sample. Do you like coffee cake?"

"Homemade?" He nodded at her assurance. "I'll eat homemade anything."

"Spoken like an actor on a diet. Come back for some cake one day. And do make sure this beautiful girl returns home safely."

"I will."

She shooed them away, so Lamont wished her a good evening.

"You didn't have to get out of the car," Nevaeh murmured.

"Of course I did. How else could I ensure I'd be the first to see you looking beautiful?"

Her eyes met his. "You're turning on the charm tonight."

"Giving you my best like you deserve."

Nevaeh studied him, then slid into the back seat. He followed, reaching for the gift he'd stowed in the car earlier.

"I wanted to get you something." He handed Nevaeh the rectangular box.

"Lamont Booker, you can't keep spending money on me. First the dresses then . . ." She lifted the lid, and it snapped to the open position. She gasped, hand shaking as she lifted the necklace from the velvet box. "Oh my word."

"Is that a good *oh my word*, or were you substituting that for a bad word?"

She laughed. "So good. It's lovely." The leaf-shaped diamonds hung in threes from the rose-gold necklace. There were also matching earrings in the box.

"Then it matches its owner."

Her gaze shifted to him. "You're in fine form tonight."

Lamont scooted over. "Let me put it on?"

She bit her lip.

"What's wrong?"

"It's all just so much," she whispered. "The clothes. The dinners. Now jewelry?"

He got it. He'd been a little overwhelmed the first time he'd seen how many zeros followed the balance in his checking account. He searched his mind for a solution. "What if you consider it something borrowed?" He gulped. "Not that we're getting married or anything. I only meant I could hang on to it for safekeeping, and you can wear it when you want to."

Nevaeh slowly nodded. "Okay."

After Lamont fastened the necklace, Nevaeh switched out her hoops with the ones in the box.

"Nevaeh?"

"Yes?" She faced him.

"There's something I've been wanting to do but kept stopping myself from."

Her eyes locked onto his. "What?"

"Kiss you." He swallowed. "Can I? I mean, do you want to . . . ?" *Ugh, this is so awkward.* He ran a hand down his face, but Nevaeh stopped his trajectory, gripping his wrist.

"Why?"

"Why what?"

"Why do you want to kiss me?"

"Because I've been dreaming about it since the day I met your parents."

Her eyes flickered back and forth, studying him as if weighing the truth of his words. Then she leaned forward and pressed her lips against his.

Nineteen

promised myself I'd keep my lips far away from Lamont Booker. Until he admitted to wanting to kiss me. Not because we were supposed to be dating, or in love, or whatever we told *Luminary*, but because he felt some kind of attraction to me. As much as I wanted to protect my heart from this fairy tale we'd built around us, I couldn't resist finding out if these butterflies were real or a figment of my imagination.

Kissing him was pure instinct and letting him take the lead an easy choice. As he tugged me closer, I followed each movement until no space existed between us. Heat filled my middle and spread into every limb as he continued the languid exploration of my mouth.

He then trailed tender caresses along my jawline, leaving goosebumps in their wake. My head swam as he brushed his mouth along each dimple before lifting his head. I stared up at him, blinking rapidly to bring myself into the present.

What was he thinking? My brain shouted various bullet points as if I'd subconsciously been taking notes.

Magnificent.

Out of this world.

Ruined any other man after this.

Did Lamont have any of the same thoughts?

"That was . . ." He leaned his forehead against mine.

"All right? Better than average? Amazing?" I replied breathlessly.

"The best kiss of my life."

I couldn't have stopped the grin from spreading even if I wanted to hide my emotions and play coy. "I'll accept that answer."

Lamont chuckled and let go of my hands, sliding to the other end of the bench seat in one fluid movement.

"We're sitting far away now?" I asked.

"Yes." He nodded. "Because I don't need to show up to the charity event looking like I was making out with my girlfriend the whole ride over."

"What if you were?"

His heavy-lidded eyes met mine. "I would not survive a car ride like that." His Adam's apple bobbed. "I know we kind of talked about boundaries in the interview, but that was before we kissed."

"What are you saying?"

"I'm saying now that we've kissed, we should revisit that talk. Like you staying over there and me over here."

I laughed. I couldn't help myself. "I'm not going to take your virtue."

"You can't." His expression turned somber. "I'm not a virgin like you, which means I could very easily use my imagination to fill in the gaps. Which is why we can't have a repeat of that"—he waved a hand between us—"too often. I'm no angel."

I wasn't either. His declaration emboldened me and made me want to erase the distance between us. The fact that this man felt the need to take a breather was heady to my senses.

Thank the good Lord there was enough sense in my brain to keep me away. Was this that escape the Lord talked about regarding temptation? If so, I needed to remain in my corner and think logically, not emotionally.

"Okay. No more kissing."

"Well, maybe a small good-night kiss," Lamont suggested.

I nodded, trying to suppress the twitch of my lips. "And hands to ourselves."

"Maybe holding hands at the event would be okay."

"Lamont." I laughed.

"Hey, I didn't mean we had to ignore each other, just maintain a little social distance until we arrive. I've been in relationships that were nothing but physical and know how quickly lines can be erased." He frowned. "Not to mention how intimacy links you to a person a lot longer than you may even realize. God put rules in place to protect us. Plus, neither one of us wants to break promises to the Lord."

His words had the effect of an ice bath. "You're right."

I was already uneasy about the relationship we portrayed— though right now, I felt very much like we were truly dating— and I didn't want to compound any lies or the guilt I'd been carrying around since I said yes to being his girlfriend. After agreeing to save his reputation, I certainly didn't want to be the one to ruin it.

I bit my lip. How had a mere kiss directed us to a boundaries conversation? *What* was I doing with Lamont? Where could this relationship possibly go? Though maybe the bigger question was, How could I keep my heart safe through the process? I *knew* a kiss would only hook my feelings in further. Now Lamont was talking about linking with a person. I'd heard talks about why abstinence was so important. Was I ready to marry Lamont in the eyes of God?

I couldn't possibly be blessed enough to ride off into the

sunset with the leading man, could I? That wasn't the current script or direction my life was going.

"You okay?" Lamont asked.

I nodded. "Thinking." We needed a change in topic. "What should I expect tonight?" I'd never done anything like this before.

"A lot of schmoozing. Some celebrities will be polite, and some will show you their true selves, which won't make you a fan."

I wondered which celebrities were snobs and which were genuinely nice. "So I should . . . ?"

"Be yourself. We'll mingle with the cast, sit through the charity dinner, and maybe even dance."

"That sounds nice."

"Then that's what we'll do."

The car slowed, and I attempted to peer out of the tinted windows. "Are we here already?"

"Looks like. You ready for this?"

With the way my insides went on high alert, probably not. Except there was no turning back. "I'll have to be."

Lamont held out his hand. "I'll be with you the whole night. We've got this."

"Then let's go." I slid along the bench seat, took his hand, and sighed.

Lamont lowered the partition. "We're ready."

"I'll be right around, then."

The partition closed, and Lamont looked at me. "There will be lots of flashes. Trick is to look down the red carpet. If we need to stop and talk with a reporter or pose for a picture, I'll squeeze your hand. If we're answering questions, I'll wrap an arm around you and respond to the question first. If it's a picture, I'll whisper, 'Smile,' and guide us into a pose. Good?"

I nodded as my mind shouted, *No, no, not ready!*

Lamont stepped out of the sedan, and immediately, flashes went off. Somehow, he ignored them, turning toward me to offer his palm. Thank the Lord I could squeeze the life out of it as I came to my feet and did my best to look unaffected. Was this why stars wore sunglasses on the red carpet? Here I always thought the reason purely egotistical, but they were probably saving their retinas from flashbulb trauma.

Lamont and I strolled down the walkway as if we had all the time in the world. Thank goodness I skipped dinner, or my stomach would have ejected the contents, making headlines for mortifying reasons.

"Lamont, over here! Lamont!"

Left and right, journalists clamored for his attention. It wasn't until a Christian vlogger—seriously, Ann Grace was shoulder to shoulder with other reporters—called out to him that he squeezed my hand and guided us over, placing his arm around my shoulders.

"Lamont and Nevaeh, thank you for stopping by. Inquiring minds want to know what your favorite Bible verse is and why that verse?" She thrust her recording device near Lamont's mouth.

"That's easy. I have Ezekiel 36:26 framed and hanging in my room. Knowing that God reformed me and gave me a new heart and spirit is a great reminder that I don't have to be bound by my past."

My heart turned over. This was why I agreed to be Lamont's girlfriend. He was shining his light for all to see.

"What about you, Ms. Richards?" The device sprang in front of me, and I blinked.

Yikes. I was supposed to tell them my favorite verse? The past two Sundays, I'd attended church with Lamont. Seeing how focused he was, how well he knew the Bible, made me question the depth of my faith. I didn't believe going to church made him better than me per se, but it had certainly given him a thorough knowledge I didn't possess. After attending services, I'd been convicted to read my Bible again, starting in Psalms. I searched my memory.

"Since I've met Lamont, he's been such an encouragement to my own faith. Psalm One, verse two, not only reminds me of how Lamont views his faith, but how the Lord wants me to see it as well."

"*But his delight is in the law of the* Lord, *and in His law he meditates day and night.*"

I really did need to take the time to think about the Word day and night. I had no problem sending a prayer heavenward, but studying the Bible had never been a priority. Maybe I'd frame the psalm and place it on my nightstand as a reminder to maintain God's priorities. Or I could write it on a sticky note and stick it on my mirror.

"Thank you."

"Our pleasure," Lamont stated. He squeezed my hand, and we started walking away.

We posed a few more times and spoke with a fashion columnist who wanted to know the designers we were wearing. Thank goodness I'd had the good sense to look at the label before dressing, granted the name written in gold script on the box cover had been a dead giveaway.

Finally, we entered the Griffith Observatory. I let out a breath and stared up at the ceiling, taking in the mural depicting the gods the planets were named after. A nearby plaque even mentioned the star of Bethlehem featured in the mural. I exhaled, letting the tension slowly seep from my body.

"That wasn't so bad, was it?" Lamont asked, leaning close and pulling me from gawking.

"It's a wonder you celebrities aren't blind."

"Give me a few more years."

I grinned up at him, but the sound of heels clicking against tile alerted us to company.

"Incoming," Lamont whispered.

I tensed as Blake Smythe strolled toward us, a model wearing impossibly high heels on his arm. The source of the clacking I'd heard. Oh, that was his new wife. The one younger than his youngest child. *No judgment, Nevaeh.*

"Lamont, good to see you here." He shook hands, then pointed toward his wife. "This is my wife, Esilda."

"Nice to meet you." Lamont slid an arm around my waist. "This is my girlfriend, Nevaeh."

"Lovely to meet you." Esilda spoke with a beautiful Spanish accent.

"Likewise." We shook hands, though she obviously hadn't gotten lessons on handshakes like my father had given me. Her palm fell against mine like a noodle to the kitchen wall.

"Do you guys know where you're sitting?" Blake asked.

Were there assigned seats? Somehow, I'd imagined us standing around trying to outdo one another in the looks department before hearing a boring speech, then being permitted to dance while spending a preposterous amount of money.

Lamont pulled out an invitation from his suit pocket. "We're at table five."

"We're at table six. Maybe we can sit near each other. Who knows what kind of bores they'll put at my table."

"How many are at a table?" I asked.

"Eight," Blake answered. "The tables are pretty big so no one will step on any toes. It's on the lower floor."

"Let's go find our seats," Lamont suggested.

I nodded.

"See you, Blake."

"We'll sit after we grab some drinks. It's an open bar, my friend."

Lamont nodded, then he placed a hand on the small of my back and guided me away.

"I'm sorry."

"What for?" His brows shot up.

"You'll have to rub elbows with him all night."

Lamont chuckled. "Not like I haven't before. At least he doesn't pretend to like you, then spread rumors behind your back like some other celebrities."

"How do you live like this?" I murmured.

"With God reminding me of my blessings and what's real. All this—" he tilted his head—"this is all just another stage. Reality is within my four walls."

Did that mean he didn't feel reality with me? What about the kiss in the car? Before I could ask, one of the leading ladies of *Sands of Time* stopped us.

"Lamont Booker, don't you look as fabulous as *People* claimed." She winked, then leaned forward to air-kiss his cheek. "Now introduce me to your girlfriend."

"Rebecca Lane, this is Nevaeh Richards. Nevaeh, meet Ms. Lane."

"Call me Rebecca, darling. I may be ancient, but I don't stand on titles. They're a bore."

"They can be."

"What do you think of the event?" She gestured around us.

I took my time staring at the gold stars hanging from the ceiling and the serving staff in their suits holding golden trays of fluted champagne. "I think the place is stunning."

"Do be sure to go outside and get a picture of the view. Your social followers will go green with jealousy, and hopefully the event will get more accolades."

Well, that was pointed.

"We were just making our way to our seats," Lamont said.

"Oh, don't be boring, Lamont. Mingle with the others before sitting down. Don't worry, there'll be a five-minute warning to get to your seats before the speeches start."

"Thanks, Rebecca."

"That was Rebecca Lane," I whispered as Lamont steered us around the room.

"Are you a fan?"

"Rebecca Lane, boyfriend. Rebecca. Lane."

He smirked, then nodded. "And there's Philip Draver. Do you want to meet him?"

"I think I'm going to puke."

"You didn't wear that offensive shapewear again, did you? If so, we're heading straight for the bathroom."

"You can't take it off me," I hissed.

"So you did wear it?"

"If you were me, you might have been tempted to double up."

Lamont rolled his eyes, a ghost of a smile flirting with the edges of his lips. "There is nothing wrong with your figure, other than you trying to strangle it every time you wear a dress."

"Booker, fancy meeting you here."

A tall man I had never seen before stopped beside us.

"Dan!" Lamont shook his hand, then introduced me to him. "Nevaeh, this is my producer for the current film."

"Nice to meet you."

Dan gave a nod, then turned, effectively blocking me out of the conversation. I tried my best not to let my emotions show all over my face, and judging from the twitch developing in my right eye, I was losing.

I scanned the room to see a few of the celebrities—ones I had seen on the news, the newsstand, and my social feed, and a tiny select few in my styling chair—staring at me. What were they thinking? Were they watching me get snubbed?

Before I could react, Lamont finished his conversation and reached for my hand. "Let's go sit."

"Are you sure? You don't want to mingle?" Not that I wanted to, but hadn't we arrived to be seen?

"Nah. We'll save the rest of our energy for dancing. Okay?"

I nodded, but was pretty sure dancing would just put us even more on display. I didn't want people measuring the size of my body and comparing it to my uber-handsome boyfriend. Right now, I wanted an oversized tee, leggings, and ice cream. Not fluted champagne, a designer dress that cost more than my last paycheck, and judgmental celebrity stares.

Unfortunately, this was the life I had agreed to. But was being Lamont's girlfriend worth it?

Twenty

Lamont opened the door to his trailer and dragged his weary body inside. This morning's taping had been brutal. He could easily picture himself in an ice bath like athletes used after a grueling game. A sandwich to get rid of the hunger gnawing at his gut also sounded like a dream.

"Surprise."

He glanced up from his leaden feet to see Nevaeh in his trailer. "How are you here?"

Her dimples winked at him. "Your mom gave me the great idea when I saw her earlier to do her hair." She held up an insulated grocery bag. "I brought you some lunch."

If he didn't close his mouth soon, flies would find a new landing pad. "Thank you so much." He trudged over to her, holding out his arms for a hug.

Nevaeh held out her palm, arm stretched out and head tilted back. "You may need to shower before lunch."

"Right." He looked down at the sweat marks on his white tee that had been under his costume. "Give me five minutes."

"Make it ten."

He laughed. "I promise I'll come out smelling clean." At

least he hadn't landed in horse droppings like he had during yesterday's taping.

"You better," she called.

Lamont rushed to the back room, where he'd stored clean clothes to change into. Judging by the low number of shirts and shorts, the stash would need to be replenished soon. He raced through the shower and came out seven minutes later.

His body ached less, but some pain reliever and a good meal should fix him up. He walked back toward the dining area and stopped. Nevaeh buzzed around the table, placing containers here and there. She had a wisp of a smile across her lips as she hummed a song under her breath. Lamont came up behind her and wrapped his arms around her, kissing her cheek.

"Thank you for this." He dropped his arms before he was tempted to turn the small peck into something more.

"Of course. When your mom said you guys would be filming in Studio City, the idea came to mind."

"You didn't have to work at The Mane Do?"

"Nope. It's a non-salon day, but I do have two more appointments."

Lamont held out a chair for her, then sat across from her. He took a pickle spear and bit into it. "Do you prefer the salon over personal visits?"

She tilted her head. "I do like travelling to the clients. Only sometimes they'll request makeup too." Her nose scrunched up.

"You do makeup too?"

"Yes, but when I work on set, it's usually hair only."

"Why's that?"

"Personal preference." She shrugged. "I don't have the passion to do someone's makeup and have them looking like a Sith or something equally detailed. I don't mind doing that as a one-off, but not day in and day out."

"But you don't mind doing hair daily?"

She shook her head. "It's fun. It's like playing with dolls."

"Oh, well, obviously that's awesome."

She stuck her tongue out at him, then took a bite of her sandwich.

Lamont chuckled at her antics. "You know, I was just dreaming of sandwiches when I came into my trailer." He paused. "How did you get into my trailer?" He always left it locked.

"Bryan saw me. Which reminds me." She got up and grabbed a stack of papers from the couch. "He has a new endorsement offer."

"That's the fifth one since the *Luminary* article."

Her mouth dropped. "You've been getting new endorsements?"

"Just offers. I haven't agreed to any yet."

"But there are some you'll agree to?" She took a sip of her drink.

"Definitely. As long as they adhere to my brand, I don't have a problem submitting to their terms. Unless they're downright unreasonable."

"Give me an example."

Lamont thought as he chewed on the turkey sub. "I had a sports drink company who wanted me to represent them. However, in their contract they listed I could only drink their products. I considered that caveat to be unreasonable and turned down the offer."

"How much were they offering to pay you?"

"Twenty-nine million dollars."

Nevaeh's eyes bugged out, and she thumped a hand on her chest as she sputtered.

"You okay?" He rubbed circles in the middle of her back.

Her head bobbed, and she gulped her drink. After a few

seconds, she spoke. "You said no to twenty-nine *million* dollars?"

"As much as a sports drink can help me combat dehydration on the set, I don't only drink those. I like bottled water, sodas, or—"

She held up a hand. "I get it. But for twenty-nine million dollars, don't you think you could learn to like only sports drinks?"

"I take it you'd only drink one product for that much?"

"Bathe in it, use it as hair dye, whatever."

He tried to suppress his amusement, but he never could around her. "I'll keep that in mind."

"So what's this deal for?"

Lamont scanned the documents. "A start-up company wants me to wear their apparel."

"That's interesting. What do you have to do, and how much will they pay you?"

"Looks like they'll pay only if they see an increase in sales."

"That seems a little ridiculous."

"Agreed. It'll go in the no pile."

"What have you said yes to?"

"I'm praying over one. It looks like a good fit, and the contract is sound. It's for a company that clothes the homeless."

Nevaeh frowned. "Then can they afford to pay you?"

"Their business model is tried and true. You purchase a clothing item, and that same item will go to a shelter for homeless." Lamont wiped his mouth, his sandwich now gone. "They have a list on their website of all the shelters they work with to provide clothing."

"Would you be a male model?"

"Something like that. Do some commercials, put their info on my website, and occasionally wear their apparel."

"You're amazing," she said softly.

His neck heated. "Do you really think so?"

She nodded.

Lamont leaned forward and kissed her on the forehead. "I think you're amazing too."

She'd come out to bring him food, she'd tolerated some snubbery the other night at the charity event, she was helping to save his reputation . . . Nevaeh was a powerhouse, but somehow humble through it all.

As Nevaeh grabbed her things to leave, Lamont pressed his lips against her cheek. "We should do this again. Maybe I'll bring lunch to the salon."

She shook her head. "And cause a traffic jam? It'll go live on social media, and random strangers will start filling the shop."

"Like the fan the police detained?"

She shuddered, and he pulled her close. "I can't believe that happened. I don't think you'll be in further danger since events like that are so rare."

She nodded. "Do you have more filming to do today?"

"Yeah, a few more hours, and I'll be done for the day." He closed his trailer door. "Why? Want to have dinner tonight?"

"That sounds great."

He glanced at his watch. "Hey, I wanted to talk to you about something."

Nevaeh shaded her eyes and met his gaze. "Something wrong?"

"Not at all. I was just wondering if you're still going to your high school reunion?"

She dropped her gaze, looking to the left. "I don't think it's a good idea."

"How come?" She'd seemed excited when she'd first asked him to go with her.

"The press around me seems a little intense. I can't imagine the people at the reunion will act any better than the paparazzi."

She had a point. "I definitely want you to be safe." He sighed, thinking for a moment. "What if we go out and do something fun that day instead?"

"Like what?" She stepped closer, tilting her head back.

Did she realize how adorable she was? He leaned forward and kissed her full lips, glad he could do that now. "I don't know. Name something fun."

"Disneyland."

He stepped back. "Really?" Out of all the things they could do? "You know I can afford to take you to more expensive places, right?"

Her brow furrowed. "It doesn't always have to be about money." She bit her lip. "We can do something else if you want, though. How about whale watching around Catalina Island?"

"Sounds perfect." Besides, roller coasters made him ill.

"See you later?"

"I'll plan dinner, okay?" Maybe a picnic at a beach to watch the sunset would be nice.

"Okay." She tossed a wave over her shoulder.

Lamont headed back toward costume design. He needed to don his outfit for the afternoon scenes, then stop by hair and makeup. Yet his mind remained on the beauty who had brought him a meal, taking time away from her own plans to brighten his day.

Lord, please help me do right by her.

His assistant met him at the dressing room doorway. "Mr. Booker, did you see the paperwork from Mr. Wilkinson? He said he gave them to Ms. Richards."

"Yes, Greg."

"Great. What should I tell him your response is?"

"No."

"Do you have any errands you need completed this afternoon?" He looked up from his clipboard.

"Actually . . . yes."

"What can I do for you, sir?"

"I need a place to have a picnic or an ocean-view dinner tonight for me and Ms. Richards."

Greg nodded. "I'll take care of it and contact you if I have any questions."

"Appreciate that, Greg."

His assistant nodded, then left the room.

Time for Lamont to get his head back into the role of horse trainer instead of dreaming of Nevaeh and a future that was beginning to look promising.

Twenty-One

I hit send for the fifth—or was it sixth—application this week for a spot on the hair and makeup teams with various film studios. Then I threw the strap from my cross-body bag over my head as I rushed through the house. The application had taken longer than I'd anticipated, and now I needed to hurry if I was going to be on time at the salon. If I didn't dawdle—as my grandma used to say—then I could still make it before my first scheduled appointment.

Nora looked up from her seat the sofa. "Going to the salon?"

"Yes. Need anything while I'm out today?" I paused at the front door, awaiting her answer.

"We're out of almond milk."

"I'll get some." I opened the door, then quickly shut it again. Only that didn't stop the shouts of my name from the snaparazzi.

"What in the world?" Nora stood, coming up behind me. "Who was that?"

"Looks like the world knows where I live." I squeezed my eyes shut. *What do I do, Lord?*

"Are you serious?" A gleam entered Nora's brown eyes. "Do you want me to go out and make a statement?"

So she could get her fifteen minutes? "No, thanks." I leaned back against the door. "How am I supposed to get to my car?"

"If I make the statement for you, you can continue on your way." She flipped her hair over her shoulder. "So what's it going to be?"

No! I opted for a serene smile and calm words. "Thank you, but no. I'm sure they'll leave once they see me departing."

Nora rolled her eyes and flounced back to the couch. I was surprised she didn't rush to her room to change and walk out with me to get her chance in the spotlight.

I grabbed the doorknob once more. "Wish me luck."

"You'll need it."

At this point, rolling my eyes at her would only expel the energy I needed to make it through the fray, so I opened the door, head down, and flinched internally at the flash of cameras. *Lord, please let me look calm and collected.* Only the bead of sweat rolling down my spine betrayed my nerves as I walked from the common area to the street curb, where my MINI was parked. The photogs followed me along the way, questions flying in the air.

"Nevaeh, are you going to work at The Mane Do?"

"Nevaeh, have you worked on any big film sets?"

"Nevaeh, are you just with Lamont for the money?"

My head jerked to the right, trying to make out who asked such a loaded question. Whether it was a nudging from the Holy Spirit or just common sense—my vote was on the Holy Spirit—I ignored the question and got in the car.

My hands shook as I fastened my seat belt and attempted to insert the key into the ignition. The reporters wouldn't follow me to the salon, would they? *And please, Lord, let the customers be there for hair care and not my personal life.*

Since that incident with the police, Monica had been complaining about the number of customers there just to take a peek at me and not actually get any styling services. If the gossip columnists followed me, would that be the last straw?

Thankfully, the drive was relatively short. Although I was no expert, no one seemed to be tailing me. I turned down the alleyway to park. I let out a breath, leaning my head against the steering wheel and battling back tears.

While Lamont was getting offers for new roles and endorsements and the media had returned to calling him a bright star in Hollywood, my life was becoming unrecognizable. How exactly had the reporters figured out where I lived? Had a neighbor been suspicious of the sedan Lamont had arrived in to pick me up for the charity event last Friday and dimed me out? That seemed the most logical option.

I quickly went inside to change into the apron before meeting my first customer. As I tied the apron around my waist, Tammy walked into the room.

Her eyes widened. "Girl, Monica's looking for you."

"What?" I froze. Was I in trouble?

"Yeah, she said for you to go to her office right away."

My mouth dried. "Did she seem angry?"

Tammy tilted her head, tapping a comb against her chin. "You know, I'm not sure what kind of mood she's in, but I can tell you it's not happy."

Rocks filled my stomach. "Thanks for letting me know."

"Good luck."

I weaved out of the room and around the corner toward Monica's office. Had I mishandled a client somehow? No one had complained to me, unless they'd said something behind my back. The turmoil that had hung around me since I saw the paparazzi outside my doorstep increased. Not to mention thoughts of all the rejections from production companies piling up in my inbox. Did no one need a stylist? I didn't need the key stylist position, just a place on the team to prove my skill.

Don't worry about that right now. Find out what's wrong with Monica. I rapped my knuckles on the office door.

"Come in."

My face contorted into a grimace at the frost in her voice. *Lord, please go before me.* I fixed a smile on my face. "Morning."

Monica looked up from her laptop screen, and her lips flattened.

Okay. So I definitely did something.

"Have a seat, Nevaeh." Monica motioned to the empty chair in front of her desk.

I sat. "Everything okay?"

"Unfortunately not."

What was I supposed to say to that? Obviously, whatever was wrong involved me, but asking questions would only reveal the depths of my troubles. Forgive me for wanting to remain in ignorance a little while longer.

"You know I think you're an amazing stylist, right?"

She was giving me a compliment? Everyone knew that a criticism or worse would soon follow. "What happened?"

Her lips pursed. "It seems our loyal clients are distracted by your presence. Not to mention the amount of people who show up on a daily basis hoping to get a photo of you. They sit in the lobby taking up space for those who actually want the hair services we offer."

"I'm so sorry. I can't believe they're still doing that." I had really hoped otherwise, but obviously that was what had brought me to The Mane Do's principal. "Do you think if we put up a sign saying *No service, no sit* that would help?"

"I had a similar thought until I noticed the paparazzi had

decided to camp out in front of my store. Who knows if the clients will even be able to get through."

This was not good. If I'd traveled the route to take me in front of the salon, I would've seen them and could've called in sick or something.

"Did you call the police for trespassing?"

"I don't own the sidewalk," she snapped. Her lips pursed, and she waved a hand in the air. "It doesn't matter. What matters is this is my place of business. As much as I like you, I have to make tough decisions in order to ensure my company runs smoothly."

"What are you saying?" Yet the question was a foolish one. It didn't take a rocket scientist to figure out what her next words would be.

"I'm afraid I have to let you go."

"Please don't fire me," I whispered. "I need this job." And the income it supplied. I didn't have enough personal clients to sustain being fired.

"You can seek unemployment benefits."

Wouldn't my freelance gig prevent me from getting those benefits? I needed to fight this. "Hasn't business increased since the first client recognized me?" Not all the people pouring through the doors were lobby lurkers, right?

"Nevaeh . . ." She sighed. "I can't have the atmosphere of The Mane Do contorted into some reality TV set. This is supposed to be a place of relaxation and tranquility, and it hasn't been since the locals figured out you work here." Her lips quirked into a half smile. "I'm sure your *man* can take care of your expenses above unemployment."

My head reared back. "I pay my *own* way."

"Hmm." She simpered. "Then I'm sure you'll find another salon job quickly . . . *if* that's what you want."

Would I find one fast enough to pay my next set of bills?

"What about a vacation? I could stay away for two weeks. Give it time to see if the crowds die down." Anything to change her mind.

Monica studied me, and I pleaded with God in heaven to intercede on my behalf. While two weeks without money from this job would hurt my pocket, it would be a lot less painful than having my revenue stream completely dry up.

"Fine. Two weeks."

My eyes watered. "Thank you."

"But if the crowds are still awful and our main clients continue to leave, then your leave of absence will be permanent, and I will gladly announce it to the world."

"I understand."

I left her office feeling like someone was sitting on my chest. I rubbed the offending area, trying to take deep breaths and assure myself that it would all work out. After removing my stuff from my locker, I slunk right out the back door without anyone seeing humiliation stamped all over my face. How could dating an A-list actor upend my life so much? This wasn't the picture of glitz and glam I'd imagined.

I drove around aimlessly for an hour before I realized it would be smarter to get home and start finding another salon to work at. Then again, maybe I should try to increase my home clientele. Could Ms. Rosie introduce me to some friends who'd rather their hair stylist make an in-home visit so they could avoid the noise and gossip of the beauty shop? Though that was what made the beauty shop the beauty shop.

God, this stinks. First the paparazzi, then the forced vacation. What am I going to do?

Should I call my mom?

I laughed. My mom would be happy I no longer had the job at the beauty salon. She'd urge me to get a "real job."

Still, I wanted—*needed*—someone to tell me all would be okay and that I didn't have to worry. I pressed Lamont's name in my favorites, then speaker phone, so I wouldn't be holding the phone while driving.

"It's my girlfriend. Just the person I wanted to speak to."

"Oh yeah? Everything okay?" *Please be okay, please be okay.*

"Everything is fantastic. Guess what?"

My lips curved on their own accord. He sounded so happy. At least one of us was having a good day. "What?"

"I got another movie offer. Think Hallmark-style but add in faith and put it on the big screen."

"Are you serious? That's amazing." There weren't enough movies that held a faith message, in my opinion.

"Yeah, Bryan's combing through the contract now to see if we want to negotiate on any of the terms."

"When would it start filming? You're not even done with the one you're working on."

"I know." He blew out a breath. "Filming is supposed to finish at the end of July, so I would be available to work again in August. However, I normally like to put in some time to rest between projects."

"You're that close to being finished?" Why hadn't I realized that? I needed to do a better job of paying attention to his schedule.

"We are. I'll have the premiere for my previous movie in a couple of weeks, and this one won't premiere until sometime next year."

"How long would filming be for the new project? Where is the set located?"

"Nine months, which is pretty standard. As for locations . . . hmm . . ."

I smiled at the soft noise. Lamont's voice had somehow

managed to soothe me. His good news outweighed my bad, or at least, temporarily allowed me to forget.

"I remember it'll start in Canada but can't remember what overseas spot they listed in the contract."

Canada? Overseas? Was this when our relationship would end? "Do you know how long you'd be filming at each location?"

"Hold on, let me grab the paperwork." Paper rustled, then Lamont began speaking once more. "Filming is in Canada, New Zealand, and then back in California for three months each."

"Then if you take the job, you'll fly to Canada in just a few weeks." It was more statement than question, but I could hear the disbelief in my voice. Should I bring up the end of our relationship? Lamont seemed to be getting everything he hoped for by dating me.

"Yes," he drew out cautiously. "Is that a problem?"

How could I say it was? Paparazzi were now following me, and my job was in a precarious state, but the boyfriend who was causing it all would be leaving the country. Would that save my job?

"I'm happy for you." I forced a smile, hoping he'd hear the happiness in my voice. I needed time to work through my thoughts before saying anything more.

"Are you sure?" he asked.

"Of course. This is your job. This is what you do. I'd cheer for real, but I'm driving."

"You know we could work it out so you can come up and visit me."

Should I tell him I'd never stepped foot out of California? I hadn't needed to. None of the film sets I'd worked on had been outside of Hollywood. "Canada now requires US citizens to use a passport upon entry." I sounded like an infomercial.

"You don't have a passport?"

"No." I held back the sigh that made my eyes water—water, *not* cry.

"We can fix that. I can pay for an expedited one if it means my girlfriend can visit me."

My lips quivered. Hadn't I just told Monica I paid my own way? Yet I couldn't remember the last time I'd used my own money around Lamont. He paid for the donation at the charity event, my new wardrobe to wear to said events, and every meal we shared together. Who knew how much he paid his driver to take us places. I certainly hadn't contributed so much as gas money. I was a leech.

"You don't have to. I can pay for that. Besides, how long does it take to get expedited?" Though I should figure out how much passports cost before deciding I could spend the money.

"Five to seven weeks."

If he took the job and we were still together, I would have it in time to visit. *If* we were still together. "Hey, I need to go." Water—*fine*, tears—was starting to spill over, and I didn't want Lamont to hear when I started sniffling.

"See you for our fun date tomorrow?"

Ugh, how could I have forgotten? There was too much going on at once. "Right." I bit down on my lip, quieting the sobs. I did *not* want to smile and pretend life was grand tomorrow.

"Bye."

I pressed end and let the sobs go free.

Twenty-Two

The sound of a text notification pinged, and Lamont put the car in park outside of Nevaeh's apartment before grabbing his cell.

Chris
How's everything going in La-La Land?

Lamont
I got a new movie offer.

Chris
Congrats. Good story line?

Lamont
Amazing story. I'm betting award winning.

Tuck
Because MTV Movie Awards and Teen Choice aren't enough.

Lamont
Those aren't Oscars.

Tuck
True

Lamont
The filming will take place in Canada and NZ for a total of six months. The last three months will be here in CA.

Tuck
How does Nevaeh feel about that?

Lamont
She's happy for me. Said she'd get a passport to
visit while I'm on location.

Chris
So you guys will do a long-distance relationship?
You don't think it's a safe time to part ways?

Lamont
You know, I really like her. I'm hoping the
distance won't be a problem.

Because he wasn't dating a celebrity, the fears of seeing
her on a tabloid magazine cheating on him were nonexistent.

Chris
Kind of sounds unrealistic.

Tuck
Was she truly happy for you? Y'all've been
dating for what, a month?

Now that he thought about it, she hadn't seemed all that
enthused.

Lamont
Honestly, she sounded down.

Chris
Sounds like you two need to have a
conversation.

Tuck
Agreed

Lamont
Great. Now I'm worried.

He slid his phone into his back pocket and headed for Nevaeh's door to find she was coming down the two front steps.

"Hey, I was going to knock on your door." He smoothed a hand down his blue polo.

"No worries." Her full lips curved into a smile. "I was ready to go."

He couldn't help but think the smile didn't quite reach her dark brown eyes. They weren't twinkling with joy like usual. "Everything okay?"

She nodded.

He leaned down to kiss her cheek. "You look beautiful," he murmured.

"You don't have to say that." She laughed. "My dress isn't designer."

She looped her arm through his, so Lamont led them toward the car.

"But you always look beautiful."

He opened the car door just in time to see Nevaeh roll her eyes. "You don't have to say that. Besides, if you say it now, how will you react when you see me in my dress for the premiere?"

He peered into her eyes. "Nevaeh, you know I think you're gorgeous, right?"

"Lamont Booker, you didn't spare me two glances before I got us in this snafu with the snaparazzi." She propped her hands on her curvy hips.

He tugged her close. "Listen to me, okay?"

She nodded.

"Yes, the media storm had me taking a closer look, but that's because I was moving at such a speed I couldn't appreciate you. Slowing down, getting to know you, shows me more and more that I'm thankful to have you in my life."

She shook her head, as if trying to loosen thoughts. "Thank you," she whispered.

He placed a kiss softly against her lips. "I want you to know that I want this relationship to be real."

"You said that before. But isn't now a good time to part ways? I mean, the media loves you once again, and you're going to be traveling."

His heart clenched, and he battled against a dry mouth to ask the question forming in his mind. "Do you want to part ways?" He wanted to say more. Ask her if her feelings weren't already involved . . . like his were.

Nevaeh tilted her head back, her gaze roaming his features.

Lord God . . . Lamont didn't know what else to say. He wanted her to choose him for him, not for his fame and not because she felt she had to.

"I'm good. My career is back on track, and no one is talking about canceling endorsements or removing me from sets. So you don't have to save me. But if . . ." He stopped.

"But if?" she asked softly.

"If you want to be with me because you like me, and you know I like you, then . . ." The ball was now in her court.

Nevaeh slid her arms around his waist. "Then let's be together. Not for the press, not for the public, but for us."

His heart double-timed, and he laid his forehead gently against hers. "For us." He kissed her gently once, twice, and moaned when she initiated a deeper kiss.

Heat rose quickly, and feelings he wanted to keep tame battled for supremacy. He broke off the kiss and motioned for her to get into the car. "Where it's safe."

The sound of her laughter was heady to his senses, and he shook his head. He rounded the car, taking his time until he felt back in control. "Let's go have fun." He slid the car into drive and headed down the 405. They had a little way to go to make it to Newport Beach for their cruise.

"How's your week been?" Maybe if he kept the conversation light, Lamont would forget the feel of Nevaeh in his arms and how right it seemed.

"Let's not talk about my week. I need a nice outing with my boyfriend to forget about my troubles."

Troubles? He tapped a mindless rhythm on his pants leg. "If I drop the subject, will you tell me what's bothering you tomorrow?"

"Do I have to?"

He chuckled at the petulant tone. "Please. I want to know what's bothering you. I'm here for good times *and* bad." History had taught him if a couple could work through trials *together*, then they were more successful. Granted, Diva had always been the cause of his trouble because she craved the spotlight.

Maybe he needed to pray that God would get through to her. He knew from firsthand experience that wanting that kind of attention stemmed from a warped view—the world's view, not God's.

"Is that a vow? Sounds like one," Nevaeh quipped.

"More like a promise. Besides, we've only been dating a month."

"Okay. I will tomorrow."

He nodded, gripping the steering wheel. "Then we'll enjoy today." When he got a moment, he'd pray for whatever she was going through and that she would feel comfortable talking to him.

"Have you ever been whale watching before?" she asked.

"No. Have you?" He reached over the console and cupped her hand, rubbing his thumb across her smooth skin.

"No. There weren't a lot of things I did growing up. My parents were always super focused during the school year."

"What about during the summer?"

"In the summer, we would go to Disneyland. Dad got season passes as a work bonus."

Ah, so that's the reason she'd suggested it the other day. "Did you go every summer?"

"We did. Now it feels weird if I let the summer go by and don't go. What about you? Did you have any summer traditions with Ms. Rosie?"

Lamont thought about it. "Well, before I was discovered, my mom would take me up and down the state visiting different cities. We went to Santa Cruz one year, San Jose the next." Life had definitely been simpler. His mom had been healthy, and Lamont had no worries. "Money was tight, so we stayed at the cheapest hotels available and drove in a beat-up car that didn't have AC." He glanced at Nevaeh.

She gave a shudder. "That's rough."

"Maybe so, but we made so many good memories. Mom told me once that she felt the need to make up for the fact that my dad had died so early."

Nevaeh held his hand. "Your mother's a great woman."

"She's the best. When I found out she had cancer . . ." He swallowed. "I've never been so thankful that I had so much money. I hoped if I threw enough money at the situation and prayed the rest of the time, that she would survive. But there was enough doubt in me to worry I'd turn out to be wrong." Now he didn't feel calm unless he saw his mother glowing with health and wearing a smile on her face.

That's not your job.

Chills covered the nape of his neck. The words hadn't been audible, but it was like his soul felt them. Was God trying to tell him something?

"I can't imagine how hard that must have been," Nevaeh said. "When she had that upset stomach, my first thought was the cancer had returned."

He nodded. "That's always mine too. She keeps trying to tell me to shake off the fear, but I'm not sure it'll ever go away. If it weren't for my faith, I would've lost hope the moment they gave her the diagnosis."

"Then maybe that's why God saved you when He did. He knew you'd need Him."

Lamont's mouth dropped. "Wow. I never looked at it like that." He squeezed her fingers. "Thank you for a different perspective."

They continued talking as they drove toward the harbor. Lamont shared about how he'd been a scrawny kid until his freshman year of high school, when he'd practically sprouted overnight. What it had been like to work on Broadway, and how much he loved being an actor. Nevaeh in turn talked about her high school years, meeting her current roommate in college, and her first on-set position.

Lamont thanked God for the great conversation. How easy it was for them to switch to different topics as they got to know each other. There were no cameras, no journalists, just the crew running the boat. Nevaeh took plenty of pictures of the whales—videos too—and they got the crew to take some pics of them as a couple.

He immediately changed the wallpaper on his phone to one. Being out on the ocean with a woman he admired made him think of his mother's warning to take a true rest. Because right now he felt completely carefree. He didn't even feel the pressing need to text his mother and make sure she was enjoying her day.

He hugged Nevaeh close as they stared out over the water. "This was a perfect plan."

She snuggled into him, and he tightened his arms around her, placing his cheek next to hers.

"I agree. Nothing could get better than this."

Lamont smiled and prayed that God would bless their relationship and do something exceedingly and abundantly better than this current moment.

Twenty-Three

Aﬀter such a lovely day surfing the Pacific with Lamont—I definitely had an inner meltdown at the sight of the yacht—I thought my sleep would continue the theme of perfection. No such luck. Last night had found me tossing back and forth, and now my nightgown clung to me.

Didn't take a psychologist to decipher my dream—or was it a nightmare? I had married Lamont, lost excessive weight, and become a person I hadn't recognized. Was it foreshadowing, or too much worrying during the day disrupting my sleep?

I threw back the covers and shuffled toward the bathroom. Hopefully Nora wasn't in there. I really needed the shower spray to wash away my unease.

"Nevaeh."

I jumped backward, stumbling into my open door. Nora stood in the hallway, facing me as if she'd just left the kitchen.

"Morning," I mumbled.

She pursed her lips. "Can we talk, or are you about to do something?"

Shower and look presentable. But apparently that would have to wait. "What's up?"

Nora motioned for me to follow her into the living room. We both sat.

She tapped her fingertips together. "I think we need to talk about the paparazzi situation."

"Are they outside again?" They hadn't been around when Lamont picked me up yesterday morning. Then again, we had left pretty early. Maybe the buzzards weren't the type to scour after worms.

"No. I haven't seen them since Mrs. Hazelton drove them off yesterday evening."

I groaned. "They *were* here?"

Nora nodded. "Mrs. Hazelton probably made the news, or if she didn't, it was because they were too embarrassed to be outdone by a geriatric."

God bless her. I'd have to remember to stop by her place soon and hang out for a bit. She deserved an in-person thank-you and maybe even a little treat baked by my own hands.

"If they're not here now, what's the problem?" I asked. Nora always had something to complain about. Not that I could blame her in this instance. I was mortified they knew where I lived.

"I keep wondering what we'll do if it happens again."

Same. "I suppose we'll deal with it then." *Lord, please let them give up.*

"What if they come back today? The next day? Then what?"

I bit back a sigh. "Is there a point you're trying to get to?" A scalding shower was in my immediate future, and I didn't want to sit here feeling worse than I already did.

"I want an exclusive."

"Excuse me?" Her words weren't making any kind of sense.

"I've been giving it some thought. The next time paparazzi

show up, I can go out and talk to them as your roommate. I've known you for ten years. I can be the source that's close to you, but obviously they can use my name." She grinned. "Once they get their story, I'm sure they'll leave. Plus, it'll give me a chance to be on the news, which is truly a win-win for everyone."

I would *not* cry at her complete selfishness and lack of respect for my privacy. My arms folded on their own accord, barricading my heart. "No."

"But why?" she whined. "First, you said no to the *Sands of Time* charity event, now you're saying no to an exclusive?" She threw her hands up in the air. "Next you'll be telling me I'm not invited to Lamont's premiere."

"Why would you be?" I held up my hand, shaking my head in tandem. "Wait a minute. Let's go through your list. I have nothing to say to the paparazzi. I've already been interviewed by *Luminary*, and that was enough. I don't have to give them every single detail of my life."

"Which is why I can do it." Nora placed a hand on her chest. "It spares you the limelight, since I know that's not your thing, and will up my who's who power for future auditions."

Ugh. Just *ugh*. I'd never fooled myself into believing we were BFFs or even good enough friends to really hang out with each other, but I certainly never believed she'd be so quick to use me either.

"My answer remains a no."

"You are *so* selfish."

I laughed. Was she serious?

"If you don't say yes, then you can't live here." Her eyes narrowed.

My body flushed hot. "Come on, Nora. You're not really serious."

"I am. I want my name in the spotlight. It's not right that yours is when you don't even want to be a star." She snorted. "Correction: You'd *never* be star material. Let those of us who shine brightly do so."

"So your real issue is this"—I twirled my finger in the air—"isn't about you?"

"It's all of it. You don't wear the right clothes. You're always doing something weird to your hair instead of styling it on trend. You're so hopeless. Can't you tell by the criticizing comments you've received? I mean, some of them are trying to be helpful."

Right, telling me to call Jenny or sign up for Noom was so helpful. For all they knew I could have a health condition giving me generous curves, though genetic coding didn't seem to be a disease, more a way of life. *No pun intended.*

"You do realize I dress for work half the time, right?" Just not today thanks to Monica's forced vacay.

You asked for time off. Yeah, but stalling was one of my skillful tactics. Too bad it wasn't working on Nora. She was showing more and more of her altruistic side—insert heavy dose of sarcasm. I no longer wanted to be associated with her.

She rolled her eyes, crossing her arms. "Why are you working when you're dating Lamont Booker? Seriously, we could be living in a better place than we are now."

"This conversation is over." I walked into the bathroom and slammed the door, my temper barely under a boil. Who did she think she was?

"I want your answer by tomorrow!" she shouted through the door.

I stepped closer to the door so she'd hear me. "But we've been roommates forever."

"And we can continue to be if you accept my terms."

Tears welled in my eyes. *Great.* I turned on the water to accompany the liquid running down my cheeks and drown out anything else Nora would say. At least she wouldn't see me lose my composure.

By the time I dressed for church—a nondesigner maxi dress without my shapewear—my makeup had been applied and all evidence of any crying jags had been artfully concealed. I waltzed through the house like I didn't have a care in the world and purposely ignored Nora.

My cell pinged just as I reached for the knob. I pulled it out of my purse in case Lamont was running late.

> Lamont
>
> Photogs outside. Act cool when I knock on the door, and I'll get you safely to the car.

My stomach clenched, and I waited for a knock. When it came, I straightened my spine before opening the door. *Lord, please let don't them follow us.* I couldn't believe they were really out here on a Sunday. Didn't they have their own relaxation plans?

Lamont wrapped his arm around me, tucking me into his side. Questions blasted us from all around.

"Lamont, over here!"

"Nevaeh, how do your parents feel about your relationship?"

"Lamont, do you plan on proposing anytime soon?"

Lamont's strides never ceased nor faltered. He guided me right into the safety of his car. It was minutes after we left the flashing lights behind that he spoke in the stifling silence.

"How long has that been going on?" His voice was low, dangerous sounding, even.

"Off and on."

"Why didn't you tell me?"

No sense in both of us having bad days. I shrugged. "You were excited about your offer."

"They've been coming around since then?"

I blew out a breath. "I hoped they were no longer an issue, though Mrs. Hazelton had to send them packing last night. I didn't tell you because I . . ." My voice wavered.

"You what?" he asked softly.

"I just didn't want to bother you. You were so happy about the offer, and then when we saw each other again it was to go whale watching, and I didn't want any bad news to ruin the moment."

"You know what concerns you concerns me, right?" He glanced at me, reaching for my hand to interlace our fingers.

"I appreciate that, but what can you do?"

"For starters, I've got Kyle looking into the situation. Believe me, I *will* do something about their trespassing."

Would that get them to leave The Mane Do alone? Not that the paparazzi were ultimately responsible for keeping me away from the salon. "If you think it'll work."

"If it doesn't, then I'll try the next thing and the next until this becomes a nonissue for you."

I squeezed his hand. "I really do appreciate that, but maybe I was trying to do things on my own." More like still process. I truly had no idea how to handle all those flashing lights. Was pride getting in my way?

"Why? I'm your boyfriend. I'm supposed to protect you and be here for you."

"Lamont, that's probably the sweetest thing I've ever heard. But maybe allowing me to figure stuff out on my own could actually help you."

"What?"

I winced at his incredulous tone.

"How do you figure?"

Here goes. "The paparazzi couldn't care less about me. It's *you* they want. They want to know everything about you, and I'm their target in lieu of the real prize. If I handle it on my own, they'll realize they can't get to you through me. But if you ride up in your Mercedes—" I paused, tilting my head to see if the interior of the car had a logo. I actually hadn't seen which car he'd arrived in. "This is the Mercedes, right?"

"The Tesla but continue."

Another car. "Right, so if you ride up in your Tesla or whatever car of the day you're driving, you become exactly the target they've been trying to trap. Surely you realize I'm just bait." Or maybe not, since it just occurred to me in the middle of my tirade.

I was the easy target in all of this. The internet trolls couldn't shut Lamont down and were probably irritated he was back to being a golden boy, so they went after me for not meeting their beauty or celebrity standards.

"Even if you are, I can't stand by and let you deal with all of this alone. We're a team now."

Oh, my heart. Why had I tried to shield myself? To believe that this was all fake? Just remembering him bringing up our relationship status yesterday took all the defenses out of my heart. "You're right."

This time he squeezed my hand. "Is there anything else going on?"

"Well, I may have to move out."

"Because of the paparazzi?"

I shifted in my seat to look at his profile. "Nora wanted to use us as a chance to be in the spotlight. If I didn't know any better, she's probably why the paparazzi came back." Which, now that I thought about it, made the most sense.

Lamont shook his head. "Is there any other way to handle the situation?"

"Moving out was her ultimatum."

"Are both of your names on the lease?"

I smiled. "Why, yes they are."

"Then she can't make you leave."

"True." I paused, thinking. "But do I want to live with someone who would use me like that?"

"Good point." He tapped the steering wheel with one hand. "Then what will you do?"

"I don't know." With my income tenuous at the salon, I either needed to find another roommate or get a stylist position on a film set.

"Do you want me to help you find a place? I had an awesome realtor."

"I'm pretty sure our price points are different."

"I could loan you some money," he offered.

"Ugh, that's exactly what everyone expects." My voice echoed in the interior thanks to the raised volume I'd used.

Lamont simply looked in the rearview mirror, put on the hazard lights, and pulled over to the shoulder.

He faced me. "You honestly care if people think you're taking advantage of me?"

"Of course I do. That's not why I decided to date you. I don't want people thinking I'm a gold digger."

"You're not." He looked like he was trying to contain his laughter, so I narrowed my eyes.

He trailed a finger down my cheek, then placed his palm on the side of my face. "You couldn't be a gold digger if you tried."

"Other people think I am."

"What other people? You know better than to listen to people sniffing for blood."

A tear spilled over, stopping at his thumb. "Monica may have mentioned it."

His brows furrowed. "The salon owner?"

I nodded. "She was going to fire me the day you got the movie offer, but I managed to turn it into an unpaid vacation." And, wow, that still hurt.

The veins in Lamont's neck became pronounced. "On what grounds?"

"Don't. Don't go white knight on me." Even though my heart upticked at the sight. "I'll probably lose composure, and my face won't be fixed in time for church."

"Church is the perfect place to ruin your makeup."

"Then take me there and let me cry. Just not on the side of the road."

Lamont placed a kiss on my forehead. "Is that it? Is that all you were hiding about your 'terrible, horrible, no good, very bad day'?"

"You only watched that movie because Steve Carell was in it, didn't you?"

"No, Jennifer Garner was the pull."

I rolled my eyes, then leaned over the center console and kissed him. Kissed him for caring, kissed him for using movie quotes all the time.

He pulled away. "I think we need to get to church." His voice sounded husky, and I wanted to cheer for making it sound that way.

But he was right. It was time to show my face at a place I wasn't sure I liked all that well. At least it wasn't stifling like the one I grew up going to. That place was so very strict and had way too many rules, including what you could wear. Oh, how I had chafed at not being able to chew gum or having to ensure my legs were fully covered at all times, as if my legs were shameful. I'd been too young to understand that they were trying to encourage modesty and decorum, and only picked up on the censure of wearing a dress to church that left portions of my legs bare.

"Should we visit your parents' church one Sunday?" Lamont asked.

"Hard pass."

"What's it about their church you don't find appealing?"

"All the rules."

"Did you try out different places during college?"

"Mm-hmm." *Too many.* "Only none of the churches near the university had congregants that resembled me. When I moved to Studio City, I tried so many that I ventured outside my zip code. I've never felt like I fit in, and none of them seemed like a safe place. So eventually I stayed home or did other things on Sunday." I wanted to meet Lamont's gaze but was also afraid to see his disappointment.

"Then I'll pray for the right fit."

And that was all he said.

The lot was full when we pulled into the parking lot.

"It's a good thing the snaparazzi gives people space at church," he said.

"'Sanctuary,'" I quoted in my best Quasimodo impression.

"*Hunchback of Notre Dame?*"

"Of course." We shared a grin.

We strolled into the building just in time to hear the opening of a worship song. I discreetly scanned the premises, checking the diversity quota today. Lamont's church had a lot of rich parishioners—you could tell by the cars sitting in the lot—but they also seemed to have some middle class as well. Jury was still out on exactly how diverse the church was. It was too large for me to count how many people walked in that fell in the shades between Lamont's lighter skin and my darker one, but I did notice other Black and Brown faces.

Maybe I could let the turmoil of the past few days roll off my back. Just sit in prayer with the Lord and somehow recalibrate. *Please help me, God.*

As the song's lyrics washed over me, I blew out a breath and lifted my voice with everyone else. At least I knew this song and didn't feel so awkward like some of the past few Sundays attending. For now I'd try to focus on God and remind myself He was in our praise and I didn't have to feel alone.

Twenty-Four

Lamont sat back in his office chair and hit the join button for the video conference call. The other participants filled his screen in a grid pattern, so he smiled.

"Thanks for having me, gentlemen," he said.

"Wonderful to have you here, Lamont," James Cannon said. "Our company is pleased to be working with you."

Lamont couldn't believe he was on a conference call with the owner of Cannon Industries. Not his assistant but the actual owner of the huge film production company.

"Well, hold on," Bryan interjected. "Nothing's been signed."

Lamont wished Bryan was beside him and not on-screen so he could kick his agent in the shin. Instead, he pushed his cheeks higher. "I don't see a reason why we won't go in that direction. I feel very good about the contract."

The owner of Cannon Industries smiled. "Glad to hear that."

"You have a great reputation, Lamont," Otto Schneider said. The director for the film wore a casual T-shirt instead of the suit Mr. Cannon wore. "I'm glad all that mess with your girlfriend was cleared up. We definitely want a clean reputation for all who come aboard this film."

"I completely understand. I keep the same mentality for whatever film I'm working on." Lamont would have to buy Nevaeh a thank-you gift. If it weren't for her willingness to be his girlfriend in the beginning—before their decision to continue to date—he would be having a different conversation right now.

"As you know, we'll be filming in Canada, New Zealand, then back in Studio City. Do you have a problem with that?"

"No." He paused. "Well, not with the filming. I did have a question regarding the morality clause listed in the contract." He understood those clauses were becoming standard, but CI's wording was a little ambiguous in parts.

"Yes?" James said. "Is there a problem?"

"I needed to clarify a part."

The men nodded while Bryan eyed him in a suspicious manner.

Lamont cleared his throat. "Is there a problem if my girl-friend visits me on location?" The wording regarding visitations almost sounded like only married actors had that right.

Otto looked at James, a wordless conversation passing between them. Then James met Lamont's stare. "I know your stance on celibacy, but our standard is to be above reproach. We don't want anyone misconstruing a hotel visit, even if she were to have her own room."

Lamont swallowed. They were essentially asking him not to see Nevaeh for six months.

"Will that be an issue?" Otto asked.

Bryan smiled. "Of course not. Distance makes the heart grow fonder, right?" He laughed.

Lamont wanted to reach through the screen of his Mac and shake his agent. He knew better than to speak for

Lamont. Instead, Lamont kept his mouth shut. He would talk to Bryan once this meeting was over. It was supposed to be a mere formality to make sure everyone's interests aligned before they moved to signing the actual contract. However, this clause made Lamont pause.

If he could suffer through the rest of the pleasantries until the video call was over, he could call Nevaeh and get her input. Surely she'd have an opinion on the separation. It was one thing to talk about the possibility of not seeing each other, but now Cannon was essentially saying it was a guarantee. Tuck's comment about making sure Nevaeh was okay with the distance reared in his mind. How had he forgotten to talk to her more before this meeting happened?

Oh yeah, the paparazzi had taken center stage.

Funny how in the beginning he thought this would all end amicably with no real feelings involved and now the thought of six months apart was enough to make him break into a sweat. What could he do about it?

He sat up in his seat. "Do you guys have a hair stylist lined up already?"

James stopped talking and looked at the camera. Oops, had Lamont interrupted something important?

"Sorry, my mind was on logistics. I didn't mean to interrupt."

"No, no." James motioned for Lamont to continue. "Your girlfriend is a stylist, right?"

"Yes. She has skills in makeup as well, but her passion lies in hair styling."

"Those positions haven't been set yet, but I see no reason why we can't look at her credentials," Otto stated. "Have her email me her portfolio, and we'll go from there."

"Great. I'll let her know." Lamont wanted to throw a fist in the air. If Nevaeh worked on set, then they could be together.

"Just so you know," James started, "if she ends up being employed on set, we don't allow coworkers to date. It's caused some problems in the past."

"But we're already dating." He blinked. "The world *knows* we're dating. It's not like we'd be doing anything in secret."

"Yes, but what if you two break up and then can't get along on set? Not to mention the staff usually resides in the same hotel as the actors. Again, perception is the issue here."

"Right, because I always argue with the costume department." He sat back, taking a measured breath. Why were they making this so difficult?

James's mouth turned downward.

Otto sighed. "If we made exceptions for you, then we'd have to make exceptions for everyone else."

Bryan stared at Lamont through his computer's camera and gave a slight shake of the head. Lamont didn't know if his agent was signaling to be quiet or something else. Either way, he'd had enough of this meeting.

Lamont propped his elbow on his desk, placing his chin in his hand, then wiped at his mouth. It was the code he and Bryan had come up with for *wrap it up*.

"Well, gentlemen, I think this conversation has been really helpful," Bryan started.

Lamont tuned him out until the other men dropped from the meeting.

"What was that?" Bryan asked.

"Come over, and we'll talk more."

"Fine." Bryan looked at his smart watch, swiping continuously. Probably trying to locate his calendar. "Give me thirty minutes."

"That's fine." Lamont didn't have to be on set for another couple of hours since they had an evening scene. He had no plans to talk Bryan's ear off.

Thirty minutes later, Bryan arrived.

"Can I get you something to drink?"

"Nah, I had something on the way over." Bryan rolled the sleeves of his shirt up. "So what's wrong? I know that tone."

"What made you think you could speak for me? Did you ever consider I don't want to go *six months* without seeing my girlfriend?"

Bryan snorted. "Please, it's not as if your relationship is real."

"Who said it wasn't?"

"Are you kidding me?" Bryan lifted his hands. "It was always supposed to be a fake relationship."

Lamont paused, working to keep his emotions in check. He didn't want to lose his cool like he used to when he turned eighteen and felt everyone was trying to control him. This was different. *He* was different. "I told you from the beginning I wasn't comfortable with a fake relationship. Besides, Nevaeh and I have agreed to legitimately date. We. Are. Dating."

"Right. 'Dating.'" Bryan used air quotes. "It's a great publicity stunt. Look how many supporters you have now, and with this movie offer, your career is golden. I told you, all we had to do was change the narrative."

"Bryan. I didn't do this to further my career but to make sure everything I've worked for didn't turn to smoke." A career in this industry could be fleeting. Lamont wanted a little more time in Hollywood so he could continue to help those who needed help and use his platform for God's glory.

"Well, now it won't. You're a hot commodity. However, turning your little outings with Richards into the real deal—" Bryan shook his head—"dangerous game, my friend."

"Why would you say that?" Lamont paced the area in front of the kitchen island, trying to get out his irritation in healthy ways.

"Because now your focus is split. Instead of thinking of your career, you're considering turning down a role because you can't be away from your girlfriend for half a year." He scoffed. "I can't even believe I'm hearing this."

That made two of them.

Lamont had always appreciated having Bryan in his corner. When his life had taken a turn for the worse, Bryan had helped pull him back. Found Lamont a therapist to help him work through the fast-changing life and the anger he'd harbored from various people trying to fill the role of father. Bryan had been different. He had informed Lamont he would be more like a mentor and a guide since Ms. Rosie was more than capable of raising Lamont. Bryan had encouraged Lamont to leave the alcohol alone and find something else to channel his energy into.

When Lamont had found God, Bryan had been skeptical until he started seeing the changes in Lamont. Although Bryan didn't believe in God, he never mocked Lamont's faith, as long as it "kept him on the straight and narrow."

Still, Lamont would continue hoping his life would be a testimony for Bryan. Only right now, he didn't recognize the man standing in his kitchen.

"I'm dating Nevaeh," Lamont repeated. "Not for publicity, *for real*. And I refuse to be away from her for six months."

"So let them hire her. You'll see her then."

"You heard him say we couldn't be together if we're both under contract with the company. That's ridiculous. If we go out for coffee, are they going to consider that a date? Fraternization?"

Bryan threw up his hands. "But you'll still see her."

"It's like you're not even listening." Lamont squeezed the bridge of his nose.

"I'm done. You're obviously not thinking clearly, and I

blame that on your 'real relationship.'" He headed toward the door. "Call me when you want to have a serious conversation."

"I am being serious."

Bryan stopped and turned back toward Lamont. "Then maybe give her the option. I'm sure she'd jump at the chance to work on another set."

Probably. But would she be choosing it to be closer to Lamont or to further her career? He swallowed and said nothing as his agent walked out. When had this all become so complicated? He didn't want to hinder Nevaeh's career, but he also wanted to know she'd choose him over it.

Lord, please tell me what to do.

He'd keep praying until he had clear direction because he didn't want to mess up his career or his relationship.

Twenty-Five

had an interview. Relief—and anticipation—held my heart in its hands as I drove toward Hollywood. A studio there had an open stylist position on a Netflix movie. My nerve endings were doing a happy dance at the idea of working on a movie set again. It seemed like forever since I'd been involved with one. Hopefully this one had blockbuster potential.

The smog wasn't so bad today, and a cool breeze was keeping the stifling temps from making me melt. All in all, it was a good July day. Until my phone rang.

"Hello?"

"Yes, can I speak to Nevaeh Richards, please?"

"Speaking." I frowned, trying to figure out who the caller was. I hadn't seen an ID on my phone but noticed the 213 area code.

"Hi, this is Nat Fine with Wonder Studios. You're scheduled for a two o'clock appointment, and I need to cancel that."

My heart dropped to my toes. "Why?" I cleared my throat. "I mean, when can we reschedule?"

"Unfortunately, the position has been filled. I'm sorry to cancel last minute."

Considering I'd be arriving in twenty minutes, *last minute* was an understatement. I wanted to rail but swallowed down my irritation instead. "All right."

"Thank you for being so gracious. Have a great day."

Ugh. Way to guilt me with the term *gracious*. I glared at my phone, then realized the green light wouldn't give me any time to pout at the traffic signal.

"Now what?" I asked out loud.

Should I just call the rest of the day a personal one and forget about job hunting? *What to do, what to do?*

I dialed Ms. Rosie.

"Nevaeh, how are you?"

"Not bad. I had an appointment that canceled and wondered if you had some free time? Maybe we could hang out?"

"What did you have in mind?"

I relayed my thoughts, and she agreed to the plan. So I made a U-turn at the next legal spot. Hopefully Ms. Rosie would enjoy our outing, and I could get to know her a little better outside of our regular appointments. When she'd first asked to have lunch, I'd been excited, then hurt, so I'd put her off. Now that Lamont and I had committed to dating for real, I was excited once more to get closer to Ms. Rosie. Plus, her company would take my mind off the situation with Nora, who'd acted shocked and affronted when I'd informed her that I'd be moving out. I couldn't care less. Our friendship was over as far as I was concerned. Now I could only pray Nora would have some kind of honor and not seek out reporters anyway.

I drove up the hills, stopping to grab some lunch for two, then continued until I reached Mission Hills, where the San Fernando Rey de España mission stood. The building had been erected in 1797 and maintained many historical architectural features that marked it as a mission of old.

I scanned the lot, looking for Ms. Rosie's vehicle. A white Mercedes pulled into the lot, parking beside my vehicle. Lamont's mom beamed at me as she stepped onto the sidewalk.

"Nevaeh!" She squeezed me in a hug, and my heart overflowed.

And my eyes tried to as well. I sniffed silently to ensure nothing would give me away, then pulled back.

"Thank you for joining me," I said.

"Of course. I'm so excited about this."

I held up the takeout. "Want to sit and eat before exploring?"

"Yes."

We walked across the street to Brand Park and sat at a picnic table.

"I'm so thankful for the breeze today," Ms. Rosie stated.

"Me too." I unpacked the lunch, sliding a food container in front of her. "I remembered you said you liked Mexican-Asian fusion food, so I got you some bulgogi tacos."

"With kimchi?" Her brown eyes lit up.

"Yes, ma'am."

"That's what I'm talking about." She shook her body left and right, pumping her arms up in the air.

I laughed. "Glad I made the right choice."

"Let me say grace."

I bowed my head.

"Heavenly Father, thank You for this time with dear Nevaeh. I pray that You would bless her coming and going and bless her with abundant plans for her life. I also pray You would bless her relationship with my son and give them wisdom to navigate those waters. And last, please help our relationship deepen in new ways. Amen."

I sniffed. "Amen."

"I didn't mean to make you cry."

My head shot up. "I'm not crying."

She raised an eyebrow.

"I'm not. I promise. But it did touch my heart." I pointed to the offender making my emotions change faster than permed hair that had just been doused with water.

"I hope you know I've been praying for you since you came into my life."

I stilled. "You have?"

"You bet. You don't pray for me?"

"Of course I do." I paused, shaking my head. "Which, I mean . . . I guess I'm just surprised you do the same for me. You're the client, you're the one who gets pampered." I shrugged a shoulder. "I'm not that special."

"But you are, dear." She reached across the table and squeezed my fingers. "Lamont finally sees it. I already knew it. And God was the one who designed you to be the way you are."

I bit the inside of my cheek. What was it today that had the waterworks so close? It was as if God knew I needed to hear those words. I'd been living in a world that had picked me apart on a daily basis for being less-than. For not being famous. For not being the right size. For not being as committed in faith. Apparently, some people thought my social media presence wasn't Christian enough. Those last comments made closing my accounts easier, and after a week of silence in that arena, I didn't have as much sadness as I'd imagined.

"Thank you, Ms. Rosie."

"You ready to call me Rosie yet?" A sly grin covered her brown face. "Or should we move on to Mom?"

My shoulders shook with suppressed laughter. "Rosie I can do. Jury's still out on that second one."

"Then I'll work on my son in that area."

I tilted my head, studying Lamont's mom. "Do you think our dating is a good idea?"

"It's a mother's dream to see her son with a good woman. I couldn't be happier." Her expression turned serious. "But please don't hurt him. Just because he has a nice house, too many cars, and a glamorous job doesn't mean he's impervi-able to harm, especially in this industry."

I thought about his breakup with Diva, the little tidbits he'd shared here and there. His life had been tumultuous with her. Could I bring him peace? Could we go the distance?

Ms. Rosie and I cleaned up our trash and headed back across the street to the mission. The archways on the long building beckoned me in. We decided to skip the museum areas with their beams filling the ceiling and headed straight for the chapel.

Goosebumps pebbled my flesh as I stepped into the sanc-tuary. How did the mission feel so holy? Like God was sit-ting here, waiting to meet someone? Tension seeped from my shoulders as I sat in the middle of the pew, Ms. Rosie following suit.

"Can you imagine going to church in the 1800s?" she asked.

I shook my head. "I still find it difficult to go today."

"Why is that?"

"I don't feel His presence like I do right now. Here, there are no distractions. Just me and the Lord and my thoughts."

"Mm-hmm. I can see that. But at local churches . . . ?"

I sighed. "I'm distracted by the people. What they look like, if they're judging me. Not to mention what the music sounds like, how the sermon is preached, et cetera. I'm so fo-cused on what I can get." I sat back, stunned by the revelation.

"That makes sense. After all, most of us attend church to be fed. We want to be filled by the atmosphere, and we forget we're there to worship God, not the other way around."

Quiet descended between us as I reflected on Ms. Rosie's wisdom. Was this why I could never find the "perfect" church? I expected the local churches to cater to my needs. To have people who looked like me, thought like me, and worshipped like me. Yet God's people had always been diverse. His heart was for *all* nations. Even though I knew that mentally, I'd failed to recognize the fact in my heart when searching for a place to visit each week.

Lamont's church had nice music, and the preaching gave me something to think about. But no matter where we sat, people near us would dart their gazes our way more than once. At first, I thought I'd been imagining things, but it became quite obvious they were paying more attention to us than to the pastor preaching. Lamont was able to ignore the looks, but for me, they were another con of going to church.

"Why do you attend the church you do, Ms. Rosie?" I didn't know exactly where she went, just knew it wasn't the same place as Lamont.

"I've made a lot of friendships over the years with the women there. They were there to make Lamont and me meals when I was going through chemo. They were there when I had the double mastectomy. Any time I need prayer, they will respond with a text, and I *know* they're lifting me to the Lord. So long story short . . . community."

Community. Had I ever felt like I truly belonged?

"Aren't we in community with the Lord?"

"We are, but He wants more for us. He wants us to be part of the body of Christ, being His hands and feet on earth. We need others to function properly. When we go it alone, we miss the help when we're in need and being a blessing when we are prospering. Alone, we're just an individual constantly seeking to belong. And that can lead us on some very dangerous paths."

She was right, and I wasn't too prideful to admit that it stung. I'd been avoiding community—church—because I didn't want to be different from others. Because I never felt like I belonged. And I needed to figure out why.

Until I got a clue, I'd keep seeking answers.

Twenty-Six

He lit the two candles on the other side of the pizza box. Tonight, he and Nevaeh would have a relaxing evening at his house with a movie on for background noise . . . or maybe they would actually watch it. It depended on how she took the news of the Cannon Industries offer.

His phone pinged, and he pulled up the text from Tuck.

Tuck
I need help.

Lamont
What's up?

Chris
Everything okay?

Tuck
Piper wants me to train her horse for the Derby.

Lamont
Don't you already train for the McKinneys?

Tuck
Not for her parents, for her.

Chris
I have so many questions.

Lamont

Same. Will the McKinneys have a problem with that?

Tuck

She wants me to work solely for her if I say yes.

Lamont

Chris

What are you going to do? Is this something you even want to do?

Tuck

She's my best friend. Shouldn't I help her?

Chris

Pray

Lamont

Agreed. If God wants you to go this direction, He'll make it clear. I get wanting to help a friend, but she's not asking you to just do something part-time. Sounds like she wants a full commitment from you.

Tuck

That's what makes this so difficult. The McKinneys have been good to me. I can't just quit and leave.

Lamont

You can if God tells you to.

Chris

What Lamont said.

Tuck

Enough of my woes. What's up with you two?

Chris

Same ol', same ol'.

Lamont

Waiting for Nevaeh to come over so I can share more details about the movie offer.

Chris
Praying, brother.

Tuck
Likewise.

The doorbell rang, so Lamont texted *ttyl*, then shoved the phone into his back pocket. He swung the door open and grinned. Nevaeh stood there wearing a T-shirt that read *Licensed to Carry* with a pair of hair scissors on the shirt.

"That's perfect for you."

"I was tempted to buy you one that said, 'Who needs hair with a body like this,' but I figured being Mr. SMA was enough to enlarge your ego."

Lamont threw his head back and laughed. "Yeah, you're probably right." He tugged her close, wrapping his arms around her. "I'm glad you're here."

She squeezed him back, nuzzling her nose in the crook of his neck. "Me too."

"You hungry?"

"'I could eat.'"

"Should we watch *Antwone Fisher* with dinner?"

"Too sad."

"But it has an uplifting ending."

"True." She pulled back. "Feed me, handsome."

Lamont interlaced their fingers and headed to the living room. "Happy to." He opened the cardboard box, plated a slice of pizza, and passed it to Nevaeh. "Your BBQ chicken pizza as requested."

"My hero." She bit into the slice, eyes closing with pleasure. "This is heavenly."

"Think they'll serve pizza in heaven?"

"I'd really like a taste of manna. I can't help but think it's the best bread around."

He chuckled. After taking a bite, he spoke up. "So, uh, Monica contact you lately?"

"Nope." Nevaeh popped her lips with the word. "An insider told me there are still people trying to get a glimpse of me. I don't think this will go in my favor."

"I might have a solution."

"Oh yeah?"

He nodded. "On Monday, I met with the owner of Cannon Industries and the movie director, which is when the solution presented itself." He shook his head. "Let me back up. There's good news and bad news. Which one do you want first?"

Nevaeh wiped her mouth. "Bad. Everyone knows the good news helps you recover from the bad."

"'Alrighty then.'"

"*Ace Ventura*," they said at the same time.

Lamont laughed. "It was an unintentional movie quote."

"Likely story but continue." She smirked. "What's the bad news?"

"We'll be filming outside of the country for six months, and since the company has a morality clause in the contract, you won't be allowed to visit, so we'd have to continue our relationship long-distance."

Her mouth dropped and relief filled Lamont. So she did feel awful about it too. "I tried to contest, but they said even if you stayed in your own place, people might assume you came all that way to do more than have dinner with me."

She said nothing, and worry tinged his heart. "You can see why I objected, right?" he asked.

"Six months without seeing each other in person?" she repeated slowly.

Lamont gave a slow nod, palms beginning to sweat.

"What's the good news?" Nevaeh asked cautiously.

"Otto, the director, is willing to look at your portfolio for a possible set stylist position."

Surprise widened her eyes. "Then we'd be able to see each other. No need for the long-distance drama."

"Well, uh"—he scratched at his face—"that kind of falls into the bad news category once more."

Her eyebrows contorted. "Explain."

"CI has a no-dating policy between staff—that includes actors."

"But we're already dating."

Part of him wanted to cheer that she voiced his same complaints, as if they were already becoming a team. Them versus the world, so to speak. "Believe me, I brought that fact up. Unfortunately, they don't want to give anyone preferential treatment."

She balled up her napkin, a glare on her face. "That stinks, Mr. SMA. Why can't you use your star power to get them to change their minds?"

"Otto said if he changed the rules for me, he'd have to do it for everyone."

"Ugh. Doesn't he realize he works with adults and not children?" She leaned forward. "I thought you said there was good news."

"You'd have a job?" He resisted the urge to fidget.

"But I wouldn't be able to hang out with my boyfriend. How could I see you at work every day and not act like we're a couple? What if I wanted to sit with you and talk—would they consider that a date?"

Lamont thought it was adorable how her bottom lip poked out just enough to be noticed. He reached for her hand. "I'm sorry it's not completely good news."

"What did Bryan say about it all?"

"Bryan was extra difficult." He explained how his agent

interjected during the meeting and made it sound like Lamont would jump at a chance to work with them under any circumstances.

"I mean, I get it. He's your agent and trying to make you look good." Nevaeh nudged his side. "Plus, he's ensuring he keeps getting a piece of the pie."

"Yeah, but I don't want to build up someone's expectations if I plan on turning them down."

She pulled back, studying him. "Am I the only reason you'd say no?"

He thought about it. If Lamont weren't with Nevaeh, he couldn't see a reason to turn down the job. Was that a bad thing? Shouldn't you be willing to let some things go for the right people?

"I am the only reason, aren't I?"

"Well, yeah," he said quietly. "I don't want to go six months without seeing you, Nevaeh. That sounds absolutely ridiculous when I say it out loud. Besides, they know my stance on relationships. The world *knows* we won't cross the line. If I end up staying at a local hotel instead of renting a place, you could simply stay at a different hotel."

"Except the perception of that lands us right back with the snaparazzi and that pic that started this all."

"True."

"Maybe you should just visit me here when you can."

He shook his head. "They want us near the set per the contract."

"Ugh." Her head fell back against the sofa cushion.

Lamont leaned back, pulling her to his side.

"Have you been praying about this, Lamont Booker?"

More like pleading with God to make a way out of no way. Did that count? "I have."

"And?"

"Other than telling you, I have no idea what to do."

"I can join my prayers with yours."

"Thanks." However, that didn't help Lamont with the looming deadline. Cannon Industries wanted his answer soon. "How do you feel about everything?" he asked.

"You tell me first."

He cupped her cheeks. "I don't want to go six months without seeing you, especially since our relationship is so new. Spending so much time apart when all I want to do is see your pretty face every day makes saying yes difficult."

She bit her lip. "Do you understand the position this puts me in, though? If I say don't go and you don't, will you regret that decision? Will I set some unknown precedent where you turn down roles because we don't want to be apart? Will you . . . will you resent me?"

He sighed and leaned his forehead against hers. "I couldn't. Not if we both feel like this is the wrong move for our relationship. It's both of us now. Not just me."

She stared into his eyes. "I get that. Truly. But I can't be the one to make this decision. Not when our relationship is fresh and considering the reasons we started dating to begin with."

"But that's not how it is now."

"Still . . ." she whispered.

He wanted to argue, but if she thought him pushing the issue would create resentment—on either side—then he'd go back to prayer.

"Do you have any other movie roles pending?" she asked.

"No, but that doesn't mean there won't be one waiting around the corner. If I say no to this one, it's not like it'll ruin all future opportunities."

Footsteps sounded in the hall, and his mom shuffled into the kitchen area, a book in hand.

"Hi, Ms. Rosie." Nevaeh stood and hugged his mom.

"Rosie, remember? How are you?"

She shrugged a shoulder.

"You two okay?" Mom arched her thin brows, gaze darting from Nevaeh's to his.

Lamont placed his elbows on his knees. "We're having differences of opinion. Though it's nothing we can't work through, right?"

Nevaeh sat back down next to him. "Right."

"What's going on, if I may ask?" His mom sat in the chair, setting her book on the end table.

"I got a movie offer, but filming will be out of the country for the first six months, and their morality clause means Nevaeh can't visit. If they offered her a job on set, we would see each other but couldn't date."

"That's ridiculous." Ms. Rosie shook her head. "Have you prayed?"

"I have. Nevaeh said she'd join me."

"Well, I will too. Maybe her taking the job is better than nothing."

True, even if he didn't like the answer.

"When do you have to give them an answer?" Mom asked. "Friday."

"I say if Nevaeh wants the job, then that's your answer."

He froze. Had he asked her if she wanted it? He turned toward her. "Do you want the stylist position?"

She swallowed. "Is it guaranteed I'd get the job?"

"No, they just agreed to look at your portfolio."

She bit her lip. "I don't know. I don't want any favoritism." She sighed. "Let me think about it."

"Okay. We'll sleep on it and talk about it tomorrow."

"Sounds like a plan," Mom interjected. "And a reminder for me to get my beauty rest. Good night, you two."

"Night, Mom."

"Sleep well, Rosie."

They tabled the talk of contracts and turned on the movie. Lamont wrapped his arms around Nevaeh and found himself praying that somehow, someway, she could go with him on location.

Twenty-Seven

My nerves strummed as I took the seat in front of Monica's desk. Tammy hadn't given me any warm fuzzies whenever I asked for updates on the situation. But maybe she was exaggerating. *Please, Lord, let her be exaggerating.*

"Thanks for coming in to chat with me."

"Sure." What choice did I have? If I wanted to get back to work, I had to come here.

"As you know, we've been assessing the situation since you took a vacation."

Unpaid vacay. "And have you come to a conclusion?" I asked. My tone was without censure and more filled with curiosity.

"That unless we make a declaration that you no longer work here, our operations will continue to be disrupted."

My stomach sank, and my hope fizzled. "So that's it?"

"I'm sorry, Nevaeh. You do good work, but like I told you before, this is my business, and I promise my clients a certain atmosphere. Your relationship disrupts that."

Yeah, well, dating Lamont had disrupted a lot of things in my life. I hadn't been able to find another apartment since I told Nora I was moving out. I hadn't found another salon job—one lady laughed when I asked her if I could work there. Another offered me the job but told me I'd basically be the salon mascot. *Thanks, but no thanks.*

While Lamont's life was looking rosier and rosier, the shine had worn off on my end. There was nothing glamorous about being a celebrity in Hollywood, and I couldn't even claim that status. What did you call someone famous because they'd been on TV—and they weren't an actor? Pretty sure reality TV star was it, and no one cared about them in the grand scheme of things. I mean, in general, not personally. I wished those people nothing but goodness and a calm life.

"Thanks for letting me know." I stood and left. No reason to stick around.

I double-checked there was nothing personal left in my locker, then got in the car and sat there.

My phone rang.

"Hello?"

"Hey, Nevaeh. It's your mom."

"Yep. Caller ID said so."

She huffed. "I wanted to invite you and Lamont over for dinner one day this week. Is that possible?"

I bit my lip. "He has a premiere coming up, so I'm not sure how busy his week is."

"Well, what about you? Could you come?"

Not like I had clients booked. Even though Ms. Rosie—*Rosie*—had agreed to ask her friends, my clientele hadn't shot through the roof. Yes, I had more personal clients, but not enough to secure rent in Studio City. Regardless . . .

"Sure, Mom."

"Great. You busy tonight?"

"No." I glanced at the dashboard clock. "I could head on over now."

"Really? Great, then you can help me cook."

"What's on the menu?"

"Lasagna."

Yum. "See you soon."

My thoughts flitted from one thing to the other as I headed to Inglewood. Since Monica fired me, and I didn't have another salon job in the works, maybe moving back home would be best. I could ask my mom while there, though I couldn't stand the idea that she could gloat or give me the awful *I told you so.*

Lord, I can't help but think that all of this is my fault. I told a lie to the entire world. Surely there are consequences. Though I hadn't ever thought that losing my job would be one of them. While I thought the lie would be helpful in the beginning, my world falling into ruins made me second-guess.

Wouldn't coming clean be worse? Because now we are dating, so how would it help?

This line of thinking made my head hurt and my heart weary. I sighed and stopped in front of my parents' house. I texted my mom to let me in, then pulled underneath the carport in the back.

I knocked on the back door leading to the kitchen. Mom opened it, apron over her clothes. She eyed my clothing. "You'll need an apron."

I shrugged. "I'm not a messy cook."

She smirked but said nothing. We worked silently for the first fifteen minutes before I broke.

"Mom, could I move back in?" I kept my eyes forward as I stirred the sauce in the pot.

"What's going on?"

"Nora wanted to blackmail me into allowing her to talk to the press about my dating life. Since I objected, she said I couldn't live with her anymore."

"You can't find another roommate or a place on your own?"

"Not since Monica fired me for bringing too much unwanted attention to the salon. People have been coming in on a daily basis hoping to take a picture of me."

Mom placed a hand on my arm. "Are you serious?"

I nodded, stunned by the look of concern on her face.

"Nevaeh, are you okay? Are you sure you want to be dating someone like Lamont Booker?"

"I thought you liked him." I set the wooden spoon down and faced her.

"Of course. He's nice, has good manners, and you two seemed to really enjoy each other's company. That doesn't mean you have to go run off with the man. His life will always be in the spotlight. Not to mention they'll look for any dirt they can and smear it on the newsstand."

That I already knew.

"Can you live like that? Can you handle the pictures, the comments, the invasion of privacy?"

"I don't know," I murmured.

"That's something you need to think about. If you can't handle this kind of life, you should break up with him before your heart is too involved."

How was I supposed to know how much was "too involved"? Was it too involved if I looked forward to every message, every phone call, every visit? Was it too involved if I had a picture of me and him from our whale-watching adventure as my phone wallpaper? Or was it too involved that I lied for a man to protect his reputation?

"As for the other issue, of course you can move in. Now might be the perfect time to think of a career change. I'm sure there are schools hiring, what with the shortage and everything."

Yeah, but I didn't want to work in the classroom. Never had. Boosting other people's self-esteem was my calling, not ushering in the next generation—not that there was anything wrong with that.

"Thank you for letting me stay."

"You know your room is always waiting for you."

Good thing she had a habit of keeping the whole house clean and clutter-free. I didn't have to worry about my room being a shrine to my youth. "Thanks, Mom."

"Mm-hmm. Just let me know when you want to move in. I'll make sure your dad hires some movers or gets some of the professors to pitch in."

"I don't have a lot of stuff. I'm sure Lamont can help." Or he'd definitely hire someone if I let him.

Of course, I didn't want him paying for something again. Since I'd entered this relationship, I'd felt so inadequate. Being just a hair stylist—an almost starving one at that—while he was Mr. Hollywood. I was an average woman rocking an average-size wardrobe, and he was Mr. SMA with muscles that made my mouth dry out. I was a sometimes churchgoer, and he never missed a service unless he was filming.

We were unequally yoked.

Maybe he should take the job with Cannon Industries. Give us time apart to figure out what exactly we were doing. Before I could change my mind, I pulled out my cell and texted Lamont a message to take the job. Then I added a second line, letting him know I was at my mom's house and would talk to him later.

Was it the coward's way out? Yes, but I didn't care.

"Nevaeh, don't forget to check on the sauce."

I blinked. "Right. Sorry."

I'd check my messages later, once I was back in my own room away from my mom's potentially prying eyes. Hopefully Lamont wouldn't be upset but thankful he had another job lined up.

Twenty-Eight

Lamont stared at the text from Nevaeh, trying to wrap his mind around her words. He read her text once again.

Nevaeh
I think you should take the job. I'm at my mom's, but we can talk more later.

The irony of her text and the drafted email before him had him shaking his head. As his eyes drifted from his cell, he focused on the email before him.

Dear Mr. Cannon,

I wanted to thank you and Mr. Schneider for the opportunity to work with you. Unfortunately, the duration on set conflicts with my current priorities. I pray you find the right man for the film and hope you have much success.

Sincerely,
Lamont Booker

He'd already cc'd Bryan on the email and had been prepared to send it when the notification from Nevaeh popped up on his phone. He ran a hand down his face. *Now what, Lord?*

This morning, Lamont had that feeling he should pass on the offer. He wanted Nevaeh to know, without a doubt, how important she was to him. Their beginning, the half-truths, they had started eating at him. He could tell she wasn't all-in on their relationship. He couldn't help but feel that being in a fake-relationship-that-wasn't-but-felt-so was actually the problem. If he said no to this job, would that put them on equal footing? Was Nevaeh's text sent out of fear that he'd resent her?

He sighed. Maybe that was all it was. Since he believed saying no was the right thing to do, Lamont hit send.

Now that he'd actually sent the email turning the role down, he felt . . . relieved. As much as he thought this movie could be an Oscar-winning film, he didn't think the benefit of doing the movie outweighed solidifying his relationship. Lamont wanted the opportunity to continue to build on their relationship and being apart for six months didn't seem the way to go about it.

Since Nevaeh didn't want to be the one to influence his decision regarding his career, he'd make this choice with a clear conscience. And whenever she wasn't with her mom, hopefully he could explain his reasoning behind saying no.

Lord, please don't let her be too upset. I'd rather she be happy I'll be here for six months versus upset I essentially ignored her yes to take it.

He rose to his feet. It was time to get out of his head. Maybe a workout would help. His phone chimed again, and he halted his movements, but it was Tuck, not Nevaeh.

Tuck
I'm going to be in Del Mar in a couple of weeks.
Any chance we can meet up?

Lamont
I'll make it happen. What dates?

Tuck
Last weekend of the month.

Chris
I don't get an invite?

Tuck
Of course you do, hence the reason I'm mentioning it in the group text and not a direct message to Booker.

Chris
Bet. I'll check my calendar. I'm pretty sure I'm free.

Tuck
The animals can spare you. Plus, that's why you work with a team.

Lamont
I'm free.

Tuck
See you then.

Lamont
If you can pull yourself from the tracks.

Tuck

Lamont walked out of his bedroom and frowned at the sight of the closed door leading to his mother's room. She shouldn't be asleep so close to dinner. He knocked, but no response reached his ears. After a few more seconds, he let himself in, taking care to keep quiet in case her afternoon nap had lingered.

"Mom?" He scanned her bed, looking for the outline of her body beneath the covers. Sure enough, she still rested, shades drawn.

She moaned, and the covers shifted.

Lamont rushed forward. "Are you okay? Do I need to call the doctor?"

"I'm just tired," she mumbled, turning her face into her pillow.

He carefully laid the back of his hand against her forehead. She wasn't feverish. But the last time she had problems with fatigue, cancer had been the ultimate cause. He wanted to wake her up and march her into the doctor's office. On the other hand, if she truly was just tired, he'd hate to disturb her rest.

God, please let it be nothing. Please let her just be tired.

Had she overextended herself this morning? Lamont vaguely recalled her leaving to meet friends, but he didn't monitor her activity beyond her health. He blew out a breath, rubbed the top of his head, and walked out of her room. Whenever she decided to rise, he'd base his next actions on how she looked. Hopefully nothing was wrong. Until then, he'd try his best not to borrow trouble.

That's not your job.

Lamont gulped. That's twice he'd felt that niggling sensation. Once, he could chalk up to a fluke. But twice?

I'm listening, Lord.

The doorbell pealed, and he winced. Okay, so he'd have to talk to God later. Hopefully the sound of the bell wouldn't wake his mom. He hurried down the stairs before whoever was at the door could ring again.

Bryan rushed in. "What kind of email was that?"

Lamont let the door close, then detoured to the kitchen to get himself a drink of water. Too bad he didn't have anything stronger in the house; his agent looked bent on an argument.

"Hello to you too," Lamont countered.

Bryan shook his head. "Forget the niceties. You told CI you'd pass on the deal."

"I did." He took a long drink of water, then set the glass

down. "There will be other opportunities." Hadn't he said that to Nevaeh? He might as well believe it.

"This one was perfect for you." Bryan threw his hands in the air. "You wouldn't have to worry about any objectionable content. Your brand would go through the *roof* with this movie. I don't understand you."

"I told you I wasn't comfortable being away from Nevaeh for that long."

"Don't make me lose my breakfast." Bryan's head dropped, and he placed his hands on his hips. "Please tell me that's not the real reason you said no."

"It is." He stood tall, refusing to let Bryan guilt him over his decision.

"Lamont . . ."

"Bryan." He moved to the sofa. Only his agent frowned, arms folding before he sat across from Lamont.

"Are you trying to turn your trajectory downward? Because if you are, it's working."

Lamont snorted. "You just emailed me this morning and told me I had another endorsement offer. If they keep rolling in, then so will the roles."

"You can't let a *woman* sway you on this."

"Let me ask you a question." Lamont placed his elbows on his thighs. "What happens if I get married?"

"To Nevaeh?" Bryan cried.

"To anyone."

Bryan shrugged. "Then you'll be a married actor doing movies."

"And if I have kids?"

"Then you'll be a married actor with kids making movies."

Lamont bit back a sigh. "You do know most actors slow down once they have a family, right? They pick and choose what roles they want because their families come first."

"Only you're not married, and you don't have kids, so why slow down now?" Bryan studied Lamont. "Do you need a break? Are you getting burned out?"

"No, not at all. I simply don't want to ruin my new relationship either."

Bryan's eyes flickered back and forth, then his shoulders dropped. "Nothing I say will change your mind?"

"No. I feel good about this." Truly, he did. Bryan trying to storm the castle made Lamont realize just how important it was to take a stance. He wanted to be able to give Nevaeh the time she deserved. She was worth it.

"Fine." Bryan opened his mouth to continue speaking, but his phone rang. He held up a finger, then answered the call. "Bryan Wilkinson, how can I help you? . . . Yes, sir, I saw. . . . We talked, and I support his stance." Bryan's gaze flicked to Lamont's, and he shook his head as if he really didn't.

Was Otto or James on the line? Lamont wanted to inch forward and listen to the call, but Bryan would update him when it was over. Lamont pulled up a message thread with Nevaeh.

Lamont
Want to go to a horse race with me?

Nevaeh
Sounds fun. I've never been. Where is it?

Lamont
Del Mar.

Nevaeh
When is it?

Lamont
Last weekend of this month.

Nevaeh
Count me in.

> **Lamont**
> Can I count you in for dinner tonight?
> Someplace fancy?

> **Nevaeh**
> Applebee's?

> **Lamont**
> 😂 Better than Wendy's.

> **Nevaeh**
> 😂 Don't we have your premiere tomorrow?

He'd almost forgotten about that.

> **Lamont**
> Yes.

> **Nevaeh**
> Then I'll relax tonight in order to prepare for tomorrow.

> **Lamont**
> Understood.

"Lamont!"

His head jerked up at Bryan's yell. "Sorry." He slipped his cell into his pocket, ignoring the vibration of a new text. "What's up?"

"That was James Cannon."

So it had been the owner of Cannon Industries. "Was he mad?"

"More resigned than anything."

Phew. Lamont waved Bryan on. "Keep talking, Bry."

"He wants you and only you for the role. He said if you feel strongly about being able to see your girlfriend, he'll make an exception and arrangements."

"What do you mean 'arrangements'?"

"Check your email. Apparently, he'll send a longer version

later, but sounds like Nevaeh can stay with him and his wife whenever she comes to visit. I'm not sure if they own vacation homes in the other locations or will rent a home for the duration of filming."

Lamont grinned. He'd get to see his girlfriend. "What if she decides to try for a stylist position?"

"James and his wife will be your chaperones for dates."

It would stink not having alone time, but he'd be able to see her. "I could work with that."

"I never thought I'd see you go bananas over a woman." Bryan shook his head.

"I'm not acting irrational. Just . . ." He paused. Had he been about to use the four-letter word? After only a month and a half of dating, he couldn't be that far gone already. Right?

"You're what? Lovesick? Sweet on her?"

"Hush, man." Lamont tossed a throw pillow at his agent, who ducked successfully.

"Well, make sure you tell her the good news. And please, don't bother James every couple of weeks with a visit. If she doesn't end up getting the job, just have her come once a month."

It wasn't perfect, but Lamont could deal with that better than going six months without seeing her. "When will filming start?"

"He said if you're agreeable, mid-August."

So he'd get two weeks of no work? A small blessing. "Okay. I'll sign the contract."

"Great." Bryan stood. "Thanks for making me more money."

"And the real reason you showed up is revealed."

Bryan rolled his eyes. "Like you don't appreciate the funds." Bryan threw up a peace sign and waltzed out the door.

As soon as it closed behind him, Lamont threw a fist in the air.

"What's got you all chipper?"

Lamont spun on his heel at the sound of his mother's voice. "You're up."

She nodded. "I think the combination of Zumba this morning and shopping with Carol did me in."

"Then you're feeling all right?" He studied her, trying to note any irregular fatigue or pallor in her face.

"Who's the parent?" She eyed him, pouring a cup of coffee.

"That's a trap." He smiled. "I'm just a concerned son."

"Humph. You're about as bad as a helicopter mom."

Ouch. Maybe that's why the Holy Spirit was trying to get his attention. But he'd joke back with his mom. "You did 'claim' I had separation anxiety as a kid."

"Claim!" Her mouth dropped. "Don't act like my memory is faulty. Trying to downplay how my one and only son would sob buckets if I attempted to use the restroom in peace. Acted like I was physically harming you."

"And look how close we are now." He smirked.

"Oh, you."

Lamont laughed, then let out a slow breath, thanking God she wasn't sick. Still, he'd have to come to terms with the very real fear that gripped him at the thought of her getting sick again. He couldn't keep reacting like this. Something had to change, and it was probably Lamont that needed an adjustment.

Twenty-Nine

Nevaeh, you go ahead and sift that flour for me, 'kay?"
Mrs. Hazelton said.

I nodded, doing as instructed. She'd knocked on
my door a few minutes ago and informed me of today's activity: baking a coffee cake for my man. Her words, not mine.

"How's the boyfriend?" Mrs. Hazelton asked.

"He's good." I bit my lip, trying to keep a grin from forming at the thought of Lamont.

Knowing he was *truly* my boyfriend still induced pinchable moments. So far, all I had were irritated arms.

"Just good?"

"He's the best, Mrs. Hazelton." I studied my neighbor.
"But I'm also beginning to worry I'll end up on the side of
the road with a stupid glass slipper." Women didn't go from
rags to a ball gown without the help of a fairy godmother.
The only person I could think of who even fit that role was
God, which made me cringe. I wasn't trying to say He'd grant
my every wish—quite the opposite. Lying to the world made
me feel like I'd land in rags, sitting on a pumpkin, because
of my own choices, not because God let me down.

Mrs. Hazelton laughed, jarring me from my thoughts. "You sure do tickle me pink, Nevaeh Richards."

"It's a gift."

"It really is. It's hard to remember to laugh some days." She tilted her head, examining me. "I have a feeling the last couple of days have been tough to laugh through. Them shutterbugs camping out and disturbing your peace." She shook her head. "They'll never learn."

"Well, they're gone today." When Nora had peeked through the window earlier, her face had resembled one who'd sucked on a lemon and discovered the sourness.

"Have they been a huge problem?"

I shook my head. "I can survive them." Plus, when I moved out, they wouldn't know where I'd gone.

"I know you can, my girl." She mixed the wet and dry ingredients together. "How come I haven't seen you wearing your uniform lately?"

"I got fired."

She gasped. "I'm so sorry. Have you ever thought of opening your own salon?"

"No. I like working on film sets more." I did *not* want to be my own boss. That was a headache I would gladly give to someone else.

"Then I'll be praying it happens."

I stared at Mrs. Hazelton. How had I never thought of that? I'd *hoped* I'd get a position on a film set, even *wished* I would. I'd spent time polishing my portfolio and had applied to various positions over the past few months since my last spot ended. Yet in all that time, I'd never thought to pray to God about it. To lay my desires at His feet and see what He could do.

Hadn't the pastor at Lamont's church preached on the importance of coming to God with everything? He'd said something like it was one of the primary purposes of prayer. Had my relationship with God always been superficial on my part?

My face heated. *I'm sorry, Lord.*

After a few more moments of silence, I finally spoke. "I'll pray the same thing."

The rest of our time went relatively quickly, and I soon left with a loaf in hand for myself and one for Lamont. Back at home, I reached for the dry-cleaning bag my dress hung in. My stomach clenched. This would be my first ever movie premiere. Jody had helped me pick out a dress I'd feel confident in, but the thought of all those flashing lights and knowing I would actually be on a red carpet had me wanting to reach for a trash can to toss my lunch in.

Breathe, Nevaeh. Now's not the time to get "crazy eyes." Unfortunately, quoting *Date Night* didn't bring me any humor. Perhaps a wig would help me channel my inner diva—not the Diva Jones variety of course. I opened my wig wardrobe and stared at my beauties. The bottom row held my personal wigs. The ones I didn't let clients use. I grabbed one with coiled ringlets. The style would look great with my designer gown.

Knowing I'd be prancing around on the red carpet had me reaching for a body shaper. I shimmied until everything was where I wanted it to be. After donning my gown, I stared at my reflection in the full-length mirror. If Lamont didn't drool when he saw me, I'd let him hear it.

My phone rang, and I smiled at Lamont's name. "Hey, boyfriend."

"Hey, beauty. Are you all ready?"

I slid a hand down my hip. "I am."

"Great. I was about to turn the corner when I saw paparazzi out here. Just wanted to let you know."

Of course they were here. Nora must be home. She had started posting old pics of her and me to gain more followers. She was pathetic, and I refused to engage in her shenanigans. "Thanks for the heads-up."

"See you in a sec."

I hung up and made my way toward the door, but Nora stopped me in my tracks.

"Going somewhere?" She arched a brow, looking down at me, even though we were practically the same height.

I stood up straighter, chin tilted to let her know I refused to be intimidated. "Lamont's premiere."

"Since you're still here, expect me to make a comment soon."

"I'll be gone tomorrow." I had originally planned to move next week, but why wait?

Nora's eyes flashed, and her mouth opened, then shut.

I wanted to say something further. To demand an apology for all the turmoil she'd caused. How could she just throw away a decade of knowing each other? Instead, I made my feet go around her.

As soon as I stepped outside, Lamont linked fingers with me, smiling at me in a way that signaled he was happy to see me. Somehow, the press faded into the background as I took in the joy on his face.

He bent down and kissed my cheek. "You look lovely."

"America's sweetheart lovely?"

Lamont chuckled. "You're in your own category."

I'd take it. We said nothing more, pressing through the snaparazzi until we slid into the back of the chauffeured limo waiting at the curb.

"A limo, huh?"

"Nothing but the best for my girl."

I grinned.

"Sorry I couldn't make the paparazzi go away."

I shrugged. "Probably Nora's doing. I told her I'd be moving out tomorrow."

"You found a place?"

We hadn't talked since I sent that text. Guess now was the time to stop running from it all. "I'm moving in with my folks."

Judging by the gaping hole created by his dropped jaw, my news was difficult to digest.

"I hate that's the only option you have. We'll be farther apart now."

"Well, they say couples start acting alike the longer they're together. Now we both live with our parents." Though I'd be living with my parents versus Rosie living with Lamont.

"I'm sorry." He blew out a breath, running a hand over his head.

Is it a shame if I envied his fingers?

"I've got some news myself."

"Oh yeah?"

"I accepted the movie with Cannon."

Now it was my turn to resemble a guppy. "Oh."

"I actually turned it down first."

My brows rose. "Before or after you read my text?"

"After. I'd made the decision, saw your text, but in the end, I simply didn't want to be apart from you for so long." He shrugged. "So I said no. Then they called and told Bryan they were willing to chaperone if I said yes to the job."

I didn't know what to say to that. Yay?

His fingers gently grasped my chin and tilted my face his way. "We'll make arrangements for when you come out to visit." He kissed my right cheek. "And if you want, you can apply for the stylist position. And expedite that passport so we can schedule your first visit."

As much as I needed a job, I didn't want one gained from nepotism. "We'll video chat?"

"Yes."

The car slowed, and my stomach dipped. "I'm not ready."

"Hey, you'll get to see your favorite actor on the big screen. You just have to walk through the gauntlet to get there."

I laughed at the image. "At least you'll be with me."

"'I'll never let go.'" He interlaced our fingers.

"You better not. I don't want to freeze in paparazzi-infested water."

We shared a laugh, then the door opened. Lamont exited first, and the sound of camera shutters assaulted my ears. I swallowed and reached for his hand again. I glanced at the red carpet beneath my feet, letting a little smile show as I walked beside Lamont.

Entertainment newscasters called out our names, some to chat with us, others to simply get a photo of us. We slowly meandered down the red carpet, and my heart finally fell out of my throat and back into my chest.

"Lamont, let's see a kiss."

My boyfriend peered down into my eyes. "Is that okay with you? I'll keep it tame."

Kissing for the camera? Thank goodness this wouldn't be our first kiss. I nodded my agreement, and he bent down, brushing his lips against mine. I sighed against his lips as my body heated from the contact. He pulled back and winked at me.

I'm not even going to lie. My inner fangirl swooned and landed *hard* on the floor. If that was any indication of the status of my heart, I was in big trouble.

Thirty

The *Star Weekly* article about him and Nevaeh left a sour taste in his mouth. Though the majority of the magazine article was glowing, despite Nora's attempt to sabotage Nevaeh, Lamont couldn't help but feel convicted.

Though a source close to the couple says they are intimate, our journalist believes that to be a falsehood. It is apparent the source is trying to seek out their own fifteen minutes of fame, hoping to eclipse Hollywood's golden couple. Our journalist and photographers have never seen Lamont Booker and Nevaeh Richards enter hotels together, spend the night at the other's homes, or anything else to indicate they're untrustworthy.

The last sentence pierced his heart. The world believed Lamont and Nevaeh were *trustworthy*. He grimaced, rubbing the stubble on his chin. Their relationship was continuing to perpetrate the lie they'd created when Nevaeh agreed to date him. Yes, they were a real couple now. Yes, the events and dates they went to were because they wanted to be in one another's company, but it was all based on a lie.

Lately the thought had been waking him up in the middle of the night. Almost as if he needed to confess. Although he was nearly done filming the horse trainer movie, Lamont felt no relief. Joy had been sucked out of him as the constant thought of repentance echoed in his head.

Only asking for forgiveness during his time reading the Bible wasn't bringing the relief he hoped for. It was almost like God wanted him to *publicly* repent. That was foolish, right? What would be the purpose of concocting the scheme of him and Nevaeh being together in the first place if Lamont had to confess to the charade? On the other hand, he'd never been comfortable with the idea of lying. Maybe that's all this was. Guilt he hadn't dealt with.

But, Lord, Nevaeh and I are really together now. Does it matter how our beginning was orchestrated?

"For God is not the author of confusion . . ."

The verse scrolled through his mind. How did it relate to Lamont and Nevaeh? He wasn't confused on anything, was he?

Nothing but the need to repent. Okay, so maybe there was confusion. Was there also confusion on Nevaeh's part? He thought their various talks on how he felt and what he wanted out of the relationship would assure her this wasn't a game. But what if he always had to prove to her that his intentions were genuine because of their beginning?

He groaned and pushed away from the outdoor table. He'd come out to the balcony this morning needing to feel God's peace after waking up repeatedly throughout the night. Tomorrow they were supposed to drive to Del Mar and hang out with Chris, Tuck, and Piper. But all he could think about was the lie used to save his reputation.

"Why was it so wrong, Lord?" He knew the basics. A lie was a sin. But when he was trying to save his reputation due to misrepresentation, why was it wrong?

Fear.

The word slithered into his brain. Lamont had been so afraid of what would happen to him, he'd acted rashly. He sat back down in front of his Bible, pulled up his cell phone, and did a search for fear and Bible verses.

The fear of man brings a snare, but whoever trusts in the LORD shall be safe.

Ouch. Proverbs didn't pull any punches. Lamont had definitely been snared by the fear of the paparazzi and news journalists. Even the trolls on the internet had given him pause. He knew for sure they had hurt Nevaeh.

"I'm sorry I didn't trust You, Lord. I should have." He swallowed. He'd placed too much care on what others thought of him. Thought for sure if he didn't do damage control, his witness for God would be tarnished.

Do I seek to please men? For if I still pleased men, I would not be a bondservant of Christ.

Lamont bowed his head as the words of Galatians washed over him. He'd lost sight of the Lord. Did Lamont really believe that the paparazzi were so powerful that everything he'd done for God could be erased? Didn't the Bible say God could use all things for good and that nothing would be wasted? Lamont hadn't trusted God's promises. Instead, he'd seen his giant as insurmountable.

What was he supposed to do now? How could he fix this?

If we confess our sins, He is faithful and just to forgive us our sins and to cleanse us from all unrighteousness.

Looked like Lamont really needed to figure out a way to confess. Not only that, but he needed to give the consequences and the unknown to God. To lay his fears at His feet and trust that God would work things out for good. Lamont hated the thought of losing favor with the public, and if he hated it more than he hated losing favor with God, then he'd made his reputation an idol.

His heart thudded.

Not only had he made the public's opinion an idol, but Lamont had failed to trust God regarding his mom's health. Lamont spent way too much time ensuring they had healthy foods in the house, that she had access to the right doctors, the right exercise regime. All to guarantee she didn't get cancer again. Instead of rejoicing that God had worked a miracle and she was cancer-free. Lamont had been too focused on what *could* happen, just like he'd believed Bryan about what *could* happen if he didn't fake a relationship.

Shame coiled through him, and he poured out words in prayer asking for forgiveness, wisdom on how to go forward, and help to rid himself of unbelief. When he was finally done praying, Lamont sat back in his seat and stared at the LA skyline.

Everything he had was because of God. He couldn't forget that and couldn't let fear hoard what was temporary. If confessing to the public resulted in loss of contracts and endorsements being yanked, then Lamont would handle it accordingly and with God's direction. Come what may, Lamont would trust God and not lean on his own understanding.

He picked up the phone.

"Hey, Mr. SMA."

"Hey, beautiful. What are you up to?"

"Just did laundry."

"Your parents treating you okay?"

"Yes, but is that why you called? You seem down?"

Lamont blew out a breath. "I've been reading my Bible and had a question for you."

"Okay."

"Where do you stand in your faith? I know you said you believe. But you also said you don't go to church that often. I guess what I'm asking is, how important is it to you?" He held his breath. He didn't want to sound accusatory, just wanted to understand her better.

And, more importantly, wanted to make sure they were on equal footing when it came to their faith.

"I've been talking to God about that actually. When I had lunch with your mom and we sat in that mission chapel, she said a couple of things that I've been chewing over."

Really? He upped the volume on his phone so he wouldn't miss a word. "What did she say?"

"I told her the reasons I had a difficult time going to church, and she told me 'we forget we're there to worship God, not the other way around.' I know mentally why we go to church, but the way she said it just struck me right in the heart. I felt convicted that I had made it all about me."

"That's powerful."

"Right? Your mom is so wise."

"So what's the other thing that made you think?"

She sighed. "This one was a little bit weightier to me. While her first tidbit made me see myself in the right light—a created being here to worship the Creator—the second tidbit made me realize I'm not seeking the right things." She paused. "She told me 'alone, we're just an individual constantly seeking to belong. And that can lead us on some very dangerous paths.'"

His mom made a point. Hadn't that been part of Lamont's problem? Seeking to belong to the masses so they wouldn't hinder his witness for Christ?

"That is tough."

"Yes, but I needed to hear that."

"Did you come to any conclusions? Did God bless you with any revelations?"

"Just that it doesn't matter what my surroundings are. What people at church look like, the style of the sermon—all of that is inconsequential to the real reason I am there: to worship Him. Not to say that the rest doesn't matter at all. I don't want to align myself with a church that isn't preaching Christ or Bible-centric messages. But I also don't have to get annoyed if the song isn't my favorite. It's not the genre of the music but the lyrics and heart posture I'm offering God."

"Wow, Nevaeh. I think I just got chills."

She laughed. "Hey, my mom just called me. Call you back?"

"Uh, don't worry about it. I'll see you tomorrow."

"I can't wait." She blew a kiss, then the line died.

Besides, he didn't need to talk to her about confessing over the phone. He could do that in person on the ride to Del Mar. He'd just have to pray that God would give him the right words and that Nevaeh would be receptive to them.

Thirty-One

sat on top of my luggage, sliding the zipper around, working to get everything stuffed into the case. My derby hat—or should I call it a Del Mar hat since I wasn't going to Kentucky?—had already been placed into the hat box that rested near my bedroom door. The tan confection had a wide and perfect swooped brim to cover an eye and draw attention to the beautiful pink-and-blue ribbon decorating the top. Hopefully people wore the big, poufy hats to other horse races besides the Kentucky Derby. But if not, I would rock mine with pride.

My knowledge about horse racing could fill a shampoo cap, and despite the articles I'd read online and the YouTube breakdown videos I'd watched, I still felt completely ignorant. God willing, Lamont would know more and could explain everything better to me.

I checked my watch. Lamont would be driving us to our hotels situated near the Del Mar racetrack. I was looking forward to meeting Chris and Tuck and seeing the dynamic between the guys. How did a famous man make friends who weren't? Although, Chris had hundreds of thousands of subscribers on his YouTube channel, and Tuck was apparently a sought-after horse trainer, so maybe they were kind of famous in their areas of work.

I dragged my suitcase to the front of the house, passing Dad, who sat in his favorite spot on the couch. He looked up from his book, a line etched into his brow.

"That looks heavy. You going to be able to lift that, buttercup?"

"I won't have to. Lamont will probably take care of it for me."

Dad nodded. "Glad he's taking care of my baby girl. Where are you staying again?"

"Best Western." Lamont had tried to make me reservations at a five-star resort, but I didn't feel comfortable with him spending that kind of money on me. Going so long without finding another salon job made me more conscious of how much money he spent.

But he has the money to spare. What's the harm in letting him pay?

I pushed my inner voice away. If she had her way, I'd be ready to say those three little words and wear a diamond on my left hand. I gave an inward shake of the head. No, diamonds seemed too pretentious. Not that we were there, especially since that would make Bryan all too happy . . . or not.

"And where's Lamont staying?"

I blinked, focusing on the current conversation. "Um, the Lodge at Torrey Pines, I believe." The place was perfect for Lamont and his famous friends.

"Nice digs." Dad stood and slipped his hands into his pockets. "Want me to help you out the door?"

I shook my head. "No need. Enjoy your book." I motioned to the paperback he'd placed on the coffee table.

"I will. Stop in the kitchen and say good-bye to your mother first."

"Sure, Dad." Since I'd moved back in with my parents, they seemed to have reverted to my childhood days. Asking where I was going, making sure I said good-bye when I left the house. Mentally, I knew they were just concerned, so I tried not to let it grate on me.

I headed for the kitchen and found my mom pulling some muffins out of the oven. "Hey, Mom. I'm heading out. Just wanted to say bye."

She turned and not so subtly checked my outfit. Her lips pursed at my long shirt and leggings. For once, I didn't let her disapproval prick my self-esteem. The outfit covered all my assets and was comfortable to boot. A win in my book.

"I hope you have fun."

"I'm sure I will." I'd be with Lamont after all.

"Don't spend too much money gambling."

I bit back a sigh and forced my lips into a smile that had my cheeks hurting as I wrapped my arms around her. "Bye."

She squeezed me tightly, then stepped back. "Please behave."

"Yes, ma'am."

She dipped her head in acknowledgment and grabbed a muffin with a napkin. "For the road." She thrust the offering in my face.

"Thanks, Mom." I kissed her cheek, then left the kitchen. I was old enough to know when to leave on a good note.

When I walked back into the living room, the front door was open, and Dad was headed down the sidewalk with my luggage. I grinned. He just couldn't help himself. But I wouldn't complain because that sucker was heavy, and I didn't need to break my back tugging the case behind me. What surprised me more was the truck idling by the curb.

I walked down the sidewalk just as Dad handed the suitcase off to Lamont, who put it in the back.

Dad shook Lamont's hand. "Nevaeh says you're staying at the Lodge at Torrey Pines."

"Yes, sir. Two of my friends will be staying there as well. I offered to pay for Nevaeh to stay there as well, but she preferred the Best Western."

"Smart of her," Dad said. "You two don't need people speculating if you're sharing a room or anything else."

True. However, my intent had been to save myself money and not depend on my boyfriend to pick up the check just because he could. I didn't want to assume he would spend money on me. Especially since I knew how to take care of myself.

Is that why you're living with your parents?

I ignored my inner voice. As difficult as it was to live back home, it was wonderful not having paparazzi here. It made me wonder if Nora had been the cause of their appearances all along. I'd thought about bringing a lawsuit against her for her comment in *StarWeekly* but quickly vanquished that idea.

"Yes, sir. We'll maintain propriety."

"Well, you two have fun," Dad said.

I hugged Dad, and he shuffled back to the house. I turned toward Lamont. "A truck?"

"Not just any truck, an electric one."

So I was semi-impressed? "Is this one of yours?"

He shook his head. "I rented it." He opened the door, and I slid in. That new car smell hit my senses, and I snuggled into the leather interior.

After Lamont buckled up, I split my muffin in half. "Want some?"

Lamont took the piece. "Thank you." He bit it and smiled. "This is amazing."

"Mom cooks when she's stressed."

"Why is she stressed?" He put the truck in drive, and we were off.

Was it terrible that I was so excited about this trip? Too bad my mom couldn't be happy for me. This was a once-in-a-lifetime-type deal. "The trip, I think."

I ate the rest of my muffin. I really didn't want to talk about my current job issues. "What's the plan once we arrive?" I asked after I finished chewing.

"The guys want to meet up for lunch."

"Will I be the only girl?" I asked. Why hadn't I asked before?

"Tuck's friend Piper accompanied him, so no. Chris, however, is flying solo."

Thank goodness. I wouldn't have to worry about feeling awkward in a group of men. My shoulders relaxed. "Good. It'll be nice to meet them."

Tucker "Tuck" Hale was a horse trainer at the McKinney farm and apparently came with his best friend, Piper McKinney, daughter of *the* McKinneys—that's how Lamont described them. I wished I knew enough about horse racing to know how big a deal they were. I mean, would they laugh at my hat and *bless my heart*, or were they low-key about their fame because horse racing was a smaller world than Hollywood? Apparently, they were the ones who'd recommended the hotel to Lamont, which had to mean they did pretty well in the racing world.

Lamont had mentioned how much Tuck and his other friend, Christian "Chris" Gamble, had seen him through hard times, and how they often chatted, whether via text or video chat.

Chris was a wildlife conservationist. I actually knew him. Well, not *knew* knew. I'd seen some of his YouTube videos. Who didn't like a good animal video? He had serious videos talking about conservation efforts, but he also had blooper reels of things gone wrong—those were my favorite.

"What do they know of our relationship?" I asked.

"Everything."

My face heated. "Piper too?"

"I don't know." Lamont squeezed my hand. "You're not embarrassed, are you?"

"Why would I be embarrassed that your friends know we only got together because gossip columnists are so out for blood, they uploaded a picture that implied something other than reality?"

"Nevaeh . . ." He sighed. "I promise they won't judge. Besides, they know it's real, and that you're the best thing to happen to me."

My cheeks warmed at the compliment.

I envied Lamont. He'd had people to talk to about the whole situation, and I only had Mrs. Hazelton. I couldn't even tell my parents the truth because of the NDA. My breath hitched. Should I have?

Maybe my concern was if I admitted the truth of our start to the people closest to me, they'd find me foolish and agree Lamont didn't want me for me. I truly didn't want to end up on the side of the road with a stupid slipper. As much as Lamont tried to assure me this was real, my mind always went to our beginning. It had started as a lie. Wasn't that a recipe for disaster if we made long-term plans? What if I wanted to say *I love you*? Would I still wonder if Lamont was acting for the paparazzi, or would it feel genuine, as he often tried to reassure me?

Maybe the reason Cinderella agreed to a magical old woman's schemes in the first place was because she had to try. She wanted the opportunity to belong and have someone care.

Three hours later, we arrived in front of my hotel. Lamont dragged my suitcase behind me.

"Good grief, Nevaeh, did you put a dead body in here?"

Wide-eyed elderly patrons looked between me and Lamont. I bit the inside of my cheek, trying not to laugh at the horror on their faces. I think their hair went whiter than it already was.

"His attempt at humor." I jerked a thumb toward Lamont.

"So crass," a woman not-so-quietly whispered to her husband. She turned with her nose up in the air.

Whatever.

"I'll check in, then come down after I've changed real quick."

Lamont perused my comfortable shirt and leggings, then turned a smolder on me. "I like this look."

I resisted the urge to fan myself. "Lamont Booker," I whispered. "You cannot look at me like that. Remember propriety."

He snort-laughed, then handed me my luggage.

"See you in a bit."

He nodded.

I lugged my overly stuffed suitcase down the hall to the elevator and through another hall. The fourth floor actually had a nice view, and my king-size bed looked like a California king. I fell back on the mattress, arms spread out as the cushion enveloped all my curves. This was going to be a great adventure. Now to pray that Lamont's friends liked me.

Thirty-Two

Tuck
You and your girlfriend are upsetting my appetite. Can't y'all stop making lovey-dovey faces at each other?

Chris
I don't know why you're complaining. I'm the fifth wheel.

Tuck
Piper and I aren't together.

Lamont
So you say. But it's odd how you guys finish each other's sentences. Also, why are we texting instead of talking to each other? We're at the same table.

Tuck
I no longer know how to communicate in person.

Chris
That's obvious by your best friend finishing your sentences.

Lamont
Maybe he has stage fright? Afraid to lose the race? Wait . . . he's just a spectator.

"Who are you texting?" Nevaeh asked.

Lamont flushed. "Um . . ." He nodded across the table toward Tuck and Chris.

Nevaeh snorted. "Put the phone down and learn how to talk to people face-to-face." She removed his cell from his hand. "You'll thank me for this later."

"Busted." Chris smirked.

"No, sir." Nevaeh wagged her finger. "You should know better. Aren't you older than all of us?"

Chris pretended to grab an arrow aimed at his heart, falling over in his seat. "That hurts."

Piper laughed. "I'm sure there are perks to being the oldest." She peered at the menu once more. "I don't see the age for senior discounts listed." She looked at Chris. "Should I ask the server?"

Chris flattened his lips in an exaggerated movement, but his eyes showed suppressed mirth. He may be the oldest at forty-one, but that didn't stop women from staring. From the moment they'd walked in the door, Chris had received his fair share of attention from the female population in the restaurant. Lamont figured the blue eyes made his friend appear suave.

Of course, Lamont was the only one to actually get asked for autographs. A few people attempted to discreetly take a picture of him and Nevaeh. If they ended up on social media again, he knew who the culprit would be.

"Hardy har har. Tuck, it appears your friend has the same humor as you." Chris shook his head.

"She got it from me." Tuck grinned cagily at Piper.

They were an interesting case to study. Tuck claimed they were only friends, but there was such an ease to their relationship Lamont wondered if the horse trainer was oblivious to the undercurrents between him and his best friend or unsure if Piper shared any feelings past friendship. Regardless, they were fun to watch as they teased one another and drew in the rest of the group as well.

"How did you get started as a horse trainer?" Nevaeh asked Tuck.

"Born into it," Tuck drawled. "Daddy was a horse trainer and my granddaddy and his daddy, et cetera."

"You didn't want to do anything else?" Nevaeh asked.

Tuck shook his head. "Couldn't even if I'd tried. Every time I thought of doing something else as a fallback, the horses would call me to the track once more. I've never gambled, but I imagine seeing them come out of the gate and onto the track is about the same high gamblers get when they beat the odds."

"Wow, Tuck, that was almost poetic," Piper quipped.

Lamont studied her for a moment. She almost had a regal look to her. Her ebony skin glowed, and the short Afro gave her face an understated look. But when she smiled, joy took over her whole face and gave her a girl-next-door vibe.

When Tuck introduced them earlier, Lamont had to keep the shock off his face. He'd heard all about Piper from Tuck. Lamont even knew she was considered Kentucky royalty since her parents, the McKinneys, were known for producing winning Thoroughbreds. What Tuck had never mentioned was that Piper McKinney was African American.

He wanted to ask questions, but he'd have to wait until he, Tuck, and Chris were alone. Lamont's gaze darted to Chris, wondering what his friend thought of those two. Chris gave a slight shrug as if he had no clue either.

"What's this silent communication going on?" Nevaeh asked, pointing between Lamont and Chris. "First, y'all are group texting—"

"What?" Piper grabbed Tuck's phone.

"That's mine," he said.

She rolled her eyes at him, typed in the PIN, and started reading the messages. "Y'all are children," she pronounced after a minute.

Nevaeh's mouth dropped. "You know his password?" She turned to Lamont. "How come I don't know your password?"

His neck heated. "We aren't at that level yet." His eyes searched hers, then he lowered his voice. "Right?"

She patted his cheek. "I don't know, are we?"

Why did this feel momentous? Should he let her have access to his phone? "If I give you my password, do I get yours?"

She nodded.

"Hmm."

"Uh-oh. Now you're considering it." But the kiss to his cheek told him Nevaeh wasn't upset.

"It's an important decision," Piper said wisely. "Unfortunately for Tuck, he has no skill coming up with passwords, and I easily guessed his."

Nevaeh laughed.

"Does he know yours, then?" Chris asked.

"Yep. I have no secrets from Tuck." Yet her eyes darting left said otherwise.

Lamont wondered if he was the only one who noticed the telltale sign of a lie.

"It's no biggie," Tuck said. "I trust her."

"Trust is good." Chris nodded. "Now, are we going to talk horse racing?" He folded his arms on the open table.

"Yes, Dad," Tuck said.

Lamont snickered just as the rest of the group joined in with their own reactions.

"What do you want to know?" Piper asked.

"Everything," Nevaeh interjected. "I'm a novice. I tried

watching YouTube videos on what it all means but"—she shrugged—"it's still Greek."

Piper's ebony eyes gleamed. "Leave it to me." She launched into an explanation of horse racing and the different tracks to get to the Derby. She explained the lower-level races and the odds. By the time she finished, Lamont figured he could watch the day's events and actually understand what was playing out in front of their eyes.

"So if you guys don't run a horse at Del Mar, why come?" Nevaeh asked.

Tuck smiled. "It's fun to scope out the competition. Not to mention there'll be a horse auction that her parents are interested in."

"Did they give you permission to buy?" Chris asked.

"No. I'll buy on behalf of them." Piper smiled. "Horses and racing are in my soul. I may not have been born a Mc-Kinney, but being adopted a few days after birth and growing up on a farm ensured the legacy seeped into my being."

Adoption. Of course. "Farms always sound idyllic to me, but I imagine they're a lot of work," Lamont said.

"Tons of work. But it's rewarding, you know?" Piper shrugged a shoulder. "I imagine it's the same with you. You spend months making a movie that will give people two hours of escape. Still, you're proud because you know the effort you put into it."

Lamont nodded. "Very true. I guess that can be said of anything we do. We spend so much time working to bring something to fruition to only enjoy it for a moment."

"Yet the memories are lasting," Chris stated. "You can't discount the legacy you could potentially leave behind as well."

Lamont grinned at the people around the table. "I'm so glad we could all get together."

"Me too." Chris nodded slowly. "Even if I am the fifth and oldest wheel."

They all laughed. Soon their food arrived, and they ate while continuing their conversation. Finally, Lamont got that itchy feeling to break away from the table. If they didn't leave now, they might as well stick around for dinner. He made sure to pick up the tab, then they all made their way to the exit.

"Thanks again for lunch," Piper said.

"Of course. See you at the races."

Tuck shook his head but gave a salute good-bye.

Lamont interlaced his fingers with Nevaeh's and meandered toward the rental. "So what did you think?"

"I like your friends," she replied.

He grinned. He'd known she would, well, rather *hoped* she would. "I'm glad. They'll make your first horse race experience fun."

She nodded. "I believe it."

"Now that we're alone, is there somewhere you want to go? Something you want to do?"

"Let's go to the beach."

He looked down at his clothes. It would be easy enough to roll his jeans up so he wouldn't track a lot of sand. "Sounds like a plan. Do you want to go back to the hotel and change?"

"No need. I can carry my shoes."

A little while later, they stood on the sand. Nevaeh had her head tipped back, sun caressing her face.

"I take it you're enjoying yourself."

She raised her head and looked at him. "The warmth feels wonderful." She turned to face the ocean. "I can't believe how clear it is down here. LA is so full of smog these days."

"Unfortunately, but I still enjoy the ocean view." They were quiet for a few minutes before Lamont spoke again. "Should we go for a stroll?"

"Okay."

The sand was cool to his feet as the water rushed to greet their steps and retreated back out. At first Lamont didn't really know what he wanted to say. He was just glad Nevaeh was here, and he was with her.

"Have you found a job?" He winced inwardly. Maybe he could have worked that conversation topic further down the line. Only he'd wanted to see her reaction in person.

Her hand tensed in his. "Not yet."

"Are you worried?" he asked softly.

"Trying not to be. My mom makes a not-so-subtle comment daily about the longevity of teaching."

"Guess she doesn't read the news about all the teachers quitting right now, huh?"

"They're academics. They're kind of removed from all of that, I think." Nevaeh sighed. "I told myself not to worry until my savings account reads zero."

"Good attitude." He didn't know if he would have the same feelings if he couldn't find another acting job and his account was hanging by a thread. Then again, maybe Nevaeh had a nice cushion of savings. He wasn't actually sure how much money she'd stored.

"Maybe God will tell me exactly what's next and I won't have to wait much longer."

"That would be perfect." Because sometimes Lamont felt like he lived in a perpetual state of waiting, like during his mother's cancer journey.

Waiting for Mom to find out if she did indeed have cancer. Waiting to see the course of treatment that would help. Waiting to see if she was in remission. Now waiting to see if the cancer would come back—though there was no reason to believe it would.

"There's gotta be a way to live well in the waiting," he said.

"Being with you helps."

He hooked an arm around Nevaeh, tucking her into his side. "Maybe life is all waiting, and doing relationships well is how we get through."

"Feeling philosophical this afternoon?"

"Something like that. I've been doing a lot of thinking recently."

"Anything you want to talk about?"

He looked out at the ocean, the endless blue. "Not right now."

"Then how about we be still and soak up the scenery and each other's presence?" Nevaeh looked up at him.

He tucked an errant strand behind her ear. "Okay. Let's do that." He placed a soft kiss on her lips, then sat down on the sand, patting the spot next to him. He didn't look at the time or count the minutes. Instead, he emptied his mind of everything except for the woman next to him.

Thirty-Three

had a face-to-face interview lined up. The excitement buzzed through me. I couldn't be happier, because I needed something to bring me out of the funk I'd fallen in since we'd left Del Mar.

Lamont had left for Canada last week, and life was blue. I hadn't been prepared for how much I'd miss him. The text messages from him made me smile but miss him more. The video chats were great, but made me miss his hugs. More than that, I missed sitting next to him and quoting movies or even watching them together.

Unfortunately, the distance between us meant I could breathe a little easier. The paparazzi didn't know where my parents lived. It was pointless for them to camp out at The Mane Do because I was no longer an employee. And, since Lamont was out of the country and I wasn't with him, we hadn't been photographed together since our Del Mar outing. Not only that, but closing my social media accounts meant no one could slide into my DMs and harass me.

Now all I needed was this interview to pan out. I'd had a few phone and Zoom interviews in the past month, but this was my first callback since the one that was canceled and

I spent the remainder of that day with Ms. Rosie. To say I was nervous about this interview would be making light of my feelings. Thankfully, Lamont had called me this morning to pray over me. Tears had welled in my eyes at his consideration, especially because I knew how busy his production schedule was. That he would take time to lift me in prayer had warmed my heart and made that four-letter word well up in my mind once more.

But I'd kept silent. Surely it was too soon to confess such feelings.

I lifted my rolling stylist case into the back of my car and got into the driver's seat. The interview was at a studio in the heart of Hollywood. Hopefully traffic wouldn't be a pain and I'd get there on time.

Still, I was leaving with ample time to buffer any traffic impediments I could run into. I clicked on a podcast Lamont had shared with me discussing the state of the church and how to reach believers who refused to affiliate with a local congregation. He had assured me listening to it would be life changing. I could only pray he was right. Attending church was important to Lamont, and I wanted to resolve any lingering misgivings I had about my need for comfort in attending.

Couldn't I be a believer and not be a member of a local church? I was nice. I didn't curse anyone out—okay, maybe I had a touch of road rage, but I always repented afterward and aimed for keeping silent the next go around. I didn't feel like I necessarily did anything in life that was horribly sinful. Well, discounting the whole how I started dating Lamont based on an untruth.

"So why is church vital?" the speaker asked.

I tuned in, leaving my thoughts alone, and focused on the question. This was exactly what I wanted to know.

"There are many reasons. There's the fact that the Bible mentions 'not forsaking the assembling of ourselves.' Or the fact that many of us learn about what the Bible says *at* church, whether it's in a Bible study, Sunday service, or Sunday school. Without those foundations, many people would walk around ignorant of its contents. But I want to go beyond those reasonings."

Really? Because they were actually good ones now that I thought about it. I'd learned about the Lord because my parents took me to church. Would I have become a believer if I hadn't grown up in the church? Not to mention Ms. Rosie's comment about being able to worship God in church.

"I'm going to say the reason it's so vital to go to church is because holiness is required. God never leaves you in the same place He found you. He's always working to transform you and make you more like Jesus. If you can't even rearrange your schedule to attend services, how surrendered are you to change? I'm going to let that sit with you awhile. I'll play some instrumental music for background noise, and I invite you to take this moment to talk to the Lord. Are you truly surrendered to Him?"

I blew out a breath. Of course I was. I loved God. We talked all the time. Of course, *talking* and *surrendering* were two different words. What exactly did the latter mean in my life? Since I was driving, I couldn't look up the definitions, but I could take the moment and talk to the Lord as the speaker encouraged.

"Lord, You know I love You, right?" I bit my lip. "What does a surrendered life look like? Does that mean I ignore what bothers me about churches?" I didn't like to judge and point fingers, but when it came to excuses regarding why I didn't belong to a local congregation, I had plenty.

"How do I reconcile the two, Lord?"

Before I could say more, the light in front of me turned yellow. Taking my foot off the gas, I slowed and came to a stop as the light turned red.

Screeeech.

The sound of squealing tires brought my gaze to the rearview mirror as a car came flying down the street. I gasped and braced for impact.

Metal crunching against metal filled my ears as my body shoved forward, then slammed back. The sound of shattering glass clanged like cymbals after a drumbeat.

When my focus returned, I noted the stillness in the car and took stock of myself. Nothing felt broken. No airbags had deployed.

What about the glass?

I looked to the front windshield, which was still intact. I peered into the rearview mirror and saw a jagged outline of broken glass. The middle of the back window was completely gone. I turned to look over my shoulder and groaned as pain shot up my neck.

"Are you okay?" Someone tapped against the driver's-side window.

Holding my neck, I gave the good Samaritan a thumbs-up.

"You sure? Does your neck hurt? Should I call an ambulance?"

"No!" I shouted. I needed to get to my appointment.

Only the sound of police sirens told me I wouldn't be going anywhere anytime soon. I groaned again. "This can't be happening," I whined.

"The cops are arriving. I'll tell them you're hurt."

"I'm fine."

But the pedestrian had already walked away. At least, I think he was a pedestrian. A glance at the rearview mirror showed the other driver still in her car. Was she okay? Her head was stooped over. Had she hit her head on impact? Had she fainted, and that was the cause of the accident in the first place?

The police officer looked me over through the window, then pointed to the car behind me. I gave another thumbs-up, choosing not to move my head if I could help it. Soon an ambulance arrived and transported the other driver away. By that time, the cop had come and taken my statement.

"I'm afraid I can't let you drive. You really should get checked out."

"Why can't I drive? I don't have any broken bones." Besides, if I got checked out, I wouldn't make it to my interview.

"Maybe not, but your rear windshield is busted, which makes the car undriveable."

I wanted to argue but didn't have the time to waste. I could still make the interview, albeit a little bit late. "Can I Uber?"

His brown eyes pierced me. "To a hospital?"

Ugh. "I have a *very* important interview that I'm running late for. If I decide to go to the doctor, I'll do so afterward."

He tilted his head. "If I make you promise, will you go to the doctor?"

"Yes, sir."

His eyes squinted, then he looked at his notepad. "Nevaeh Richards," he muttered. Then his head shot up, and his eyes widened. "You're dating Lamont Booker."

"Y-yes." What was it with this obsessive metro area I'd chosen to live in?

"I'd be happy to give you a ride to your appointment, then to the hospital afterward."

Okay, that was really weird. Was he doing this to earn points or make the news? "Can you do that?" I asked cautiously.

He tucked his pen into his pocket. "I can today."

I thought about it for a moment. I really wanted to make the interview, and police officers were supposed to be safe. *God, please let this man be safe.* "Um, okay. Thank you." I didn't know if he was hoping for an autograph, but regardless of his intent, I would take the free ride and remember his badge information to see if Lamont could send him a signed poster or something.

He lifted my stylist case from my car and put it in his trunk. "Where are you headed?"

"Paramount Studios," I answered.

His eyes widened again. "Were you on the way to meet Lamont Booker?"

Had I sounded that giddy whenever I said Lamont's full name before we'd dated? I suppressed a laugh. "No, I have an interview for a spot with the hair and makeup team."

"Oh, nice."

We drove in silence. Partly because I had no capacity to think past the pain in my neck, and partly because I was focused on the upcoming interview. When we arrived at the gates, I gave the guard my name. He gave a head nod to the police officer driving me, but said nothing else, merely waved us forward.

The cop—he'd introduced himself as Officer Perez—grinned the entire way as I directed him to the building I'd been told to go to.

After he got my case out of the trunk, I peered at him once more. "Are you *sure* you can wait? I have no idea how long the meeting will last."

He glanced at his watch. "If it takes longer than thirty minutes, I'll probably have to leave. If you come back out before that, I'll take you to the hospital."

"Thank you, Officer Perez."

"Good luck."

I dragged the case behind me, holding in a wince at the twinge in my shoulder. Was I just sore from the crash, or was it something more?

Worry about that later, girl. You've gotta rock this interview. The spot was for a TV show that had just been greenlighted. Their pilot had been a success, and they'd earned themselves a spot on prime time for a full season. I walked into the studio, stated my name, and took the lanyard.

I took a seat, mentally giving myself a pep talk. *You've done this routine before. You know how it goes.* They'd hand me a script, tell me the look they wanted for the specific character, and give me space to interpret the rest. It was up to me to bring their thoughts to life.

The script they gave me was funny. I genuinely laughed out loud a time or two. By the time they called my name, I had an idea of how I thought the actors should look.

When I walked into the HMU room, the person conducting the interview looked up at the number showing on my lanyard. "Number 42, you're here to ready these two. They're stand-ins for the actors that play Jace Gordan and Annette English. You're aware that you'll be doing both hair and makeup, correct?"

"Yes, ma'am." I was confident in my makeup skills for a contemporary TV show. No sci-fi characters to go wild with.

"Good. You have an hour."

I tried to hide my nerves and stalked over to the actors. I circled the guy first, noting he was bald, but his character was supposed to have curly hair and a smooth face. This guy had a five o'clock shadow. After doing the same perusal of the woman, who had long blond hair and not the dark bob the director wanted, I opened my case. I knew exactly who these two were and what the studio wanted to see.

I started on the guy since he'd be the easiest to transform.

I pulled out the perfect hairpiece for him. A quick shave and some liquid color correct helped ensure no sign of his stubble existed. Some finishing powder would take away the shine the liquid corrector would create.

Twenty minutes later, Jace Gordan was ready for his first take. He left the chair, and the interviewer's assistant began taking Polaroids. I assumed they'd be labeled with *42*, to tell the interviewees apart.

That was neither here nor there. I still had the character of Annette to make over. I grabbed an angled-bob wig and went to work on the lady. Her character was supposed to be an ice queen, so I went for a pale look on her face. The colors I chose helped create an image of perfection. Before shutting my YouTube channel down, I'd done a tutorial on this specific application. Creating her look took the remaining forty minutes, and I stepped back just as the interviewer called time.

"Thank you so much," she said. "We'll call in a couple of weeks if you get the job."

"Thank you."

After ensuring the pictures of the looks had been taken, I took back the wigs from the actors and put my stuff away.

As I walked out of the studio, adrenaline left me, and aches assaulted me. The officer's vehicle remained parked. I'd thought for sure he'd be gone. I offered my thanks as he once again handled my case, and I eased into the seat. My body was really starting to hurt.

"Ready for that trip to the ER?"

I blew out a breath. "I think I am."

He nodded and drove out the gates of Paramount. I wanted to look back, to send one last plea to the Lord, but my eyelids were growing heavy, and I gave in to the exhaustion.

Thirty-Four

Horror filled Lamont as he stared at the text from Nevaeh.

Nevaeh
I was in a car accident. No broken bones. At ER getting checked as a precaution.

His mouth dried, and he exited her text thread to ask for prayer.

Lamont
Nevaeh's been in a car accident. Please pray for her.

Tuck
Is she hurt?

Chris
Praying

Lamont
Nothing broken. She's in the ER.

Tuck
Hope it's nothing. What did she say?

Lamont
IDK. Gonna call her now.

Tuck
Praying for her. I'll tell Piper, too, if it's okay with you.

Lamont
Thanks, fellas.

He FaceTimed Nevaeh and paced back and forth across his hotel room while he waited for her to answer. Her beautiful face filled the screen, and a measure of relief brought his panic down a notch.

"Are you okay?"

She grimaced. "I hurt. The pain reliever isn't touching this."

"Have you seen the doctor yet?"

Just then a man in a white coat walked in.

"Can I call you back?"

"Could I listen please? Support you via FaceTime?"

"Okay."

He listened as the doctor explained Nevaeh had a case of whiplash. Why did this have to happen when he was in another country?

It's not about you. She's the one hurt.

He tensed as the doctor prescribed some painkillers, anti-inflammatory steroids, and rest. Would Nevaeh's mother take care of her? Both of her parents worked, so who would be around during the day to help her? Lamont could ask his mom to watch over her, but would Nevaeh consider that annoying? He needed to look at his calendar and see when he could schedule a visit ASAP.

"Do you work outside the home?" the doctor asked.

"I'm a hair stylist."

The doctor frowned. Lamont wished Nevaeh would focus the camera on herself and not the doctor. Sometimes FaceTiming was difficult.

"I don't think you should work for the next two weeks. If

you can reschedule clients, do so. Your body needs to take it easy so you won't have to deal with any further complications."

"I understand."

"I'll send in a nurse with your discharge instructions. She'll go over everything with you."

Lamont's heart pounded as he considered everything that had happened.

"Thanks, Doctor."

The doctor nodded, then left. The camera flipped, and Lamont breathed a sigh of relief as he took in Nevaeh's features. He could see the pain in the wince she tried to hide, the darkening of her eyes, and the overall weariness dragging her features down. He needed to be there. To make sure she'd be okay.

It's not your job to fix it.

But if he didn't, how would he be assured Nevaeh would be okay?

He stopped walking around the room and sank onto the bed. "Is there anything I can do for you?"

"Of course not. You're in Toronto." She pouted.

He blew out a breath. Wasn't there something he could do despite the two thousand miles that separated them? "Maybe I could hire a masseuse? Do you think that would aggravate things or relieve tension?"

Nevaeh rubbed her forehead. "Don't worry about me. My mom will be here soon."

"Will she take time off to care for you? If not, I could ask my mom to come over."

"I'm not a child. I don't need someone to hold my hand."

Okay, so she got grouchy after car accidents. Understandable. Lamont bit back a sigh. "Where did they tow your car?" He could pay for that if her insurance wouldn't cover it. Or he could bypass them wholly and take care of her car stat.

"I don't know, but the officer gave me the information."

"Take a pic of the towing company's info and text it to me. I'll handle everything . . . *please*."

Her lips pursed, but she gave a short nod, then winced. "Fine."

"Babe, I'm so sorry this happened. If I can do anything—"

"You know, I don't feel like talking right now. I just want to go home and crawl in bed. Maybe we can talk tomorrow or something."

He tried not to feel brushed off, telling himself she was emotional due to the day's events. "Of course. If you need anything at all, please let me know."

"You'll handle it from Toronto?" she asked skeptically.

"My assistant will if I can't." Greg was back in LA taking care of other matters for the time being.

"All right then. Bye."

Her face left the screen before he could formulate a reply. *What just happened?* She'd never been that curt with him before. *She's also never been in a car accident before.*

Right. *Right.* This was all from the accident. She was in pain, and he was in another country.

His phone chimed with an incoming text, and he opened the message from Nevaeh, showing a photo of the towing company's business card. At least this he could handle. He dialed their number, waiting for someone to answer the call.

"Yes, I'd like to have a car that arrived at your place today towed to my mechanic." Surely his guy would take care of Nevaeh's car.

"What's the make and model?"

"MINI Cooper."

"Ah, the red one with the busted-up bumper and no rear glass?"

Lamont grimaced, imagining how hard the impact must have been to bust out the glass. "Unfortunately, that's the one."

"Yeah, I can tow it, but most likely the insurance company's adjuster is going to deem the vehicle a total loss."

"I thought that only happened when airbags deployed."

"Or when the car's value is below the cost of repairs. I'm telling you, buddy, buy a new car."

Lamont bit back a groan. "I'll have my mechanic determine that, thank you."

"What's the address?"

He rattled off the address and gave his credit card info for payment, then Lamont called his mechanic to tell him the situation.

"I appreciate you thinking of us for business, but if that's a 2010, it's probably a total loss."

Lamont wanted to pound his fist in frustration. "There's nothing I can do to save it?"

"Sure, but it's a hassle. It'd be faster and easier to just buy a new vehicle."

Why did this have to be so complicated? "Okay, then keep it in your shop for now. Let me talk to my girlfriend and see what she wants to do."

"Will do."

Lamont texted Nevaeh.

> **Lamont**
> You still at the hospital? Can I call real quick?

> **Nevaeh**
> Yes to both.

"Hey. The mechanic said your vehicle's probably a total loss. Want me to have Greg pick you out a new one? If so, he can deliver it to your parents' house by tomorrow."

"Are you kidding me!"

He knew she loved that car, but the level of outburst shocked him. "Unfortunately, I'm not."

"This is unbelievable," she shouted. "You can't be in here!"

"What's going on?" Lamont gripped the phone, his heart pounding.

"A freaking paparazzo just came into my room."

"Call the nurse and tell them to call security." His blood boiled. "And stay on the phone. I want to make sure you're okay."

"You know what? I can't do this anymore! I need a break."

The call ended.

Lead filled his gut as he stared at his cell. Now he felt like the one with whiplash. Did she just break up with him? He pinched his nose, hating the burning feeling creeping up his throat and making his eyes water.

Lord, what just happened? Please don't let that have been a legitimate breakup.

He stood there, mind reeling, trying to connect the dots. What was he supposed to do all the way in another country? Resolve filled him. He knew exactly what to do. He put on his shoes, grabbed his room key, and headed for the elevator. It would take a quick internet search to find a flight and get him on the first one back to LA. He could *not* let them end on a break.

Thirty-Five

The squeak of the door hinges interrupted my blank stare at the door. The one I had been staring at since I'd walked into my room and sat on my bed, trying to ignore every muscle that stiffened in protest of today's events.

"Nevaeh?" Mom whispered. "How are you feeling?"

My gaze shifted from the door to her face. "I hurt."

She grimaced. "Would you like some tea? I can get you a heating pad or ice."

I just wanted to be left alone. I still couldn't believe that gossip-rag photographer had the nerve to break into my ER room and get a few pictures.

"I'm fine."

"I doubt that." She walked toward me, then sat on the chair in front of my vanity. She brushed a hand along my hair.

"Spring me from this neck brace." Already, I itched and couldn't stand the constraint.

"I don't think so. I want you to get healthy."

"Then I guess I'll take a heating pad. Or maybe ice." I sighed. "Whichever is easier."

"Do you want some dinner too?"

"'I could eat.'"

She nodded. "Good. I'll bring you a tray."

Tears gathered in my eyes. Lamont would have caught the movie reference.

Lamont was in Toronto.

Since we'd started dating, part of me had felt alone. Alone in the mess the paparazzi made of my life. Alone in the online attacks from haters. Alone in being fired. At the same time, I had to make red-carpet appearances, smile while we ate in public places, and pretend to be the perfect Christian dating a Hollywood celebrity.

As much as I cared for Lamont, I didn't care for the life I'd been thrust into. And today, being at my most vulnerable and having the snaparazzi invade my privacy, it had all been too much. I thought moving to my parents' place would give me time to find another job and apartment, and life would get better. But I also thought living here would give me space from the media attention.

Only now, it was quite evident that I would never escape the media. All Lamont's suggestions for ignoring them, my own actions of closing my accounts, none of it seemed to help. The world wanted more of me, and I just wanted to fade from the limelight.

You were meant to shine.

I blinked, my gaze searching the room to ensure I was alone. Had I heard those words?

"I was meant to shine?" I asked softly.

"Let your light so shine before men, that they may see your good works and glorify your Father in heaven."

I could vaguely recall disagreeing with that verse the first time I read it. After all, I didn't like the limelight. It was one reason I craved being behind the scenes. I loved the atmosphere on a movie set, but I didn't want any camera pointed my direction.

Just like I hadn't whenever Lamont and I attended an event, knowing there would be more comments on my looks than I could handle. I was not cut out for a life in the spotlight. God hadn't made me that way. *Right, Lord?*

"Wow, that's an intense look." Mom put the tray of food on my vanity. "You want to talk about whatever put that frown on your face?"

"What's there to talk about? My life has gone down the drain thanks to dating in front of the public. Not to mention I have no job. No place to live. And now I may have accidentally broken up with Lamont." Though when I said I needed a break, I'd been shouting at the paparazzo.

Hanging up on Lamont had been an accident as I reached for the call bell with one hand and attempted to switch to video on my phone to show the guy invading my privacy. Only Lamont hadn't called me back. Was he upset? Was he happy to be rid of me and all the drama dating each other had brought?

"Life has been a little hectic for you lately."

I snorted. "A little? It's been nuts, and it's all because of the paparazzi."

"I'm sure dating in front of the world isn't easy. But you can't blame everything on the paparazzi. I've read the articles about you, seen you two interact in person, and can tell you guys are the real deal. Don't let the publicity drag you down."

"That's just it," I cried. "It wasn't real. It was all fake, but then it was real, and now it might be over."

Mom gently lifted my chin. "Explain."

So I did. I told her about the stupid photojournalist hiding in the tree, the resulting scandal, and Bryan's plan to fake it until Lamont could be assured his career remained intact. Of course I explained how my feelings had become real, and how Lamont wanted to date for us and not his career.

"Only thanks to our beginning, I always feel iffy about our now. Does he truly like me? Is he merely playing a part? How can I trust that what we have is real when it all started because his career needed saving?" I sniffed, tears spilling down my cheeks. "Not to mention I lost my job and my home thanks to Nora hating that the attention wasn't on her, and now I don't even have a car." I gulped at the enormity of the situation. "I have nothing."

"You have everything."

I blew out a breath. "What are you talking about?"

"Nevaeh, Nevaeh, do you know why I named you that?"

"Because you thought it was pretty?"

"That it is, but I wanted you to remember where you belong and who you belong to. Your citizenship is not earthly but heavenly. You belong to a God who would see you enjoy nothing but an abundant life. But dear girl, you've been chasing dreams for so long, I don't think you know what's what anymore."

More tears fell, and I berated them for making my eyes even puffier than they already were. The truth of my mom's words convicted like a punch to the gut. I always thought *Nevaeh* was a religious nod toward *heaven* but held no real substance. Hearing Mom explain the heart behind the name made a huge difference.

"I don't think God's too pleased with me either," I mumbled, swiping at the tears dripping down my chin.

"He delights in you, sweetie."

"Why? I haven't done anything momentous. I *lied*."

"You don't have to do anything big to be noticed by Him. Just be who He created you to be." She looked down at her hands, then back at me. "I want to apologize. I've been trying to mold you into a teacher, but you've never been interested in education like your father and I are."

297

"I get it." I tempered my desire to shrug, the body aches hanging on me like a shroud. "You wanted a stable life for me."

"I did. Still do. But I should've given you room to soar and been a safe landing place if you needed one."

I wrapped my arms around my mom, careful not to knock the neck brace against her face. She nestled her arms around me, rubbing small circles on my back. I inhaled the floral scent that was distinctly hers, and soon my tears settled and a calm enveloped me.

"Sweetie?"

"Yes?"

"If that lie is tearing you up inside, confess and repent. It's as simple as that."

Maybe not as simple as she made it sound. I had no problem confessing to God and asking for forgiveness. But what did I tell the world I'd lied to? I'd signed an NDA, which meant I couldn't admit my deeds to those who followed the story. My moment of weakness may have impacted them in ways I couldn't fathom.

I sighed. *Lord God, please forgive me for lying. And please show me how to clean up my mess.*

Warmth filled me. I might not know the next steps, but for this moment, I could feel peace and hope for a better tomorrow.

* * *

Chris
What's the word on Nevaeh? How's she feeling?

Tuck
I was just getting ready to ask the same thing. Piper's been breathing down my neck wanting updates.

Chris
I asked my parents to pray too.

Tuck
Yeah, I'm sure Piper got the whole church
prayer group sending up petitions as well.

10 min later

Chris
Seriously, everything good?

Tuck
Are you on set? Should we track down your
assistant's number?

Chris
Why don't we have that number?

Tuck
Because we have Lamont's. Why use the
assistant's?

15 min later

Chris
They don't give you breaks at work?

Tuck
I make my own. Usually the amount of dust in
my mouth tells me I'm in need of a water break.

Chris
That's why you breathe through your nose.

Tuck
Real helpful there, ol' man. Hey, how did y'all
contact friends in need in the stone ages?

Chris
Pager or we knocked on their door.

Tuck
The horror.

Thirty-Six

W e'd like to be the first to welcome you to Los Angeles, where the local time is one a.m. Please stay seated with your seat belt fastened until the captain turns off the seat belt sign. If you have a connecting flight, your bags will be checked through to your final destination."

Lamont tuned the rest of the flight attendant's spiel out. As soon as the seat belt sign turned off, he'd jump in the aisle to get off the plane first. He hadn't packed a bag, just left everything back in Canada, so there was no need to pick up luggage. Greg had arranged for Lee to see Lamont home.

During his flight, instead of sleeping, he'd been planning his next steps. Then he'd taken those plans and surrendered them to God. In order for things to work out, God had to be at the forefront. Lamont had to trust that God had good things for him. He couldn't focus on the consequences of his plan because there *would be* consequences. Telling the truth and trusting that Nevaeh would understand his grand gesture made him wish for a bottle of antacids. But it needed to be done.

The seat belt sign chimed, and immediately the aisles filled. Thank goodness he was in first class and not all the way back in economy, where he'd have to wait forever. He slid on his shades and ball cap and weaved his way down the jet bridge and into the airport, following signs for customs, then, finally, baggage claim.

Lee waited near the first carousel. "Welcome back, Mr. Booker."

"Thanks, Lee."

"Car's parked right out front."

Lamont nodded.

"Did you have a long flight?"

"A little bit."

"I understand you want to go to Mr. Wilkinson's home before yours?"

"That's right." He needed to talk to Bryan. Let him know his plans so he'd be prepared to handle the fallout.

"Then settle back and grab some shut-eye." Lee closed the door, and Lamont did just that.

Thirty minutes later, Lee lowered the partition. "We're here, Mr. Booker."

"Thanks." Lamont straightened his tee, then exited the vehicle to stroll up the steps leading to his agent's house.

Bryan lived not too far away from him, which made coming and going to his house easy. Lamont would head to his own place next, before going to Nevaeh's parents' home. At least, that was the plan.

He knocked on the door, sliding his hands into his pockets. A dog barked in the background, and Lamont smiled, thinking about the Goldendoodle Bryan owned because his kids considered a dog an essential part of growing up. Bryan had quickly caved.

The door wrenched open, and Bryan squinted at Lamont.

He rubbed his face, then stepped back, motioning for Lamont to come in.

"Why are you here?"

"Flew back to take care of some business."

"Otto and Cannon gonna like that?" Bryan glanced at the clock hanging on the wall.

"I got their approval beforehand. They understand I had some things to take care of."

"Why are you here so late?"

"Took the red-eye."

Bryan flopped onto his couch, then winced. He shifted onto his right side and pulled a toy from behind him and tossed it to the side. "Have a seat." He gestured toward the empty room. "What's so pressing that me or Greg couldn't take care of things for you?"

Lamont said a prayer before speaking. "Nevaeh was in a car accident. I think she broke up with me. And I'm hoping that coming clean will right things and be a little bit of a grand gesture."

"You should *not* have woken me up in the middle of the night." Bryan ran a hand down his face. "Start over. From the top. Wait." He held up a finger. "I need coffee before I hear whatever harebrained scheme you came up with on the red-eye."

Lamont held back his chuckle. He rarely saw Bryan so out of it.

"What's up with Nevaeh?"

"She got rear-ended and has whiplash." It took everything within him not to pull up his cell phone and check on her. He'd even ignored the messages from Tuck and Chris. He hadn't figured out a way to tell them his plans yet.

"Ouch. Is her car really messed up?"

"Totaled, according to my mechanic."

Bryan shook his head. "That girl can't catch a break."

Lamont winced. "Yeah. I kind of feel like I ruined her life. It's one of the reasons I want to come clean."

"After all we've done?" Bryan sat down, took a few sips of coffee, then sighed. "All right. What's this nonsense about coming clean?"

"I lied, Bry."

"You gave an alternate truth to keep the public happy. I told you, perception rules in Hollywood."

"It does. But that doesn't fly with God. In fact, I didn't even give Him a chance to help me. To be my defense." *I'm so sorry, Lord. I'll confess. I'll do what I have to do to make it right.*

"You're going to lose supporters."

Lamont nodded slowly. "I figured."

"There's nothing I can do to change your mind?"

"No. The world needs to know. Nevaeh needs to know that regardless of how we started, I choose her. I'm thankful for her. I . . ." He took a deep breath. "I love her."

"Ah, kid. I figured you were gone on her." Bryan shook his head. "So you need me to do damage control when the news hits the fan?"

Lamont laughed. "As much as you're able, but don't lie."

Bryan's lips twisted. "Fine."

"Thank you." Now Lamont could do the next thing he needed to do.

"How are you going to do this?"

"Do you really want to know?"

Bryan looked in his cup, then shook his head. "Not enough coffee yet."

"Ha. Then go drink more coffee so you'll be ready."

"It's gonna be a long day," Bryan muttered as he shuffled back to his kitchen.

Lamont jogged down the steps of the house and jumped back into the car. "Take me home please, Lee."

"You bet. Everything okay?"

"It will be." Lamont had to believe that. He didn't know what would happen. How God would work out the details. God had healed his mother of cancer and kept her healthy. God had saved Lamont from a selfish life.

God would do exactly what He said He would do.

Lamont just had to remember that.

He opened his text messages. It was time to get the fellas praying.

> Lamont
> I could use some prayer.

> Tuck
> Everything good? Is it Nevaeh?

> Lamont
> She's fine. I'm going to tell all. Explain how Nevaeh and I really started dating.

> Tuck
> Whoa. What does agent man think of that?

> Chris
> What brought this on?

> Lamont
> Bry's not happy, but he agreed to stand by me, and he's prepared for a media storm. I need to come clean. Need to confess. I'm also hoping Nevaeh will see it as a grand gesture.

> Tuck
> Y'all having trouble?

> Lamont
> Maybe?

> Chris
> Praying.

Tuck
This might be genius.

Chris
Or might be a disaster.

Lamont
You're telling me there's a chance?

Chris
Dumb & Dumber

Tuck
Dumb & Dumber

Lamont
I knew there was a reason we were friends.

When he walked into the house, it was after three. For his plan to work, the world needed to be awake, and even those who lived on the East Coast were probably still sleeping. He set an alarm on his phone and fell back on his bed.

Lord, please let this work.

* * *

He had to be delusional to think this would work. The conviction he'd felt early this morning seemed to have waned after his brief snooze fest. Or maybe it was the fact he was doing this live instead of recording it in multiple takes before uploading it to his social media.

Beads of sweat popped up along his forehead. *Lord, give me strength.*

In order to build something better in his life, Lamont had to expose the lies. The only way he could do that was to be honest with the world at large. Hopefully they would understand, and Nevaeh, well, hopefully she would give him a chance to further explain his feelings. He couldn't expect the video to do *all* the work.

"You ready?" Mom held Lamont's cell phone, having volunteered to be his videographer.

"I'm ready."

She held up five fingers, then counted down to one.

Lamont's mouth dried. "Hey guys, thanks for joining me here, live. I'm sure many of you are wondering what I could possibly have to say, considering I've never done one of these before." There was something nerve-racking about confessing live. Hopefully his deodorant would hold up.

"I've been thinking about my life, about my faith, and what God asks of us, and I have come to some conclusions." He resisted the urge to rub a hand over the top of his head or the back of his neck.

"In June, I hit the spotlight when a picture of me and my girlfriend, Nevaeh Richards, went viral. People questioned my stance on celibacy and if I was a hypocrite or actually living the faith I claimed to be part of. The only problem was, that picture didn't tell the whole story. So let's clear up some details."

He took a deep breath. "Here's what's true: Ms. Richards was hired as a personal stylist to care for my mother's hair during chemo and after. But at the time the photo went viral, we were *not* dating." He paused to let that sink in, glad he couldn't see emojis showing whether people were upset with his comments.

"At that time, Nevaeh and I had only exchanged small talk. That fateful day, I thanked her for going the extra mile for my mom, who had a stomach bug. Nevaeh made my mom homemade soup, even though cooking was not part of her job description. As a thank you, I offered to help her with her stylist case, which is huge by the way." He shook his head. That was neither here nor there. "She almost fell off the front stoop, so I caught her to keep her from hurting herself. That picture was taken as I asked if she was okay. Apparently, there was a photographer hiding in the trees who snapped the moment for posterity. That is the real story behind the picture."

Already his chest felt lighter, and his shoulders weren't near his ears. *Keep talking.* "When that photo hit social media, threats were made to cancel me without even allowing me to tell my side of the story. I admit the pressure and fear of being canceled caused me to justify my next actions. I wanted to keep my reputation as a true and reliable Christian in a culture that doesn't always show the best sides of humanity. So I concocted a scheme to date Ms. Richards. I told myself that if we started a relationship, then I wouldn't actually be lying to the public. I figured I could claim her as my girlfriend without the guilt of deceiving folks." Shame heated his face.

"I'm sorry for lying. I'm sorry for being hypocritical and justifying the sin of lying in order to help my career. The truth was, Nevaeh and I were essentially strangers when we told people we were dating.

"Despite how we started, I fell in love with her for real." He stared at the camera, praying she would somehow be watching this live, in this moment. "Nevaeh, if you're watching this, I'm sorry I didn't tell you sooner. Because of how we started, I was afraid you wouldn't believe me. I know living this life isn't easy. The harassment you've had to endure from the public, the columnists, losing your job, all of it couldn't have made you my number-one fan."

But man, he hoped she could see past that.

"To my fans, I know this all might be hard to hear, especially for those of you who have cheered me on from my very first theater role. Some of you would never use your words carelessly or knowingly lie, and that's exactly what *I* did. I thought if I changed the narrative to ease my conscience, then I could stand right before you and before God. But God convicted me. I have confessed to Him privately, and now I'm confessing to the world, including my fellow believers." He swallowed. "I ask forgiveness from my colleagues, those I have contracts with, my fans, the reporters, and Nevaeh."

Lamont stopped for a moment, searching for the right words. He focused on the camera. "Nevaeh, please know that nothing means more to me than you. Not my career, not my reputation, nothing. Meeting you has shown me how empty my life was before you. I love you, and I truly hope we can have another chance. A new beginning from the lies."

He stared at the camera, then made the signal for his mom to end the video. Lamont dropped his head and let out a small groan. It would probably only take seconds for the backlash to commence.

Even though James and Otto knew he was coming to LA, they believed it was just to check on Nevaeh. Lamont fully expected them to remove him from the movie. He knew the morality clause backward and forward. Though he hadn't crossed any lines in their dating policy, lying about his relationship in the first place probably belonged to some retrograde clause he'd missed.

"Thanks for your help, Mom." He took his cell phone back and enacted do not disturb except for his mom, Nevaeh (God willing), Bryan, and Otto. Everyone else would have to wait until he had the energy to wade through the copious notifications to see what was legit and what wasn't.

"I'm proud of you, son." Her arms squeezed him around his waist.

And for once, he didn't think she was too frail. He wrapped

his arms around her and held on tightly. Mom hugs were the best hugs.

She patted his back, then stepped back. "Now go see about our girl."

"Pray for me."

"Always."

Thirty-Seven

Studying the Bible was never really my forte. Just getting into the daily habit of reading the Bible was only something I'd done upon dating Lamont and seeing how dedicated he was to his faith. Now that I had plenty of time on my hands and had been ordered to rest, I was attempting my first ever Bible study. I'd found one that would help me discover God's plan for my life.

Choosing one hadn't been easy. There were countless studies on being a woman of God and what beauty really meant. All of those sounded like things I needed to read, but after prayerful consideration, I'd finally chosen a study on God's plan for me. After reading the table of contents and some lauding reviews, I'd downloaded the ebook.

So here I sat, reading through the study and highlighting in my Bible. My mom kept darting glances my way, an occasional smile on her face. I wasn't sure if she was happy my Bible was open or that I knew how to use a highlighter.

She hadn't said much since I'd brought my stuff to the dining table. Just offered me a drink and something to snack on. Mom had gone through a transformation, and I wasn't really sure what to make of it. Should I trust that she'd finally accepted my decision that I didn't want to be a teacher? Maybe me being in an accident had shaken something loose within her. I really didn't know.

She was also baking a lot, reminding me of Mrs. Hazelton. I grimaced. I hadn't visited her since moving back in with my parents.

"Hey, Mom, do you remember what the doctor said about driving?"

"He said after two weeks of rest you could do so. Why? Do you want to go somewhere?"

"Yes. I need to check on my old neighbor. Would you like to come and meet her?"

She studied me, taking a sip of her coffee. "You want me to meet a friend of yours?"

"Yes. She's elderly and doesn't have anyone. But I think you'd like her." I met Mom's gaze, hoping she understood my olive branch.

"Then my day is all yours."

"Thanks, Mom."

She nodded. "We can go after you're done with that."

"All right."

After a few minutes, Mom broke the silence. "Have you heard from Lamont?"

"He's probably on set this morning." It's not like he could leave and visit me. And of course there was the confusion with the paparazzo, so surely that explained why I didn't have a text waiting for me this morning to wish me a great day like all the other mornings since he'd left.

My heart warmed when I thought of Lamont. It always did. I was pretty sure I loved him, I just didn't like all the other things that went along with dating him. Was he worth the headache of paparazzi invading my life and people viewing me with a magnifying lens? Sure, I didn't like the spotlight, but before dating Lamont, I was also usually comfortable in my own skin.

Lord, please guide me.

My phone chimed, and my pulse picked up speed as the internet alert for Lamont's name filled my status bar. I clicked the notification and gaped.

What in the world was he doing?

What in the world was he *saying*?

I watched, partly horrified as I thought of all he could lose and partly fascinated that he'd been brave enough to confess to the world that our relationship had been fake. Now they knew we had lied. Though Lamont didn't say I lied. He specifically confessed his own sins.

Oh my word.

My eyes remained fixed on the feed, tearing up when he spoke directly to me, and heaven help me, he loved me.

Lamont Booker, Mr. Sexiest Man Alive, loved me. Me, Nevaeh Richards. Jobless Nevaeh Richards. Curvy Nevaeh Richards.

To say my heart swooned . . . I couldn't believe my eyes or the fact that Lamont would actually tell the world about our start, middle, and . . . new beginning?

While he'd talked, I'd glanced at some of the comments. Some people were shocked, some not at all surprised by the paparazzi's role in the whole thing, and some stunned me with their gracious response. A few repented of their catty remarks and admitted to forgetting celebrities were real people. Of course, there were those trolls who continued their tirade and apparently were willing to die on that hill.

For the first time, I saw them for what they were: a deterrent from living a life God had tailored for me. I wasn't a skinny Hollywood starlet because God hadn't given me that path. He'd given me a love of making women feel beautiful. He'd given me a faith—even when I didn't attend church faithfully (pun intended)—that saw me through difficult times. He'd given me a mom willing to apologize and a boyfriend willing to accept the public's backlash. Instead of counting all my losses, I should have been counting my blessings.

Lamont loved me. The surety of his declaration and the belief that flowed through me erased all past doubts. It helped that I'd been on a similar path. That the guilt of our lie had me repenting and seeking ways to rectify my mistakes. I'd been reading the Word, asking God to help me, and transforming my focus from myself up toward the Lord.

I doubted I would ever be one-hundred-percent comfortable in my own skin, but I certainly didn't have to let people who didn't live my life dictate what I wore—oh, I was throwing that shapewear away—or who I dated.

"Mom, I need to catch a flight."

"Yes, you do."

I looked up, wincing at the pain in my neck. "How long have you been looking over my shoulder?"

"Since I heard Lamont speaking." She smirked. "Guess we know what he's been up to."

I stared at the screen once more. "Wait, that's his living room. Is he here?"

"How can you tell?"

I waved a hand. No need to get into that now. Instead, I dialed Lamont's assistant.

"Hello?" Greg said cautiously.

"Please don't say my name if Lamont's nearby." Greg was notorious for his impeccable manners, which is why he always referred to me as Ms. Richards. "Is he nearby?"

"No, he isn't."

"But he's in LA." It was more statement, but it should have come out more of a question.

"He is."

"Oh, thank goodness. Do you know how long he'll be here?"

"He flies out tomorrow."

Then I had time. I thanked Greg and walked to my room.

"What are you doing?" Mom asked.

"I need to change. Do something to my hair."

"You were in an accident yesterday."

"And that means I have to go see my boyfriend"—was he still my boyfriend?—"unpresentable?"

"Who cares?"

I stopped. She was right. Hadn't I just said no shapewear? I took in my black leggings and light blue tank top. "You're right." I was in an accident, which meant I didn't have to change or do my face. If Lamont loved me, he'd love me in loungewear.

"Let me at least grab my purse," I said.

"I'll get mine and the car keys."

Dad walked into the hall. "What is going on in here? You two sure do know how to make a ruckus."

"Lamont just declared his love for me live on social media. Mom's driving me to his house so I can tell him I love him too."

Dad raised his eyebrows, looking between me and my mom. "Do you really love him? Can you handle the paparazzi following you everywhere?"

Well, I could always do like I did yesterday and send the police to handle them. But it was a good question, a very fatherly question.

I walked toward my dad, grabbing his hands. "Sometimes we have to deal with hard things in order to get the rewards. Lamont is my reward."

Mom sniffled.

"Then I wish you luck."

"Thanks, Daddy." I hugged him, then grabbed my purse out of my room. Mom nodded that she was ready, and we left.

As she drove, I opened my text messages and typed up a new one.

> Nevaeh
> Is Lamont still at home?

> Ms. Rosie
> He is.

> Nevaeh
> I'm on my way there. Can you make sure he doesn't leave?

> Ms. Rosie
> I'll stop him. He just headed to the garage to come to you.

I bit my lip, waiting, hoping she would give me some sign that she'd stalled him. Then again, if she had, she couldn't very well text me and alert Lamont to what was going on.

Lord, please let her keep him from leaving the house. Please see us safely there. Amen.

What was I going to say besides those three words? Would he be happy? Did he think we were over? He'd mentioned a second chance, but he had done nothing to need a second chance.

I sighed. So many questions, and the car moved so slowly. *Stop thinking. Trust God and see what happens.*

Thirty-Eight

The garage door opened, and Lamont put the car in reverse.

"Lamont!"

He froze as his mom appeared, waving her arms to get his attention. He put the gear in park and lowered the passenger-side window. "Everything okay?"

"You need to come see this."

"What is it?"

"It's on the news."

He blew out a breath. He really wanted to see Nevaeh. His plan was to avoid all of that until they talked. Strengthening his resolve, he shook his head. "You can tell me about it later."

"Son, you really need to see this. You're going to be shocked."

"Give me the CliffsNotes version."

"It's about Nevaeh."

He turned off the ignition, hopped out of the car, and headed to the living room. His heart pounded. He hadn't meant his confession to cause Nevaeh any more pain.

He immediately looked at the TV that projected a landscape picture when it wasn't in use. But there was nothing on it that showed Nevaeh, just the local weather. He turned to his mother.

"What's going on?"

"I needed to get you out of the car." She shrugged, a sheepish grin on her face.

"Okay. Why did I have to get out of the car? You know that going to see Nevaeh is important to me."

"Of course I do, but maybe you should let her come to you."

He snorted. "I'm pretty sure she broke up with me. Well, at least halfway sure."

"Why would you think she broke up with you? I doubt the thought ever entered her mind."

"Maybe I put it there. I told her in the beginning we would date, then amicably part ways."

His mom shook her head. "That's ridiculous. Why would you do something like that?"

"Because I didn't want to tie her to me for something the paparazzi took the wrong way."

"And now?"

"Well, I asked her to date me for real, but then the accident happened." Lamont rubbed the back of his neck. He wanted to know she was okay. See her with his own two eyes, face-to-face, with no cell phone camera marking the distance.

"Maybe she's not up for visitors just yet."

"Mom, I'm not any ol' visitor." He lifted up his hands. "I thought you liked us together."

"I really do. I have from the beginning, and it was my hope and prayer that you would stay together despite how you started."

"Then again, I ask you, Why did you stop me from leaving?"

"Because I asked her to."

Lamont whirled around, and cool air entered his mouth before he slammed his jaw shut. Then he opened his mouth to try to make sense of the woman standing before him. Had he really been talking long enough for her to come down from Inglewood to Beverly Hills?

"Wow, who would have thought I could make a guy like you speechless." Nevaeh's dimples winked at him.

"That's my cue to leave." His mom wiggled her fingers at Nevaeh, then walked up the stairs.

Lamont rushed forward, then stopped, noting the neck brace. He couldn't swoop her up in a hug. What if she was still in a lot of pain? "You're here. Are you okay?"

"A little neck pain but I'll live, and that's what really matters."

He cupped her cheek. "I'm so happy you're here."

"Are you?" she asked softly. "You didn't think 'we were on a break'?"

"No way I'm going out like Ross."

She chuckled and wrapped her arms around his waist. He sighed, tucking her under his chin and relishing the feel of her in his arms.

"I saw your live feed." Her words warmed his chest. Literally.

"What did you think?" He took a step back so he could see her.

"I'm glad you confessed."

"Really?"

"I've been feeling like I needed to do the same thing. It was just a thought at first, but then it seemed to gain momentum and took over my entire being." Her nose wrinkled. "Does that make any sense?"

"It makes perfect sense. So you're not mad that the whole world knows?"

She shook her head slowly, but he saw the wince.

He took hold of her hand and led her to the couch. "Did you drive here?"

"No. My mom dropped me off."

"Good." He gestured to the couch. "Please sit. Do you need any pain reliever?"

She chuckled. "I'm okay, Lamont."

"I'm sorry. I can't help but worry."

"You were so worried you didn't text me?"

"Well, I was on the plane for some of that time, asleep for a little more of that time, and putting my plan into action to win you back the rest of the time."

Nevaeh scooted closer to him and wrapped her arms around his neck. "Lamont Booker, my SMA, I love you for you. Always."

"I love you too. And I'm so grateful you feel the same. But I do have to ask you a question."

"Okay."

"Can you handle the spotlight? I'm sorry for not realizing how badly it was affecting you. I don't want our relationship to bring you down. I'm willing to move out of Hollywood if that's what it takes."

"Are you serious? No. I . . . I've realized I need to do better at ignoring those who have no authority in my life. My focus needs to remain on God and us. You don't have to leave a career you love just to make me feel better."

"Are you sure?"

"Absolutely positive."

"Will you tell me if it gets to be too much? We can always reevaluate and make new decisions."

"I promise to let you know if anything changes."

"Bet. Can we kiss and be happy now?"

She chuckled. "Yes, please."

Lamont placed his lips softly against hers, loving the way her hands cupped the back of his head.

Nevaeh sighed. "I've missed you."

"I missed you too. Want to fly back to Canada with me? That is, if I haven't been fired yet."

She chuckled. "How can you joke about that?"

"Because I'm trusting God with my future."

"So what do we do now?" She peered up at him.

Lamont pressed a kiss to each dimple. "Let God write our next chapter and trust Him to guide us."

She laid her head on his chest. "I like the sound of that."

Thirty-Nine

I got the job.

I stared blankly down at my cell phone as the words echoed in my ears. Despite interviewing minutes after an accident and suffering from whiplash, I, Nevaeh Richards, got the job. I couldn't believe it.

Not only did I land a spot on the hair and makeup team, but due to unforeseen circumstances for the initial key stylist, I was offered the lead position. I didn't know whether to let the scream building in my chest free or to fall on my knees and thank God.

Okay, falling to my knees and praising Him was the obvious answer.

A few minutes later, I sat back on my bed, stunned. Despite Lamont's confession, despite my circumstances when I interviewed, I was now the key stylist. If I hadn't finally clued in that making all the plans in the world meant nothing if God didn't bless and order my steps, I'd still be banging my head against the job board.

My yesterdays had been spent living without direction, working on my own merit, and putting faith in blind hope that something great would happen if I just did what I was supposed to do. I had never really understood the Source of my blessings.

A knock on the door sounded.

"Ahhh!" The scream flew from my lips, and not a jubilant *I got the job* type either. I placed a hand over my heart just as the squeak of the opening hinges greeted my ears.

"What in the world, child?"

"You startled me." I placed my phone on the nightstand and rose to my feet. "Did you need something, Mom?"

"You have a visitor."

"It's not Lamont, is it?" He should be filming in Toronto. I had come back Monday, and only two days later, I was aching to go back.

"No, it's Monica from The Mane Do?" My mom said the last part as if she wasn't sure that was the right name.

My brows rose. "What does she want?"

"She said she needs to talk to you. She's waiting in the living room."

I blew out a breath, then nodded. "Fine."

"I'll be in my room if you need me," Mom said.

"Thanks." I gave her a smile and headed for the living room.

What could Monica possibly want? Did she regret how things ended? Was she going to offer me my old job back? And most importantly, how would I react to whatever she had to say?

Monica stood gazing at the bookcases lining the wall. Despite my parents being staunch academics, they had a fair amount of fiction on their shelves in addition to the nonfiction related to their fields of study.

Lord, please give me the words.

"Hey," I said.

Monica whirled around, and her ruby red lips lifted into a

half smile, as if unsure of my reception of her. "Hey, Nevaeh. Hope you don't mind that I came by."

"Kind of wondering how you knew where I was."

"I stopped by your old place, and Nora said you moved back home. She reluctantly gave me the address after much pleading."

Nora shouldn't have given out that information regardless of who asked for it, but that was neither here nor there. I didn't miss that friendship as much as I thought I would.

"Would you like something to drink?" I asked.

"No, thank you. Can we sit?" She gestured toward the sofa set.

"Sure."

I sat on the love seat while she took the longer sofa. I was tempted to jangle my leg up and down in impatience, but something told my spirit that whatever happened, I'd feel peaceful afterward. Now to tell my mind that. I inhaled, then exhaled.

"What did you want to talk about?"

"It's about the day I let you go."

You mean fired me. I nodded.

"Nevaeh, I should never have dismissed you like that. It was unfair to expect you to know what to do about the paparazzi. Not to mention the publicity *was* beneficial for the salon for a bit. I'm sorry."

Was she sorry now that the media had admitted to their fault in the whole situation? The photographer who'd snapped the infamous photo in the first place had come forward, apologizing for invading our privacy. Then in the same breath, he'd mentioned how he had to feed his family, and photos were always worth money to those interested.

It wasn't a system that would be fixed anytime soon, but I had made peace with it. I opened a new social media account, a professional one. One where I could share tips for hair and makeup. My personal photos, well, they were on my laptop for me and Lamont to enjoy. No need to share them with the world.

Focus on Monica. "Thank you for your apology." The words came freely, and I realized that I actually meant them. The apology loosened something inside my chest and released tension from my shoulders.

"I only wish I would have said it sooner." She shook her head. "No, I wish I hadn't fired you in the first place."

"It's in the past. We can leave it there." Because I didn't want to revisit it. Not with a job as a key stylist in my future.

"Thank you for your grace."

I gave her a genuine smile. We could all use a measure of grace on a daily basis.

"There's just one more thing before I go." She leaned forward. "Is it possible you would consider coming back?"

My mouth dropped, but she rushed on.

"Not simply as a stylist but also as a partner."

"Partner?" I echoed.

"Right. You'd be my business partner and have equal share in the decision-making process."

"As well as have a chair?"

"Yes."

Why was my heart pounding so hard? Surely it was the surprise and not . . . intrigue at the possibilities before me. Still, the swallow I tried to take to moisten my mouth and let me speak seemed ineffective. "For real?" I squeaked.

She laughed. "Yes. Don't give an answer today. But if you could have one by next Monday, that would be great." She stood and ambled toward the door. "Thanks for talking with me."

"Sure."

I locked the door, then turned, leaning against the frame. What had just happened? I'd awoken this morning thinking it would be just more of the same. Instead, I had two incredible job offers, and it wasn't even lunchtime yet.

What was I supposed to do? I'd always thought a key stylist position was my dream, but honestly, running a salon didn't sound too shabby either. Maybe it was just the allure of the offer and not really what I wanted. If I went for it, would Monica revert back to her old bossy self or truly treat me as a partner?

I needed to start praying. This was too much for my brain to handle.

"What happened?" Mom asked, coming into the living room.

"Monica offered me a job."

Mom's eyes widened. "Is that a good thing?"

"She wants me to be a partner."

"Are you serious?" Her voice rose a couple of octaves.

I let loose a laugh full of unbelief. This was such a surreal day. "Not only that, but I got a job offer on a new show airing on prime time."

"Honey, that's amazing. Is it a steady job?"

"It's the head stylist position, so I would be running the hair and makeup team."

"So essentially both opportunities give you time to be in charge?"

"Yes." I pushed off the door and headed for the kitchen. I needed coffee.

"Do you know what you're going to do?"

"Nope." I smacked my lips for extra emphasis and selected a K-Cup pod for the Keurig.

"Which opportunity interests you the most?" she asked.

"The key stylist is all I've ever wanted." I grabbed the cup and headed for the table near the kitchen window. "But co-owning a salon sounds enticing as well."

"Well, if the stylist position is what you've been working toward, shouldn't you take that?" Mom grabbed the banana bread and held up the loaf. "Want a piece?"

"No, thanks."

She cut herself a slice while I thought about the question.

"I'm just going to pray that God makes the decision for me. I don't want to choose the salon just because it's the new shiny object. And I don't want to be so closed-minded by feeling like I've obtained my dream and choose that because I have tunnel vision. I want to pick the place God wants me to be."

"Then I'll pray He makes it clear for you." She took a bite. "Want to go shopping today? Clear your mind?"

Mom must have forgotten how much I hated shopping, but I knew she was trying. "Um, shopping for what?"

She laughed. "Not clothes shopping. I was thinking of redecorating. Maybe updating the furniture. What do you think?"

I thought I was in shock. She remembered I didn't like shopping for clothes? "That sounds like it could be fun."

"Great. Grab your purse, or whatever you need, and let's go. I'll drive."

Fine by me. I hadn't gotten behind the wheel since the accident two weeks ago and really wasn't too eager to do so. So far venturing out as a passenger was enough for me.

The sun shined bright in the August day, but it was a little hotter than I'd like. Still, it was nice to be out and about. Lamont said he'd come visit this weekend—Cannon Industries was being more lax about allowing their actors to travel on non-set days—and we'd get a new car for me. I had objected, but he sat me down and explained that he was loaded, and it made no sense for me to spend money I needed to save when he was capable of spending it and not hurting his balance.

I had to admit he made sense, so I finally agreed.

But now I wanted to call him and get his opinion. Only he was on set, so I shot him a text.

> **Nevaeh**
> Got two job offers. Key stylist position and partner at The Mane Do.

Lamont
That's amazing, babe.

> **Nevaeh**
> I thought you were on set.

Lamont
Food break. Everyone was starving. They bought hoagies.

> **Nevaeh**
> Which one should I pick?

Lamont
What does your gut say?

> **Nevaeh**
> Pray.

Lamont
What does your heart say?

> **Nevaeh**
> Pray.

Lamont
Have you prayed yet?

I chuckled.

> **Nevaeh**
> Yes.

Lamont
Then wait on His answer.

I sighed. He was right. I needed to take the time to let God guide me. It was something I was working on. It's the reason I had gone to church with Mom—still didn't care for it, but I'd been able to worship and focus on God. Then I went back to Lamont's church on my own. A few people actually spoke to me and congratulated Lamont on being honest. They'd even invited us to join their small group. I wasn't sure if that was something Lamont wanted, but it was nice to be invited.

I probably would always be a little uneasy in a church space. Churches weren't perfect and weren't meant to be. Like my mom had told me, they were a place for sinners in need of a Savior and run by redeemed sinners. There were bound to be issues with that combination. But when I took the time to focus on the Lord and not my comforts, it made all the difference in the world.

Lord, thank You for two job offers in one day. I pray that I have the patience to wait on Your answer. I pray I have the ears to hear You clearly. And I pray that I always seek Your guidance first. Amen.

EPILOGUE

Tuck
It's a shame I had to read about your
engagement online.

Chris
I saw it on The Cheese. You?

Tuck
StarGazer. That's a nice-size ring you got her.
Piper wants to know why you didn't get a
diamond.

Lamont
My girl isn't a fan of diamonds. Had to go with
something that suited her.

Chris
The amethyst looks nice.

Lamont
She thought so.

Tuck
This is Piper. How did you propose?

Lamont grinned. Piper had taken to commandeering Tuck's
phone a lot more to interrupt their chats. But Lamont knew
for a fact she and Nevaeh had started their own thread.

> Lamont
> You didn't ask Nevaeh already?

> Tuck
> I did, but she's not answering. Is she with you?

Lamont squeezed Nevaeh around the waist. "Piper's asking about how I proposed. Want me to tell her, or are you going to text her?"

She sat up and glanced at his phone, then grinned. "You've got more messages."

> Chris
> Yes, we all want to know.

> Lamont
> This is Nevaeh. He's feeling shy so I thought I'd share how it all went down.

> Tuck
> I'm all ears, even Tuck, though he's pretending not to read over my shoulder.

> Chris
>

> Lamont
> We decided to act like tourists for a day and went to Santa Monica pier. Apparently, he paid the Ferris wheel operator to stop with us on top. As we looked over the skyline, Lamont turned to me and said, "I don't have a token, a shoe, or dirty cargo pants with a hidden ring. But I do have a heart that's ready to love you and a ring I hope you'll love a little less than you'll love me."

> Chris
> A token?

> Tuck
> While You Were Sleeping proposal scene.

Chris

How do you know that? Oh, wait, Piper, is that still you?

Tuck

No, it's me, but that was her. She's crying happy tears. What's the shoe?

> **Lamont**
> Ever After

Chris

And the cargo pants?

> **Lamont**
> He's Just Not That Into You. Geesh. It's like you two never watch movies.

Tuck

Only the ones Piper makes me. I have seen Ever After but didn't get that.

> **Lamont**
> I did.

Chris

Congrats, you two.

Tuck

Yes, congrats. From me and Piper.

> **Lamont**
> Thanks, fellas. From me and Nevaeh.

ACKNOWLEDGMENTS

Each time I get to the acknowledgment part of the writing process, I feel so grateful that I have another one to write. There are so many people I want to thank, so please bear with me.

Thanks to my awesome agent extraordinaire. Rachel McMillan, you always know the right things to say when I'm panicking over a story. I'm blessed to have you in my life.

I would love to thank the ladies on my street team. Your help in naming characters and giving me names for some of the gossip magazines is so appreciated. Thank you to Ami Coote, Candy Holbrook, Jaycee Weaver, Gretchen Garrison, Debb Hackett, and Allyson Anthony.

Special thank you to Corrine Lussier and Carrie Schmidt for your invaluable advice on making this story better after reading the first draft. Your support and encouragement got me through days of doubting whether this story was good enough. I appreciate you more than I can say.

Thanks to my brother, Michael Scott, for letting me ask questions about LA and acting. Love you!

Of course, no acknowledgment would be complete without thanking my critique partners. Andrea Boyd and Sarah Monzon, you ladies are awesome, and I love you.

Many thanks to the entire Bethany House Publishers team. You guys blow me away. I'm so thankful for the editing skills of Jessica Sharpe and Kate Deppe, the design team, and everyone else who comes alongside me to make this story a success. Thank you for making my dreams come true.

Last, I'd like to thank my family. Glenn, thank you for putting up with me and my various moods over this story. I appreciate you listening to me vent and supporting me. To my boys, thank you for listening to my playlist in the background over and over until it annoyed you.

For more from

Toni Shiloh

read on

for an excerpt from

In
SEARCH
OF A
PRINCE

Brielle Adebayo's simple life unravels when she discovers she is a princess in the African kingdom of Ọlọrọ Ilé and must immediately assume her royal position. Brielle comes to love the island's culture and studies the language with her handsome tutor. But when her political rivals force her to make a difficult choice, a wrong decision could change her life.

Available now wherever books are sold.

one

Ah, summertime in New York City. Could there be anything better? The greenery of the trees made me smile. Unlike others, I was a fan of the heat and thrived under the warmth beaming on me. I wanted to take a moment to soak it all in, but my mother expected punctuality, and I was already ten minutes late. I glanced down at my Apple watch. Okay, fifteen minutes.

As one of NYC's top pediatric surgeons, my mom had to squeeze me into her fully packed calendar. But when she could, I considered it a win. I bumped into a man in a suit arguing on his Bluetooth and sidestepped a mom pushing her kid in a stroller. Finally, I broke free of the crowd and lengthened my strides.

Nonna's came into view, and I sighed in relief. The Italian restaurant would most likely be packed at this hour, everyone attempting to grab lunch before heading back to their offices. Fortunately, it was a school holiday, and I didn't have to worry about rushing. I bounded up the steps of the stone-marble building and through the automatic doors. An air-conditioned breeze welcomed me with a *whoosh*, and my arms pebbled with goosebumps as I headed for the hostess podium.

"Do you have a reservation?" The cool disdain on the hostess's face would have put a damper on my mood if it weren't for the fact that most hostesses in the city had that practiced bored look.

"Yes. It should be under Marie Bayo." I smiled, hoping kindness would chip away at her bad mood.

She scanned the readout before her. "This way." She pivoted on her heels and strolled through the busy dining room. As if Moses led her way, the other waitstaff moved, making the aisle clear for her procession. The restaurant was filled with families, businessmen, and couples bonding over Italian dishes.

A nervous energy filled my gut as I followed the hostess to the second dining area. Mom only ate here when she wanted to share important news. No matter how hard I'd tried to think of what she could possibly want to talk about, my ideas fizzled.

The hostess came to a stop and motioned toward a table for two, then made her way back up to the front of the restaurant.

My mother stood, a grin covering her face. "Brielle, I'm so happy to see you." She wrapped her arms around me.

"Me too." I returned the hug, resting my chin on her shoulder, and soaked up the contact. Two months had passed since I'd last seen her, but the time seemed to span further. She pulled back and kissed my cheek before breaking the hug altogether.

We stood the same height—five feet five inches—though my mother's flats put her at a disadvantage to my wedges. Our thin eyebrows (courtesy of great threading), pert noses, and full lips resembled each other's. But my mother had a great chestnut color to her skin, and mine resembled a lovely shade of espresso. Our long hair did hold the same wave, though mine was black and hers dyed a light brown shade she spent hundreds on in the salon.

I lowered myself into my chair and spread a maroon cloth napkin across my lap. "So what's the big news?"

My mother's dark brown eyes flashed before she gave me a *no-no* signal with her pointer finger. "First, tell me how the end of the year is going. How are your students?" She smiled, the crow's feet around her eyes crinkling.

I shook my head at her diversion tactics but complied. I loved talking about teaching—the joys and pitfalls of eighth grade civics. "They're antsy, ready for school to end. Hopefully the Memorial Day holiday will ease some of their jitters." I sighed. "I can't wait for our summer vacation."

Mom laughed. "You just like the beach."

Understatement of the year. The ocean was my happy place, and our yearly vacation to Martha's Vineyard centered me. I couldn't wait to return.

"You do too." I rested my elbow on the table, propping my chin on my hand. "Have we done enough small talk now? We could have discussed our vacation over the phone." Not that I didn't appreciate seeing her face-to-face, but I wanted to know her big news.

A grimace stole across Mom's face, lines framing her mouth. Her brow wrinkled, marring her smooth skin.

Unease churned my stomach. "What is it?" The words seemed to stick on the unexpected lump in my throat. Was she ill? Her features held no signs of sickness. No pallor. No jaundice. But who was I kidding? I wasn't the doctor, she was.

"I have a story to tell you, Bri, and I need you to listen without interruption." Mom licked her lips. "I promise to answer all the questions you have at the end. Can you do that for me?"

I nodded, my heart knocking against a wall of fear. Was it worse than being sick? Was she . . . *dying*?

"After graduating high school in Jersey, I came to New York to get a college education. To become a doctor. I'd dreamt of being a doctor since I was a child. I used to pretend to heal my dolls and stuffed animals."

Where was she going with this? I'd heard this tale more times than I could count. My mother enjoyed retelling the story as an example of the importance of perseverance and hard work. It was why she'd encouraged me to be so passionate in my studies growing up. It turned out I didn't have the fortitude to work around blood like she did, but teaching fit me.

Before she could continue, our server appeared with two glasses of water and their complimentary bread-and-oil platter. He took our drink and entrée orders, then moved on to the next table.

My mother's gaze met mine. "My studies were all I thought about until I met your father. He didn't see my dedication to my degree as an obstacle but a challenge." She paused and reached for the bread plate in the center of the table, dipping a breadstick into the small saucer of herb-infused olive oil.

Her languid movements got under my skin. I wanted her to jump to the point, but no one could rush Marie Bayo.

"Your father believed we could be together and still have enough time to devote to our courses." A wistful smile curled her lips. "He passed me notes in the classes we shared, took his meals with me, and studied in the library simply because I was there." She blinked. "Before I knew it, I had fallen in love with Tayo Bayo."

Her nostalgia and the rhyming of my father's name brought a smile to my lips. I used to wish my mother had carried on the tradition with me instead of naming me Brielle, but once she told me it meant *God is my strength*, I'd fallen in love with my name.

My father came from a small island off the coast of West Africa and passed away before I was born. My mother didn't share many details about him with me. It was as if everything about him was too painful to repeat, too unbearable to relive. Which made her words now all the more captivating. I leaned in, eager to hear more about my father.

"As you know, we married one weekend." She swallowed. "Pure spontaneity, and an occasion I still marvel at. It was totally unlike me. We got a license one day and said *I do* the next." Mom exhaled. "I was so happy, Bri. Until—"

"Until he died," I said, breaking my silence. I knew how the rest of the story went.

What would life have been like if I had known him? Growing up, I'd make up reasons he was away, preferring imagined dreams to the truth of his death. I'd pretend he was a spy who needed to save the world from imminent doom. Even an astronaut studying the heavens. Or simply away on a visit to his native country, unable to come to us for whatever reason my mind could conceive. My mother had never taken me to see his birth country, and the desire to visit remained a constant one, but a teacher's salary wasn't conducive to world travel.

"Actually, no."

I blinked. "What?"

"I was happy until he sat me down in our five-hundred-square-foot apartment to tell me there was something important that I didn't know about him."

My breath hitched. What did that mean? Why hadn't I heard this part of the story before?

"His full name was Naade Tayo Adebayo." My mother took a sip of ice water. Then her eyes met mine, piercing me with their sorrow. "And he was the crown prince of Ọlọrọ Ilé."

My breath whooshed out of my body. Time slowed as my pulse pounded in my ears. I stared at her, trying to gather my wits. "Are you saying . . . my dad was a prince? Like, an heir-to-a-throne type prince?" I forced a laugh. Surely she was joking.

Instead of the mirth I wished for, she simply nodded, gaze somber.

"That can't be right. You wouldn't have kept a secret this big from me." Would she? I swallowed. "Did he even really *die*?"

Tears sprang to her eyes. "Yes, baby. But let me back up to that moment in our apartment." She shook her head, her brown hair swaying against her shoulders. "I was livid when I managed to move from disbelief to realizing he was telling me the truth." She pressed a hand against her forehead.

I gripped the napkin in my lap. This was insane.

"I told your father to get out. To leave. And after weeks of me ignoring every form of contact . . . he did just that. He left the country and returned to his homeland without me." Mom's lower lip trembled. "I found out about his departure from a college friend and realized the cost of my pride. I called the phone number your father had left for me, hoping we could work things out, only his father, the king, answered. After I explained who I was, he told me Tayo had died two days before my call." Her voice broke, and tears spilled down her cheeks.

My heart ached, torn between wanting to comfort my mother and fury that she had kept a secret of this magnitude.

She took a sip of water, then dabbed the napkin against her cheeks. "I went to the funeral and was permitted an introduction to the king." Her jaw tightened. "He informed me that he would arrange to have the marriage annulled. Apparently, I should never have been permitted to marry Tayo."

I gasped. How many more twists could there be? I wanted to run away, hands over my ears. But the trembling in my stomach told me to keep listening. To hear the *whole* truth.

"What your grandfather didn't expect was you." Mom traced the condensation on her water glass as a soft smile covered her lips. "When I told him I was pregnant, it changed everything. He agreed to keep the marriage intact and filed paperwork to make our union legal in Ọlọrọ Ilé as well. Although, from my understanding, he kept all that information secret. He then wrote me a check to cover any expenses you could ever possibly have." She paused. "And told me never to contact him again."

I blinked, thoughts whirring faster than a blender. Which controversial subject did I dissect first? "He didn't want to know me?"

"He blamed me for your father's death. Accused me of driving his son to a depression."

"I thought he died in a boating accident," I accused.

"He did, but your grandfather said he was an excellent swimmer and should never have drowned."

I covered my mouth at the image my mind immediately conjured. Could all this really be true? I'd had no reason to doubt my mom before today, but now . . .

"When you were five, your grandfather called to apologize, only I . . ." Mom looked away, sorrow etched into every line on her face.

"You said no, didn't you?"

She nodded.

"And the money? Are we talking about enough to cover clothing expenses?"

"Whatever you needed, Brielle. I tried not to spend it, but . . ." She shrugged.

Certain things began to click into place. "Is that why you

pressed me to do cotillion and debutante balls? Language lessons?" She'd known I would need to move in a world I'd never imagined was a possibility.

She nodded. "I used the money to pay for all of those things." She swallowed. "Plus your college education. The rest I placed in an account for you."

Disbelief filled me. "Why?" I whispered. "Why tell me all of this now?"

"The king is dying." Her gaze met mine. "And you are the heir to the throne."

Toni Shiloh is a wife, a mom, and an award-winning Christian contemporary romance author. She writes to bring God glory and to learn more about His goodness. Her novel *In Search of a Prince* won the first ever Christy Amplify Award. *Grace Restored* was a 2019 Holt Medallion finalist, *Risking Love* was a 2020 Selah Award finalist, *The Truth About Fame* a 2021 Holt Medallion finalist, and *The Price of Dreams* a 2021 Maggie Award finalist. A member of American Christian Fiction Writers (ACFW), Toni loves connecting with readers and authors alike via social media. You can learn more about her writing at tonishiloh.com.

Sign Up for Toni's Newsletter

Keep up to date with Toni's latest news on book releases and events by signing up for her email list at the link below.

FOLLOW TONI ON SOCIAL MEDIA

Toni Shiloh, Author

@tonishiloh

@tonishilohwrite

ToniShiloh.com

You May Also Like . . .

Brielle Adebayo's simple life unravels when she discovers she is a princess in the African kingdom of Ọlọrọ Ilé and must immediately assume her royal position. Brielle comes to love the island's culture and studies the language with her handsome tutor. But when her political rivals force her to make a difficult choice, a wrong decision could change her life.

In Search of a Prince by Toni Shiloh
tonishiloh.com

Fashion aficionado Iris Blakely dreams of using her talent to start a business to help citizens in impoverished areas. But when she discovers that Ekon Diallo will be her business consultant, the battle between her desires and reality begins. Can she keep her heart—and business—intact despite the challenges she faces?

To Win a Prince by Toni Shiloh
tonishiloh.com

After Ingrid Erikson jeopardizes her career, she fears her future will remain irrevocably broken. But when the man who shattered her belief in happily-ever-afters offers her a sealed envelope from her late best friend, Ingrid is sent on a hunt for a hidden manuscript and must confront her past before she can find the healing she's been searching for.

The Words We Lost by Nicole Deese
A Fog Harbor Romance
nicoledeese.com

The summer of '77 was supposed to be the best of Summer Wilde's life. But those plans never had a chance when a teenage prank went awry. Now thirtysomething with a failed music career, she returns to the place where everything changed and where she must face a reckoning with her past and the friends she lost to gain the closure she needs to move forward.

The Best Summer of Our Lives by Rachel Hauck
rachelhauck.com

Printed in the USA
CPSIA information can be obtained
at www.ICGtesting.com
LVHW051816040823
754291LV00001B/1

9 780764 241857